UNDER THE EYE OF KALI

AN ANITA RAY MYSTERY

Under the
Eye of Kali

Susan Oleksiw

FIVE STAR
A part of Gale, Cengage Learning

GALE
CENGAGE Learning™

Detroit • New York • San Francisco • New Haven, Conn • Waterville, Maine • London

GALE
CENGAGE Learning™

LIBRARY OF CONGRESS CATALOGING-IN-PUBLICATION DATA

Oleksiw, Susan.
    Under the eye of Kali : an Anita Ray mystery / by Susan Oleksiw. — 1st ed.
        p. cm.
    ISBN-13: 978-1-59414-871-2 (alk. paper)
    ISBN-10: 1-59414-871-6 (alk. paper)
    1. East Indian American women—Fiction. 2. Americans—India—Fiction. 3. Missing persons—Fiction. 4. India, South—Fiction. I. Title.
    PS3565.L42U53 2010
    813'.54—dc22   2010003986

First Edition. First Printing: May 2010.
Published in 2010 in conjunction with Tekno Books and Ed Gorman.

Printed in the United States of America
1 2 3 4 5 6 7 14 13 12 11 10

To
Eva Ray

AUTHOR'S NOTE

The Government of India and local political parties have introduced "traditional" names of major cities. For example, Bombay is now Mumbai. In Kerala, Cochin is now Kochi, Quilon is Kollam, and the capital city Trivandrum is Thiru-vanantapuram. Residents and visitors of these cities alternate between the two. I have used the shorter form throughout for the capital.

CHAPTER ONE

Guests from various foreign countries began filling up the Hotel Delite dining room, taking every seat at the main table—this was a small hotel, only eight rooms, with the owner's, Meena Nayar's, suite on the top floor, and that of her niece, Anita Ray, above a separate garage. Tired after being woken in the middle of the night by festival drumming from a nearby temple, Anita sat at a small table along the wall and only half-listened to the guests placing their orders and asking the usual questions. *What is this? What does it taste like?*

"That was some crowd last night." A woman slid into a chair at the long table and looked around expectantly, waiting for someone else to take up the conversation. In her early thirties, not much older than Anita, she gave her long, flowing top a little shake as she sat down. She had matched a purple top with maroon pants, a variation on the khurta and loose pants tourists favored at the resort. "The drummers. They must wake the dead. And they're going to go on drumming almost every night this week as part of their temple festival. They take the god down to the beach for a swim. That is so cool!" She looked around, pausing. "I'm Emily. My friends aren't up yet. Last night was too much for them, I guess."

"Didn't hear a thing," one of the other guests said. "Jean. I'm Jean." She was a robust woman, about fifty, with short, wiry gray hair, wearing a loose-fitting, rough cotton blouse and slacks, everything beige and colorless except for her red cheeks and a bright green neckerchief tied loosely around her neck. "Slept like the dead. Great place to catch up on one's rest." She nodded to her companion. Anita recalled that Jean and her friend, Marge, had reserved two private rooms after almost a month of emails flying back and forth—Jean was particular. "Got too much on my mind to be distracted."

"Well, you've come at the best time," Emily said. "The festival goes on all week, and it's amazing. They take the image of Kali down to the beach and everything."

"Hmm." Jean didn't seem impressed. "I suppose we're supposed to be tolerant of superstitions while we're here, but really." She continued to work on her breakfast.

"I slept like a log last night, but the festival sounds interesting." Jean's friend delivered her opinion with barely a glance between bites. "I'm Marge. How do you do?"

"I took drumming lessons like that last summer at this place in South Tucson. I'm Candace," another woman said, smiling at everyone around the table. "Well, Candy my friends call me." She had arrived a few days earlier and was one of those tourists who establish an instant rapport with just about everyone, even if most of it was one-sided. Candy's technique seemed to be to just start talking, whether anyone else was interested or not. Her odd haircut, which looked like someone had left a wiry brown bowl over her head, probably helped disarm her intended victims, and her row of shiny, fake stone pierced earrings climbing up her ear could blind them.

"South Tucson? I know South Tucson." Marge stopped eating long enough to take a good look at Candy. Marge looked like a fairly typical middle-aged American, in a print blouse and jeans, ready to hop in the car and head out for her Saturday morning errands. But she also looked worn out, almost beaten down, as though beneath the tourist persona was a woman who desperately needed a rest. "We used to work there, in that clinic." She nodded to Jean.

Jean gave a firm bob of her head, tugged her green neckerchief into place, and Anita imagined that her handshake would be firm if not bone-crushing. "Nice little clinic." After a brief pause, she added, "We're both nurses."

"Oh, how cool! We're all from Tucson. Maybe you can help me." Candy sat up straighter.

"Actually, I'm from Pennsylvania, King of Prussia," Emily said.

"Never been there," Marge said, but even though she smiled, it was obvious she didn't mean the conversation to go any further. Candy glanced at Emily, turned away.

"I've been thinking about nursing school," Candy said. "I'm finishing up my BA and have to get serious now. You know how it is. But I did a lot of volunteer work at a shelter and food pantry, and you can really see how important good health care is, so nursing looks like something I might really like. I'd love to talk to you about it." She leaned forward with a glittering eye and eager smile.

Marge said sure, and looked a little daunted by all this enthusiasm, but Jean took it all in stride. "We won't be here very long," Jean said. "Off to Thailand." She lifted her eyebrows with a knowing smile.

"Oh, how exciting!" Candy leaned toward Jean now.

"Very!" Jean winked at her. "I have friends meeting me there. They're going to smuggle me across the border into Burma— Myanmar." She looked inordinately pleased with herself and reached a spoon into the serving bowl, drawing out a large portion of stew. Everyone had chosen the Indian breakfast, appam and vegetable stew, but only Jean was devoting serious attention to it.

"Oh!" Emily seemed to have forgotten everything else in the face of this news. "Why are you going there?" This was the same question Anita wanted to ask, now that she was fully alert. She and her aunt usually occupied one of the small tables by the windows, so they could avoid being drawn into conversation with the guests at breakfast. The hotel dining room on the terrace was open to the general community, leaving breakfast in the small inside dining room as the main opportunity for intimacy among hotel guests.

"I was invited." Jean looked even more smug. "Friends." Her voice softened, so that no one beyond the immediate group could hear her. She looked at the faces staring expectantly back at her, all except her friend's. "I've been to this particular village before, and I managed to help them out a bit. They invited me back." She made a dive at her appam and stew and stuffed a healthy spoonful into her mouth.

"Last year," Marge added. Anita noticed that she sat very straight and continued her meal throughout the conversation, somewhat remote, on the fringe, and yet, perhaps the most alert of them all.

"I've been raising money for the village," Jean said. "I've done quite well, if I do say so. I've raised enough to dig a few tube wells, repair a school building, bring in some things for a clinic, and have something leftover to travel around a bit. I did very well indeed."

"So if you have friends there, can't you just go like any other tourist?" Emily frowned as she tried to grasp Jean's plans.

"Well, not really." Jean snorted. "The government would never let me in with what I'm carrying, and they'd never let me near the villages."

"Oh, I see." But she didn't look like she meant it. "How did you get this gig?"

Jean looked across at her, as though she'd just noticed her for the first time, and her eyes seemed to dull, as though she were coming back to earth and the reality of what she'd just been telling them. "A friend turned me on to the village." Her voice was suddenly flat. "Is there more tea?" She picked up the teapot and held it out, looking around for a bearer to take it from her. Moonu, a young man who had worked for the hotel for many years, swooped in from the doorway and grasped it in both hands, cradling it close to his chest as he loped away to the kitchen.

"Well, I think it's exciting!" Candy said. "And important too. That's the thing around here—you see such need. You know, just driving here from the airport you can see all those people living in hovels along the side of the road by the airport, and then down that highway. Why are the cows up at that hour?" She swung around to face Anita, who wasn't the least bit disconcerted. She'd had this question at least a thousand times. Didn't they have cows in America?

"They get restless, like anyone." Anita shrugged. It never occurred to her to wonder why the cows and their herders were sometimes awake in the middle of the night. People just were around here—and everywhere else in India for that matter.

"What were you studying?" Marge asked Candy.

"I'm ashamed to say I've been totally frivolous. I didn't go to college thinking in practical terms—not me. I had to see the world, study literature, get to know myself." She laughed, and sent forth a ribbon of giggles. "Officially I was studying English literature. But really, I was only interested in one thing. Poetry." Candy hung her head for a second in mock contrition, then popped it back up again. "Do you know the poet who won that big award? I studied with her in Vermont, and with some other poets in San Francisco."

"I've read—" Emily began but stopped when Candy gave her a blank look, then a tight smile, and turned again to Jean.

"And all those poetry bookstores in California! Just think of it! Mecca!" Candy screwed up her face in a paroxysm of ecstasy, shut her eyes, and murmured Mecca again. Jean looked like she was about to reach out and pat her on the head, but the teapot called as it clattered onto the table. Jean thanked the bearer in her firm voice and reached for it.

"My favorite bookstore is Readers' Rookery," Jean said. "Wonderful place."

"Oh yeah, so funky," Candy said.

"And what about the Poe's Pals Bookshop," Emily said.

"Do I need any special courses to get into nursing school?" Candy said, ignoring Emily. "I mean, if I were going to try it as a career."

Marge's spoon paused in midair as she studied Candy. The older woman began to look more run down, as though Candy were draining her of whatever energy she had left. "Well, sciences, of course. Biology, anatomy, chemistry."

"Oh, sure." Candy was undaunted. "Is it a long period of study? I'm thinking about how I'm going to pay off my student loans."

"Pretty awful, they are." Jean took a long sip of tea and set the cup in the saucer with a clank. "Didn't have to worry about those things when I was in school but can't see how anyone gets through without them today—loans and debts. Awful society we've created. Do you know, in Burma people still live in this perfectly balanced culture—balanced with nature. Nothing is wasted, nothing poisons the environment, not from the villagers, anyway. It's only the outside world that insists on bringing in corruption. It's our Western culture—we're destroying everything we touch."

"So true," Candy said. Her head bobbed up and down as Jean spoke, her eyes never leaving the other woman's face.

"But the medicines are good," Emily said. "You're bringing some, you said." Candy shot her a venomous look.

"You're so lucky to be going there, to see all that." Candy continued to nod. "And brave. Really brave."

Jean looked like she was about to say something, seemed to think better of it, and began to look uncomfortable. In a moment of tactfulness Anita wouldn't have thought Candy capable of, she switched topics. "Do you specialize in nursing school? I mean, like choosing a major like HIV or disabilities or something?"

Marge smiled, still sitting ramrod straight. "You develop your skills according to where you work. HIV is just one disease among many now, but if you work in a city hospital, you learn a lot about bullet wounds."

"Oh, my." Candy shook her head, apparently in awe. "Yeah, I guess that must be true. Oh, my. You have to be so brave to be a nurse, don't you? Gutsy, too."

CHAPTER TWO

Aunt Meena rustled into the dining room, nodded to each guest at the long table, offering them a wide smile, and spun around to face Anita.

Poor Auntie Meena, Anita thought. She's probably found that order for flowers for the temple. Or maybe the clementines for the special tourist luncheon. Or maybe the candles for the Catholic church. Anita tipped her head back and offered her aunt the most innocent of smiles.

"This was on the desk, right next to the registration book." A blue envelope, opened and spread out, peeked out from under her beringed fingers; nervously, she began to rub the letter back and forth on the table. Ever since Anita had moved into the hotel to help Aunt Meena after her husband's untimely death, Meena had been obsessed with managing Anita's life and ensuring that as the nearest aunt she produced the ideal Hindu woman. Since her own daughter had failed to live up to these perfectly reasonable standards, in Meena's view, she was determined not to fail with Anita. So Anita's parents lived in the States, so her father was an Irish American, so they let Anita do whatever she wanted, so they ignored Meena's late-night telephone pleas, so Anita refused to take life seriously and insisted on wandering around with a camera, so what?

"For me? Thanks." Anita reached for the letter. When Meena failed to release it, Anita glanced up at her. "Auntie?"

Meena leaned forward, glanced from side to side, slipped the

16

envelope across to her, then whispered, "It is from Anand."

"Oh! Anand!" Anita swiped the blue sheet away from her aunt and quickly read it through. "Oh, how sweet." She looked up at her aunt. "We're going to a Kathakali performance together later in the week. Auntie, what's the matter? You look ill."

"But he is, is . . ."

"He's what?" Anita glanced at the letter, then at Meena, feeling more and more puzzled by her aunt's behavior. Anand was a delightful man, well educated, with a good job, and—something especially important to her aunt—single, and not opposed to matrimony. Anita had met him at another relative's house, and they had hit it off at once. What was wrong with her aunt—she should be ecstatic. "What's the problem?"

"He is, ah, well, unsuited."

"Unsuited to what?"

"To you."

"You must be joking, Auntie. Have you forgotten the men you have tried to marry me off to? The dregs of our society—a lawyer who speaks neither Latin nor English and only wants two or three cases that he can drag out for the rest of his natural life, living on the fees; a business man who only wanted me to sponsor him in his application to emigrate to the States so he could open a chain of motels; a Tamil landowner who wanted to know if I had friends who would redirect the railroad near his land, so he could sell it to the government."

"You are too particular."

"Why don't you like Anand?"

"He doesn't suit you." Meena snorted, telling Anita that here was something her aunt felt strongly about but would not or could not put into words. It was impossible for Anita to be angry with her aunt—she did mean well and only wanted the best for Anita, even if that meant a way of life that had driven her own mother, Meena's older sister, far away to America, where she followed her own choice of a husband—a man of Irish ancestry who never had any intention of returning to the old sod, an irrepressible sense of fun, and complete tolerance of a slew of relatives on both sides that once led him to design a bunker for the backyard, his own escape hatch. Meena, however, was determined that Anita would not make the same mistake her mother had, even if the woman did insist she was happy overseas. Meena simply didn't believe it, and she was prepared to do battle against Anand and every other man Anita might be drawn to, so that her own, Meena's, choice might prevail—when she found him.

"Auntie, I like him." Anita reached across the table and squeezed her aunt's hand. "Give him a chance. You'll like him too."

"No, I won't. I will never like him. And neither will your mother." Meena gasped. "Don't tell her, please, don't tell her. You mustn't say a word. Oh, what will I do? Your mother will be angry with me." Meena clutched her arms to her chest and hurried out of the room.

Anita pinched off the camera lens cap, slipped it into her pocket, and headed up Lighthouse Road for two hours of seeing and snapping. For her this was the best part of the day, any day, no matter what else was going on, the one time when she could be entirely engrossed in her world, her thoughts, her feelings. She was a little late this morning, but no matter. She felt refreshed, herself once again.

She passed up the steep incline, responding to the many greetings of Good Morning, and occasionally smiling at the new autorickshaw driver offering her a ride at a very good price, madam, very good.

Anita kept walking. When she next looked up, Jean was striding down the hill toward her. She stopped dead in front of Anita, stamping her right foot beside her left, like a soldier coming to a halt on a parade ground. Anita couldn't bring herself to offer a welcoming smile—this was much too aggressive an encounter.

"You disapprove of me." Jean stuck her chin out, but kept the quizzical smile on her face. "I saw it this morning at breakfast. You disapprove." She slapped her hands together behind her back and let her feet move farther apart. She apparently was digging in for the duration—of what? An argument?

"I don't recall offering any disapproval." Anita tipped her camera lens upward and rested it against her shoulder, as though it were in danger of being struck if left facing outward. Like a weapon, she thought; I'm shouldering my camera like a weapon.

"Oh, come now. It was obvious. You disapprove of my work in Burma."

"Oh, that." Anita looked away, down at the ground, then over at the bougainvillea pouring over a nearby wall in a cloud of color and fragrance. "I wouldn't say disapprove."

"I would."

"Yes, and you did."

"Let's have a coffee." Jean took Anita by the arm, to Anita's surprise, and led her to a little shop offering coffee. The café had a few shelves of goods for tourists and two chairs, which Jean promptly claimed by sitting in one and motioning Anita to the other. She called out her order, and Anita accepted a glass of milky coffee. "All right. Why? What's your problem with what I'm doing?"

"What does it matter how I feel about what you're doing?" Beneath this pleasant tone, Anita was afraid she was giving way to the hostility she was trying to conceal. "I mean, so many people come through our hotel I couldn't possibly have an opinion on everything they're doing."

"Of course you could. And unless you're a fool, you do have an opinion." She took a large gulp from her glass and banged it on the small table between them.

"Okay, I'm a fool." Anita quickly realized just how tired she was of this woman.

"I don't believe it." Jean sipped her coffee. She leaned forward. "I'll tell you what I'm doing."

"I heard what you're doing, remember? You told everyone at breakfast."

"Ah." Jean leaned back and smiled at her. "So that's it. I was indiscreet."

"Very good." Anita was impressed. "Very quick of you."

"All right. Yes, I'm indiscreet. Look at me." She held her arms out wide, as though calling on everyone there to take a good look at this large, brash American woman dressed in plain rough cotton. "I could hardly be otherwise. I'd look ridiculous pretending to be modest and self-effacing."

Anita began to laugh. "You're right about that." She began to like Jean for her honesty.

"And what I'm doing is not quiet and self-effacing. It can't be. Too much is at stake. Certainly I will have to be careful when I get to Thailand, but this work is important. People there in Burma need us to notice them, to hear them when they call for help."

"I don't disagree, Jean." Anita let her camera rest on her lap.

"So, it's only the indiscretion?"

It was a fair question. What exactly did Anita feel about this loud, brash woman who spoke openly about a risky, illegal plan to enter a foreign country, possibly endangering not only herself but anyone associated with her, especially the villagers she was supposed to be helping, and the laborers who were going to be helping her cross the border?

"Well?" Jean clasped her hands on her knees and tilted her chin upward.

"How did you get into this?"

"I have a colleague from Burma who talked to me one day about their hardships. The medical conditions are deplorable. I thought I could help. That's all there is to it."

Anita waited. There had to be more to this, even if Jean wasn't aware of it, or didn't want to admit it.

"They're Christians, Baptists, actually," Jean added, "and that's not a good thing to be over there. She rarely hears from her family or even about them indirectly."

"Does she plan to go back?"

"Oh, no, it's much too dangerous for her and her family. And besides there's nothing there for her."

"What about you?" Anita asked.

"Me?" She laughed. "Oh, I'll be all right. If they catch me, they'll just try to frighten me and throw me out."

Anita couldn't help smiling at the idea of a slight Burmese soldier trying to frighten the sturdy Jean. It was a comic image, but not realistic—she'd be met with weapons if she was spotted and soldiers who would weigh their actions against the unanswerable question—would foreign governments really care what happened to her. "So you're going in her stead."

"Yes. The family has moved away from the village—they've been driven into the jungle."

"So what good will you be?"

"Do you have any idea what the conditions are? They need medicine and help setting up a clinic, and—"

"I got it," Anita said, breaking in as Jean's voice rose and she sat bolt upright, her eyes widening as her outrage grew. "I got it."

"But you disapprove." She eyed Anita. "Or at least you think it's foolish."

Anita wasn't sure how she wanted to answer this question. The extent of her ambivalence surprised her. "It doesn't matter what I think. You and your friends lived through it the first time, so you'll probably live through it the second time."

"Living through it is the easy part."

Jean marched off, swinging her arms forward and back as she strode down the hill, head high, legs outstretched. It was odd, Anita thought, that even though Jean had insisted on telling her more about her plans, reviewing her earlier success, Anita felt more troubled than ever. And what did she mean about living through it being the easy part? Well, she meant what she said. It wasn't Anita's business, and she wasn't going to make it so.

Anita resumed her walk up Lighthouse Road. Near the top, on the left, was the lane to the small Balabhadrakali Temple. She hadn't meant to take it—of course, she never meant to go anywhere in particular when she set off to photograph—but its tidy look, recently swept, drew her. She turned onto the lane and began sighting her camera. It was still early, and the morning sun was soft on the red soil. Most of the tourists wouldn't be up and about for another hour or more.

The wall along the left side of the lane opened onto a platform, where a set of steep steps ushered devotees down into the temple compound proper, which had been partly dug out of the surrounding hillside. It had been quite the event four years ago when the digging began and was completed in time for the annual festival.

Below her Anita could see the temple priests finishing up after the morning puja. The last devotee was long gone; a sweeper was swinging her reed broom rhythmically over the hard-packed dirt ground, building a little pile of debris; two children played nearby, leaping up to reach a root sticking out of the steep walls—its bright iron-red soil still rising straight upward, not yet melted under decades of monsoons. Across from Anita, almost at eye level, a path led into a grove of trees, the morning light flickering through the branches like an invitation to a magical, secret world. Anita sighted her camera, manipulated the lens, and into view came a woman in a sari. She came down the path, then jerked her head up and to the side, as though looking over her shoulder at the place she had just left. She drew the end of her sari from her shoulder up and over her head. The pallu covered her head and draped down over her forehead, so that as she leaned over, following the path along the edge of the compound wall, her face was hidden from view. She looked up when she came to a break in a wall opening onto Lighthouse Road.

Anita squinted through the lens and snapped the shutter several times, but the woman disappeared before Anita was satisfied. She lowered the camera and stared at the hole in the wall where the sari-clad figure had passed through. The woman looked vaguely like one of the guests at Hotel Delite, but Anita didn't recall seeing Candy in a sari that morning, or any other morning since her arrival last week. This Western woman, if such she was, tied the sari well, draping the pallu over her head, concealing her hair and part of her face. The dappled light distorted the color of her bare arms. Anita looked across the compound to where the woman had emerged. There were a number of private homes back in there, small houses that belonged to local fishermen or tradespeople, now pressed by hotels climbing the hillside and shops popping up along the road. It wasn't an area she knew intimately, since she'd had no reason to explore it. Apparently there was also a path down to other hotels and the beach. Anita reminded herself she shouldn't be surprised at that—the resort was changing daily, with new guesthouses going up, restaurants expanding, lanes branching off into old rice paddies.

Anita lowered the camera. A light breeze ruffled the branches of the palms above, the smell of the dirt rose around her, musty, thick, sensuous. She stepped away from the platform, where she was about to descend into the temple compound, and looked about her. No one was nearby to comment on what she had seen, to say yes, that probably was a Western woman coming up from the beach or a hotel.

"You can always tell an Indian woman," a man once told her. "By the way she walks, just by the way she walks."

I wonder if that's true, Anita thought. She turned again to where the woman had passed through to the road. I can't tell. I can't tell if that was an Indian or a Westerner. She concealed too much.

"Nothing here today, madam." A bearer hurried up to her with a pile of colorful folded cloths on his head. He nodded to the empty temple compound, then swung open a gorgeous red-striped cloth. "This good wrap. Good for walking to beach modestly, for shading the sun, for lying on the sand. Look, such colors!" He flipped open another one he had been carrying, laying it across his forearm, keeping the stack balanced on his head.

"Sorry, I'm not shopping right now." She introduced herself and his face turned gloomy.

"So much competition." He deftly refolded the wraps and draped them over his forearm again. "Few peddlers in Varkala but also few tourists. One resort is like another, but for size. So I am coming here. My family is still—" He broke off when he saw another likely prospect farther down the lane. He hurried down to the cluster of women, calling out his wares as he went, but the women ignored him.

Below, Emily separated herself from the crowd of women and entered the temple compound, turning in at the original gate.

She held a piece of folded paper in her left hand and fanned herself with a hat in her right. When she reached the cement platform on which the temple stood, she stopped and looked around uncertainly. No one paid any attention to her—the sweeper, the priest tidying up, the children playing, and a workman who came from behind the temple with a pair of bamboo rods. Anita started down the steps, which brought her to the foot of the temple.

"Is it open now?" Emily spoke directly to the priest as he walked toward the now-closed doors of the inner sanctum, but Anita knew he didn't speak English and probably wasn't paying much attention anyway.

"Come on, Emily." The calls came from a group of four women waiting near the gate. They too were guests at Hotel Delite, all five of them bunking together in Room 8, the largest room available at the hotel, and the one usually filled by a family or a group of backpackers. This group looked like a medley of professional women who could easily have afforded single rooms with private baths.

"The morning puja is over," Anita said when she reached Emily. "Morning and evening pujas are the only times to see the image."

"Oh." Emily turned to Anita, then looked around the compound. The flowers left by devotees on the temple shrines raised on small platforms at the cardinal points were beginning to sag in the heat, and someone had left an empty water bottle by the gateway. "I was talking to some girls from Australia outside a café on the beach and they said this was a really pretty temple, so I thought I'd come take a look." She glanced upward at the brightly painted frieze. It was a pretty temple, especially now, since the annual festival had begun this week—it was the main event of the year—and the temple had been freshly painted and decorated with lights and garlands of palm strips strung across the facade.

"If you come this evening, maybe between five and eight o'clock, you'll see the temple the way we think of temples—with lots of activity and music." Anita turned to the empty compound. "This isn't what a temple really is—just a pretty building in a compound."

Emily repeated the time and nodded as she did so.

"Are you interested in Hinduism?"

Emily shrugged. "I'm mostly just curious. We're trying to see as much as we can. We have this really cheap ticket that lets us see seven countries in seven weeks, so we're really trying to pack it all in and still have some fun." She broke into a huge smile and turned back to the gate. "We were on our way to get beach chairs when I thought I'd make a detour to the temple, but I guess I'll have to wait until tonight. Back to the beach." She waved goodbye and headed out to the lane, hurrying after her friends, who had started down the hill without her. Anita watched her go, then turned to the sweeper.

"Lots of tourists this year?"

The sweeper straightened up, pressed her open hand against the small of her back as she stretched one way, then another, and tipped her head toward Anita. She had the eyes of a woman who had a good nature but would quickly grow tired of foolishness. "The usual."

"Do they bother you?"

The woman glanced at the gate where Emily had passed through, shrugged. "They come, they look, they try to sneak photos of Kali, they get in the way, but what do they know? It is their karma to be born so far away from Kali. This moment here might save them from being reborn a dog in a future life, so who am I to complain? Let Kali decide who to bless."

An hour before noon Anita strolled down the lane toward her

gallery. The beach had filled up—she could catch glimpses of the sand from the higher lanes behind some of the hotels—dotted with colorful umbrellas and towels, the occasional dog wandering among the tourists sunning themselves, hoping for a handout, or at least a forgotten remnant of a snack. The mere sight of the animals made Anita cringe—who knew where they'd come from and how sick they might be. The few dog owners she knew around here didn't let their dogs wander free.

Anita unlocked the corrugated shutter of her photography gallery and gave a tug, sending it sliding upward. The expected blast of heat bowled past her as she climbed up onto the platform and began the process of opening up. She heard the familiar sound of Peeru's feet running down the lane.

"You are late this morning, madam." Peeru stood on the lane, leaning against the platform, looking both injured and insulted. "The tourists will pass you by."

"It won't be the first time, Peeru." Anita came toward him carrying two easels, one in each hand. They were light enough for her to manage, but the minute Peeru saw this he jumped up and took one from her. She could never remember how Peeru had come to attach himself to her and the gallery, but he was a devoted boy and she had come to trust and like him, though she knew nothing about him.

"Am I sitting here? Do I not have arms and hands?"

Anita unlocked the small, air-conditioned closet, and left him to it. Settling into a chair, she watched him drag out easels, set up photographs, pull out bins with more photographs, set up a small table with a cash box, arrange brochures about interesting art venues in the area, and then grab a reed broom and begin sweeping the entire place. For a boy barely twelve years old, he had enormous diligence—instead of wearing himself out or growing bored, he stuck to a task until it was done to his satisfaction. And sometimes he was far pickier than Anita ever was. She liked Peeru—his good nature, his eagerness to learn, his old-fashioned dismay at the way Western men and women behaved, his great care with anything considered her property.

"What's the rush?" Anita said, looking at her watch. She was suddenly aware that she was hungry.

"We must be ready, madam. Ready."

"For what?" Anita glanced around at the lane that was empty in both directions.

Peeru had such hopes for her career—he was as bad as some of her relatives, who couldn't decide if they wanted her to hide her photography and get into something respectable or at least make a go of it so they wouldn't be so embarrassed when asked about her. It was a dilemma her relatives could not solve, swinging wildly between the stark, sharp poles of mortification at the sight of her camera and unbridled ambition that someone, anyone, in the family might be a success in the arts, and that Anita might be a success at anything. Unfortunately, Anita had no ambition to succeed and even less to try something else. The success she did have—selling her photos on the Internet—she kept to herself. It would never do for her family to take her seriously. That would take all the fun out of life.

"Today is not that sort of day," Anita said.

"What sort of day is it?" Peeru looked concerned, as though he had missed something important.

"Today is a *vai nokki* day." People watching is my favorite pastime, Anita would have added, if Peeru had looked just a little less disapproving. "All right, Peeru, I'm hungry."

"Yes, madam. I will get."

"I think today I feel like fish."

"Yes, madam. I will get."

"Lots of fish."

"Yes, madam. I will get."

"And fruit. Lots of fruit. Today is a fruit day."

"Yes, madam, I will get."

Anita pulled out her purse, rummaged among the coins and paper, and pulled out a wad of rupees. She smoothed out the bills and handed them to Peeru. "And tea. I think I would like some tea also."

He nodded vigorously and ran off. Anita heard a grumbling nearby.

"I heard that!" she called out, not leaving her seat. An old man stepped onto the lane from the next shop and walked toward her, then sat on the platform, stretching out his legs into the lane. "I heard that. He has never stolen from me."

"He is just waiting until you give him a big sum. Then you will see. He will be gone forever."

Anita laughed. "I see you are in a good mood, Chinnappa. Tailoring is profitable today?"

He threw up his hands. "Shivayashivoo! Pants, pants, pants. I make the same every day. And for what? Do they wear these things when they are at home? No, no, I am certain they do not."

"But why not? What an odd idea, Chinnappa." Anita leaned forward, waiting to hear what he would say.

"Here all is sunshine and soft sand. The foreigners sweat like standing in a shower. Such weather is too much for them, and our clothes barely make it tolerable for them. Such pants are cool and comfortable. But where there is cold—a place where they must wear sweaters and even coats over them, I am told—will these pants be enough? Imagine, such cold! Will they be warm in what I make for them? No, never. They forget what their own country is like. And in this way they waste money." And in case someone might not know how Chinnappa felt about wasting money, he flicked his fingers and added a few choice phrases under his breath.

"So you have too much work and not enough leisure," Anita said.

"Precisely so." The old man leaned back against the wall and closed his eyes. In a moment he began to snore.

By late afternoon Anita had eaten lunch, had a nap, sold a few small photographs, and settled in for a quiet hour at the end of the business day. Those who had fled the beach, beaten down by the midday sun, were making their way back again, tempted by the softening shadows and gentle waves. This was also visiting time.

Tourists who had earlier purchased something from her or another vendor liked to stop and chat, fulfilling the human need to be connected even to a stranger in a strange land while on vacation. Anita often received postcards or chatty letters from some who spent one or two days choosing the right photograph to send home to friends or keep for themselves. She explained at length where this or that image was taken, what it meant, if it had any meaning, and how she felt about it. These contacts, by postcard, sometimes by email, less often by snail mail, rarely continued past six months. Those that did usually came with requests that she could not fulfill—research in a private library, a small purchase, tracking down an ex-pat in India—and left her wondering if the tourist had forgotten who she was.

The more interesting postcards sometimes made it onto a bulletin board that was propped up on an easel at the back. Tourists sometimes spent a good half hour reading the notes, commenting on the people who passed through Kovalam and their views of it. Sometimes a visitor from England recognized a name from an encounter along the trail of tourism, or a guest on her way home came across a note from a friend who had originally encouraged her to visit South India. Those were fun—the discovery of a mutual friend thousands of miles away.

She was rambling through these thoughts when a group of tourists clambered onto the gallery platform and began rummaging among her shrink-wrapped photographs. Anita lowered her newspaper, to give the illusion of approachability in case anyone had a question. When a woman about her own age, wrapped in a silky sarong and overblouse, held up a photograph of Munnar and turned to Anita, she rose and walked over to answer questions. The purchase was made, and Anita accepted payment. She handed over a few rupees in change, and met the surprised gaze of one of the guests at Hotel Delite.

"Hello, Marge."

"I didn't realize this was your place." She looked about her, an amused look on her face. "I heard about it from a sari shop at the other end of the beach."

"They said nice things, I hope."

"Sure did." Marge attempted to give a little bow, but unbending seemed to be not her style. She strolled over to a bin of photographs and watched another browser flip through the offerings. Apparently not finding anything to her liking, she turned to the bulletin board, and began to read the postcards. They were fun, Anita thought as she glanced at her, before turning to another sales transaction. Before she was finished she heard a crash—the easel holding the bulletin board had fallen against the wall. In a second Peeru grabbed the easel and repositioned it. But that didn't concern Anita—it was the look on Marge's face that held her.

"Marge?" Anita rose from her chair, a wad of rupees in her hand. "Marge, are you all right?"

Marge turned at the sound of her name, but her eyes were unfocused, settling on Anita but not recognizing her. Her face was stretched in a look of bewilderment and shock, then gradually collapsed into fear—that was the only word for it, fear.

"Marge?" Anita whispered. In a moment, Marge seemed to

awaken to where she was and whom she was with.

"Oh, I'm sorry, really." She took a step back and looked around. "I guess I wasn't paying attention. Sorry."

"It's fine, no harm done." Anita touched her arm. "You just looked a bit confused. Is everything all right?"

"Yes, no. I mean . . . Is there an Internet place around here?"

"Just down the lane a bit." Anita nodded to the lane. "Not far."

"It's just that . . ."

"Yes?"

Marge stared at her. "What?"

"Something wrong?"

"Nothing. Sorry, nothing. I'm sure it's the heat, and I'm so tired. I took a trip into Trivandrum on the bus, and it really speeds right along. I began to wonder if it was safe. I'm just rattled, is all." She gave Anita a wan smile, then turned away, stumbling awkwardly down from the platform, a mere ten inches above the lane. Anita noticed that she went in the direction for the Internet café, and kept looking up at the signs as she walked along before disappearing on the other side of a wall of hanging, shimmering handmade goods. Anita reluctantly returned to her customers.

Later, when she was again alone in her gallery, she turned to Peeru. "That woman who was here earlier. The one who knocked over the easel with the bulletin board. Did you see what happened?"

Peeru gave her his most serious look. "Yes, she is coming and looking and going. Not buying." He hung his head in sorrow; he seemed to consider failed sales his personal responsibility.

"Did she say anything?"

He shook his head.

"What did she look at?"

Peeru gave this considerable thought, then walked over to the bin of black and white photos matted and shrink-wrapped. "Here she is looking."

Anita joined him at the bin, and slowly flipped through them. Most were seascapes, some of rocks and sand—more abstract than scenic—and a few of the people she had met in the resort. "I don't think this was it."

Peeru looked about him, then skipped over to the bulletin board with its riot of colorful postcards. "Here! She is looking here." He was now pleased with himself and stood like a guard, with his feet close together and his arms rigid at his sides.

Anita again joined him. "Something here really upset her." She scanned the postcards, catching a name, a phrase, recalling a fleeting friendship. "But what? They're all so innocuous."

CHAPTER THREE

The evening sounds were all around her now—the call of touts trying to entice strolling tourists into their restaurants, the hawkers hoping to make one more sale before giving up for the day, the soft, whispered whine of the beggar woman. Anita closed her eyes, letting the sounds wash over her.

"You could easily be mugged," a familiar voice said. Anita opened her eyes. "If a man were so inclined." Anita gave him a broad smile.

"On a night like tonight?" She pushed herself away from the wall opposite her gallery, now closed and shuttered. She'd been passing the time earlier chatting with the bookseller whose tiny store with its meager offerings on the second floor opposite her often left him time to watch the foreigners walking by. He gave up just before seven o'clock, after a day of poor sales, and went home. "At least I will get a meal and no one will ask me in French or German for a book about the fishermen in English."

Anand returned the smile, stood close to her for a moment, then turned away. "Let's eat at the new restaurant in Bamboo Village. I think they're having music tonight."

"Good idea." They turned away from the beach and headed inland along the lane.

"I stopped at the hotel, just in case you returned there," Anand said as they passed other couples out strolling. Anita felt a little clutch in her stomach. She prayed he hadn't run into Auntie

Meena. Anita was mystified by Meena's reaction to him.

"I went back earlier, had a quick shower, and came back to the gallery." She ducked beneath a row of swaying blouses hanging along the edge of the lane. "You ran into Auntie Meena, didn't you?" I might as well get it over with, she thought.

"She doesn't like me very much, does she?"

It was inconceivable to Anita that anyone could not like Anand. He was gorgeous, sweet, kind, but also he had a sense of humor, knew his own mind, and liked the way the world was changing around him. He was courteous, in a surprising way, to Auntie Meena, even appearing to be courting her in the manner one used with a new and important relative. But she would not warm up to him. She took whatever he offered her with a careful right hand, barely letting whatever it was move deeper into her hand than the tips of her fingers; her eyes flitted over the object, and around Anand's face, but she never settled her gaze on his eyes. The whole experience left Anita as unsettled as she imagined Anand to be, though he gave no sign.

At first, she had hoped Anand hadn't noticed, but that was too much to ask. Anyone would have to be blind not to see how Meena felt about Anand. But why? It stumped Anita, frustrated her, and stunned her. Meena had a stone wall around her when it came to her feelings about him. When they first met, Anita and Anand, he was only a friend of a cousin's husband, a man who was invited to attend a family ritual at the end of Sarasvati Puja this past October. Meena had even consulted him at length about how the puja might affect her niece, Anita's, success as a photographer, and took consolation and hope from Anand's replies. And then came the change in attitude. Anita and Anand lost themselves in a quiet conversation on the veranda, and when it was over, she looked up to catch just a glimpse—but an undeniable one—of Meena's look of distress and disapproval.

"She can be moody, Anand. Sometimes she doesn't like me either."

Anand laughed. "Nice try, Anita. She adores you; that's why she doesn't like me."

Anita gave him an exasperated look. "Well, just imagine what will happen to her if I start taking her advice. Think of it! She'll have to become circumspect in what she actually says to me if there's a chance I'll really do it. This could ruin her life."

"Now you sound as odd as Meena," he said, shaking his head. "Over here." He led her along a sapling fence defining the grounds of a miniature village comprising individual cottages set around a pond and fountain, a bridge crossing a narrow channel, and an open-air restaurant with a small stage. The line was short, and they joined it.

"Nonsense," a large woman said, pushing past the line to the lane outside the restaurant. "You worry over nothing, Marge. I refuse to waste time on this."

Jean stepped onto the lane and looked both ways. Anita was about to offer a greeting but decided against it when she saw the look on Jean's face, a mix of exasperation and determination. Behind her came Marge, looking just as scattered as she had earlier in the day. "I don't feel very well, Jean. I think we should be careful—you never know."

"This is ridiculous. I came here to enjoy myself, and I'm going to do just that." She spun around and leaned in close to her friend. "And so are you. I see no reason to do otherwise. Now come on." She spun around again and marched off, pulling on the sleeves of the aqua sweater draped over her shoulders. Marge took a few tentative steps after her, paused, watching her friend walk away, then took a deep breath and fell into step behind her. Jean drew farther ahead, but Marge kept walking at her slower pace. Anita watched until both disappeared from view.

"What?" Anita turned to Anand. "Did you say something?" "I said several somethings. Mostly about food."

"Oh, sorry. I was thinking about those two women." Anand followed Anita's gaze to where the women had walked into the night. "They're staying at Hotel Delite."

"Do you always worry so much about your hotel guests?" The tables and chairs of the restaurant were reminiscent of a North Indian safari, all canvas and dark wood and linen under the moonlight. Voices were swallowed by the evening air, and the slightest drift of a breeze brought fragrances so rich they left the guests feeling intoxicated. Anita let them mix with the fragrances of her meal and felt enveloped in their warmth and beauty.

Anita pulled her thoughts together and looked up at Anand. "I'm awful company tonight, aren't I? I can barely pay attention, and, you know, Anand, I've been looking forward to having dinner with you all week."

"So what am I playing second fiddle to? You're not still fretting about your aunt, are you?"

Anita shook her head—she'd put Meena out of her mind for a while. After all, life was here and now and it was a beautiful, glorious evening. She leaned back in her chair. A waiter hurried by, hoisting a tray bearing three bottles of beer. Another waiter swooped up to their table and grasped her plate. Just as she opened her mouth to protest, she changed her mind, nodded, and the plate was scooped away. "Delicious, even if I didn't eat every morsel."

"So it's not the food."

"What? Oh, no, not the food." She leaned forward, her hands between her knees. "I heard the oddest thing this morning, at breakfast, and I guess it's stuck in my head."

"You live in a hotel with a lot of foreigners, Anita. Of course you hear lots of odd things at breakfast. What was so odd this time?" He continued to work on his curry, making a tidy ball of rice and vegetables with his right hand that he then popped into his mouth. He was a slow eater, taking his time as he savored each item, now and then interjecting a comment on the ingredients into a conversation on books or the foundation for a new hotel.

"A woman said she was going to be smuggled into Burma—to do charitable work in a village." Anita spoke softly, aware that diners at nearby tables were chatting away but not loudly.

Anand raised his eyes and studied her but kept on eating. "She's done it before, she said."

"Stupid woman." He popped another rice ball into his mouth. "If the military catches her . . ."

"Yes, I agree. But maybe I'm just timid." Anita leaned back and studied her hands, her long fingers and short nails, kept that way so they wouldn't interfere with camera work or make a rattling sound when she typed. She hated long nails—they always seemed to get in the way. "Maybe it's really courageous to be doing what she's doing."

"If it were courageous, she wouldn't be bragging about it at breakfast." He pushed his chair away, stood up, and went in search of a sink to wash his hands in. The waiter swooped by again, cleared the dishes, and returned with a brush for a quick cleaning of the table before dropping in front of them two dessert menus.

"Did you mean that? You don't think something like that is courageous?" Anita asked when he returned.

"Do you?"

Anita paused, watched the waiter usher another party of diners, this time three men and a woman, to a table at the far end of the open grounds. "No, I don't. I'd love to do something like that because I like adventure, but I think she's taking risks she can't possibly understand. She could be getting the villagers into trouble they can't handle."

"But if they're willing to take the risk?"

Anita considered this. "I wish I knew, Anand, I wish I knew. I mean—Burma is a dangerous place for those who aren't on the right side. And no one with any conscience wants to be on the same side as the generals." She shrugged. "I didn't speak to her closely, so I don't really know what she knows or doesn't know."

"You're very conservative, aren't you?" He gave her a warm smile, not expecting an answer.

"Some risks are foolish. If it were me, I'd be getting supplies to villagers but not going in—the villagers could pay a high price for that kind of help." She sighed. "I don't know anything about it, anyway, do I?"

"Not a thing."

CHAPTER FOUR

The music drifted down the hill, meeting Anita and Anand as they strolled along the back lanes of Kovalam, along the narrow canal, over the short bridge, and up a set of steps onto the hillside.

"I thought the puja would be over by now," Anand said, following Anita along the narrow path.

"They're not very strict," Anita said, turning around and glancing at his white slacks and blue short-sleeved shirt. She was wearing a light yellow-print salwar khameez, so her outfit was more acceptable to a temple than his. Far more, she knew. But for this temple, tolerance was a necessity.

"Meaning, it's not like some of the temples I'm used to." He winked and smiled.

"Something like that, I suppose. It's an Ezhava temple, founded by someone's grandmother, with lots of descendants among the fishing families. Shall we?"

He nodded and they followed the cement path past a number of guesthouses and little shops, some still open and illuminated by small hanging lanterns or even a row of candles set out on the counter. The shopkeepers nodded and smiled as they passed, but none took them for customers. The music grew louder as they reached the lane running up to the temple, past the vacant lot where speakers harangued the faithful to vote, actors performed traditional dances to jaded peasants and confused foreigners. Up ahead Anita could see a number of Westerners lining the stairs as they watched the events within the compound below.

The two moved among the crowd until they had wended their way across the ground to the left side of the temple, near the small block of offices. Here Anita could view the people up on the lane and the stairs watching the puja winding down, as well as the foreigners gathered among the devotees. Anand stuffed his hands in his pockets and watched attentively while Anita scanned the crowd looking for familiar faces. She nodded and smiled at some villagers she recognized, including one whose relatives occasionally worked for Hotel Delite, and counted the number of foreigners who looked like new arrivals, craning their necks to see around those standing in front of them.

"That's one from the hotel," Anita said, nudging Anand. She looked back toward the crowd, where Emily had moved to the front, her hands pressed together in anjali, her eyes on the young priest. Just in front of her were two others Anita recognized— Jean and Marge. Jean couldn't seem to stand still, moving from one side to the other, her camera poised just below her chin, not satisfied with the pictorial quality of the scene in front of her. Finally, she jerked away from Marge and pushed her way up to the outer pillar. Bracing herself against the stone, she raised her camera and began to take photos of the priest as he turned from the inner sanctum, a small oil lamp in his hand.

He walked along the crowd of devotees, holding out the flame so that they might brush their outstretched hands over the flame and then over their eyes, purifying themselves. Jean and Marge ignored the lamp, but Emily stepped forward and let her hands rest over the flame for one or two seconds before raising them to her eyes. She looked so earnest, watching the priest as he moved away, then turning her gaze again to the inner sanctum. There, in all her finery, sat Balabhadrakali, Kali as a young girl, a form of the deity rarely seen, yet long the presiding deity here.

It struck Anita then that Emily had the same warm openness as that of the Kali image, a youthfulness and sweetness she hadn't noticed before. Her round, smooth face matched that of Kali, her dark eyes also like those of Kali, and her warm, sweet smile, again that of Kali. As Anita watched, Emily seemed to grow younger, more youthful in body and expression. Anita took a step toward her, drawn by what she was seeing. She opened her mouth to speak, to draw Anand's attention to the scene, but found no words. Perhaps there were none.

The priest finished his circuit of the devotees but at the last minute a hand reached out and swiped the air above the flame. Candy had found her way in at the last minute. She had a bright smile, and glanced over at Marge and Jean, giving them a vigorous wave, then what looked like a giggle and twist of her shoulders. What a lark, she seemed to be saying.

"I think we should go," Marge said, looking around. Anita and Anand were standing a few feet away, but as Marge and Jean had moved to the back of the crowd, Marge had become more insistent, until their argument was easily overheard.

"Oh, stop it. This is too annoying. You're being ridiculous." Jean thrust out an elbow to her side, forcing Marge away, and went on studying the record of shots on her digital camera. "I really want to get this. I'm not coming back here, you know." Jean marched off toward the rear of the temple, toward the smaller shrines now covered with flowers from the earlier pujas. She stopped, held the camera to her eye, and snapped, then marched forward two steps before stopping for another shot. Jean was a recorder of events, not a seeker of a beautiful or moving image—practicality rather than creativity ruled her photography.

Marge took a step, then hesitated, and slowly looked around

her. She was still spooked, it seemed to Anita, still edgy the way she'd been at the gallery in the afternoon. Anita kept well behind her, moving a few inches as Marge moved, so she could observe her and remain unnoticed. She glanced up when a wave caught her eye. She was surprised to find Anand watching her, waving his hand in a wide arc.

"Remember me?"

"Sorry." Anita blushed and joined him by the administration building.

"What was that all about?" Anand took another glance at Marge before turning to Anita.

"That woman—her name's Marge—she's staying at Hotel Delite."

"Didn't we see them earlier?" He turned again, tipping his head one way, then another. "At the restaurant. Yes?"

"We did. But I saw her even earlier also. She came into the gallery this afternoon, and she saw something—I think in the postcards on the bulletin board. Whatever it was, it really upset her."

"Did she say what it was?" Anand pulled a white molded plastic chair away from the administration building and pushed it toward Anita, then drew another over for himself. He pushed it back closer to the wall, and sat down. Anita slid back into her own seat. A few feet away sat the temple astrologer, a few members of the temple Board of Directors, and an elderly devotee who had donated the oil for the evening puja.

"No, not a word. Whatever it was, it really confused her, startled her, I guess." She sighed and looked out on the crowd of devotees, only a dozen or so remaining. "I went through the postcards as soon as I could."

"Did you find anything in them?"

Anita shook her head. "Not a thing that was obvious. At least to me."

"Maybe it was just a coincidence that she was looking at the bulletin board when she became upset. It could have been someone passing by on the lane, or perhaps she overheard something." Anand crossed his legs and rested his arms on the chair. For him, it would seem, the problem was solved.

"Maybe," Anita said. "But it was odd."

"Isn't this cool?" Candy rushed up to her with a handful of folded leaves—prasadam, the food cooked for and offered to the deity, then distributed to the faithful. "The priest just gave me these." She shoved one at Anita, Anand waved her off. Candy hurried over to Emily, who took a leaf envelope, cradled it in her hands, and just stared at it. "You can eat it, Emily. It's good. I've had some." Emily's friends waved Candy away, like a gnat. They seemed to be listening to Emily but abruptly turned and headed up the steps, leaving Emily behind. Candy hurried after Marge and Jean, still talking loudly.

"Don't be silly," Jean said, when Candy stuck out her hand with just one envelope left.

"I didn't think she'd take it," Anita whispered to Anand. "She's like you."

Anand raised an eyebrow. "She's an American."

"You know what I mean."

"Well, perhaps. At least I hope you meant that as a compliment."

"Always." Anita smiled, thinking of Marge and Anand in the same boat, so to speak. There are two sorts of people who never take prasadam at this temple—Catholics and now other devout Christians, and Brahmans, especially Nambudiri Brahmans, the highest of that caste, and considered to be the most ritualistically pure even after centuries of interaction with others. Anand was one of them.

"Hmm, I wonder how I should feel about that," Anand said, trying to suppress a smile. "There are a lot of assumptions in that statement. Okay, tell me this. Would you take communion in a Catholic church?"

Anita laughed and shook her head. "No. I used to go with my dad to mass, when I was very young, but I was never expected to be part of that. He was pretty angry with the church."

"But you'll take anything a Hindu priest offers," Anand said, his intonation partly a question. "Any priest."

"You're dead on, Anand. Dead on."

The devotees were all gone now, the oil lamps being snuffed out and the lanterns removed, and the remnants of the evening being swept into little piles. At the top of the stairs Candy and Emily chatted a moment, then both moved away into the night. Anita and Anand made their way slowly up the steps and along the narrow lane to Lighthouse Road. They stood for a moment at the step onto the road, now fading into darkness, the shops farther up the road shuttered, and the others closer to the shore in the process of closing. Voices drifted on the night air, a single autorickshaw whined away in the night. Anita and Anand turned to walk down the hill.

"Don't you ever get tired of it?" Anand said. He waved an upward open palm at a row of shops and a hotel along the lane, and a sign for a restaurant perched on the edge of the road.

"Of what?"

"Living in a hotel, talking to foreigners, never knowing the same people one month to the next."

She could feel his eyes on her, though he seemed to be looking straight ahead. But every now and then she saw his head turn just a bit to the left, his eyes fix on her for a second or more, before he turned his sight back to the road. She wondered if there was a right answer to this question, if there was something more behind it, or another, more important question hitched to it like a toy train.

"It's my life, and even if it seems strange, I have chosen it." She heard a pebble tumble down the road, and wondered if someone else was walking nearby. A dog trotted along the lane going up the hill, slowed and began to slink along the shoulder, moving cautiously away from them. "I came here to help my aunt after her husband died—that was quite a few years ago."

"Doesn't she have a daughter?"

"In America. She couldn't stay here after the funeral." She laughed. "I can imagine what you must think of that."

"Perhaps I'm not as judgmental as you think."

Anita stopped walking and turned to him. For a long minute she studied him, the way his short dark hair had only the slightest wave, one that caught the light and brought out the brown tinge in his hair, the way his soft jowels reminded her of ancient cave paintings in Tamilnad—pictures of men and women surrounded by gigantic lotuses—the way his ears and earlobes sat close to his head. "I don't think I've been worrying about you being judgmental in quite that way." She smiled and resumed walking. "But I'm glad to hear it."

"Isn't that one of your guests?" Anand nodded to a woman standing at the stone wall at the end of the road, staring out through the palm trees to the vast Arabian Sea beyond. The resort went to bed early for the most part—villagers went home to their families and a late meal, guards prepared for a long night of listening and nodding off, guests read and planned their next-day adventures. Anita rarely met anyone out late. She studied the woman up ahead, growing uncomfortable with her solitariness at the late hour.

"Her name's Emily. She was at the temple this evening." Anita lowered her voice as they drew near. "Good evening, Emily."

They were right behind her now, but the woman didn't speak or move.

"Emily?" Anita moved closer, leaning in toward the stone wall so she could get a look at her. "Emily? Are you all right?"

Emily blinked and stepped away. "What? Oh, sorry, yes. I'm fine." She gave Anita a weak, sloppy smile and just stared at her.

"Good." Anita stepped away and glanced at Anand. "We're just on our way to the hotel. Will you join us?"

"It's so beautiful here," Emily said.

"Yes, it is." Anita looked out over the sea; she had to agree, it was beautiful. "But it is late, and the resort is pretty much closed now. The night guard wants to lock up the compound. Anand's just going to get his car and go." Anita stepped aside, indicating that Emily should join them for the short walk to the hotel. Whether she was slow to grasp the point, or just sluggish this evening, Emily hesitated, then stepped forward and walked with Anita and Anand down the lane to the hotel.

A few minutes later Anita said goodbye to Anand and locked the office door, ready to lock up the main hotel building and leave everything in the hands of the guard Sanj, and return to her suite over the garage. The only sound was Anand's mini driving up the hill. She reached out her hand to turn off the lights but stopped when a shadow moved. She peered into the darkness and recognized the figure of Emily standing once again, this time in an open window, staring out to sea. Something had happened to her, Anita knew—she could sense it, feel it, she knew it. She had known it the minute she saw her at the temple standing in front of the image.

Anita crossed the sitting area and stood next to Emily. "Do you want anything?"

"Kali isn't at all what I was expecting." Emily stood a few inches shorter than Anita, with her wide dark eyes and shiny pink skin.

"What were you expecting?"

"Something fierce, you know, like the pictures in the guide books—with fangs and blood and gore, that kind of thing."

Anita laughed. "No, she's certainly not like that. Our Kali is sweet."

"She's special. I never understood before how I fit in the world, but I saw it tonight. Kali showed me how I fit. I have a place." Her wide-open face and dark eyes sparkled in the moonlight. "And I owe it all to her. She came to me and called me. Me. Emily Terrapia." She turned again to the sea, placid this night, with the lights of the fishermen lining the horizon, making it look like Kovalam had an opposite shore lined with houses and well-lit streets. When she'd first been here, Anita had sometimes caught herself glancing out at the ocean late at night and thinking how many people were still up over there— until she reminded herself that "over there" was open sea and those lights were the kerosene lanterns the fishermen used to attract schools of fish on their small boats bobbing in the darkness.

Anita gave Emily's shoulder a gentle squeeze. "Good night, Emily."

CHAPTER FIVE

Anita pushed herself up in bed and reached out for her bathrobe. It slid to the floor and she grabbed it and held it up one way then another till she found an armhole, and thrust her arm into it. She heard the thin cotton rip, and she swore lightly under her breath.

The guard called out her name a second time, but not so loud that anyone in the hotel across the lane could hear. By the time she reached the door, she was tying the waist cord. She opened the door and looked into the guard's face, ready to ask him not to wake her except in a dire emergency. But she never got the chance.

"A guest—she is unwell, in great pain and looking most worried. You will come." The guard stepped back to let Anita pass. She slid into her sandals and hurried down the stairs. The moon still lit up the parking area and the interior of the garage bays beneath her small flat; the hotel car was parked along the far end, nearest the coast, in the darkest part of the garage. A small cot was set up nearby, with a blanket neatly folded at the foot. It felt to Anita like she and the guard were the only two people alive in Kovalam, and perhaps that's what life feels like to the seers and prophets of the world—being fully awake while the world around them dozes—she heard only her feet scraping across the lot, her own rapid breathing as her thoughts coalesced around the anxiety in the guard's voice. Sanj was waiting for her inside the hotel. Above her she could hear soft moans.

"Who is it?" she asked Sanj. He stood at the bottom of the staircase, his face still puffy from sleep, looking worried as he glanced upstairs and back at Anita.

"The American nurse, Marge. She is unwell for an hour or more."

"Okay, I'll go up. Is Auntie Meena awake?"

"No, I have not dared . . ." Sanj shook his head.

"That's a blessing. Poor Meena would probably have a stroke." Anita mumbled the last words as she took the first step. "Thanks. Let her sleep."

At the top of the stairs, her mind on what she might find, Anita turned to walk to the left, until she realized her mistake. A sliver of light sparkled along the floor at Room 4, which meant someone else was up at this late hour. Too tired to wonder who it was, Anita turned to the right and Room 6. The door was ajar. Anita pushed it open and looked in. Marge lay on her side, on the twin bed nearest the door, curled up like a woman in cold weather trying to conserve body heat. Out of this bundle came a soft moaning and a twitch as her hands and arms pressed tighter against her stomach.

"Marge? What's going on?" Anita knelt down beside the bed and slipped her fingers around Marge's wrist. Marge's pulse was racing, her breathing uneven, her body soaked in sweat. Anita picked up the phone on the bedside table and ordered the car readied to travel to the only hospital she was sure was open all night—Anandabudhi Hospital near Chokka, on the other side of Trivandrum.

By the time Anita had dressed, Sanj and a maidservant had half-carried, half-dragged Marge down the stairs and settled her in the back of the car. Anita clambered into the front seat, leaning over to keep her hands on Marge lest she tumble off the seat. She had thrashed when the maidservant had tried to arrange seatbelts around her.

"Hurry."

Joseph, the driver, hurried, speeding up the hill, onto the highway and into Trivandrum, through the roundabout, and onto the highway north—a rough drive made tolerable by the driver's skill. Anita barely noticed the potholes he missed, the curves he cut through—she didn't dare take her eyes and hand off Marge. When the sickly woman stopped moaning, Anita half clambered over the seat to check her pulse, nudged her to stay awake, urged her to listen to her. But Marge moaned, sank into silence, protested painfully when prodded. She was sinking, and there was nothing Anita could do about it. The driver honked sharply and swerved around a man sauntering across the road, the car jolted to one side and Marge's head struck the armrest, but she remained unresponsive. Anita ran her hand up and down Marge's arm, urging her to stay awake.

Lights glimmered at the hospital entrance, sparkling on the thick paving stones, brightening a dull black night that enclosed the rest of the world. The driver pulled up close to the door. A guard in red turban, blue military pants, and white shirt with gold buttons and epaulets skipped down the steps to the car, took one look at Marge, and barked out an order. A pair of orderlies appeared with a gurney, lifted Marge onto it, and carried her inside. Anita followed, wondering how long it would take to register her, pay for a membership card, and get a doctor. She'd never been here on an emergency before—just regular medical visits, nothing this extreme. By now Marge was breathing heavily, growing clammy, and barely responsive.

A tall woman in a neatly pressed green sari and matching choli emerged from an office and went immediately to Marge, giving her a cursory examination. She spoke rapidly in Malayalam to the woman clerk at the reception desk, turned to the orderlies and gave them additional orders, then led the way down the long hall into the back of the hospital.

"Oh, shit," Anita mumbled when the clerk asked the patient's name. "I know almost nothing about her." She pulled out her cell phone, flipped it open, and called the hotel. "Poor Auntie Meena. She's probably dreaming about retirement in Australia about now." She glanced at her watch—just after 3:15 A.M. "And I'm going to ruin it all."

"Drink this. Please. For me." Aunt Meena pushed the teacup closer to her niece. Meena was waiting for Anita when she returned from the hospital. Tea and information was Meena's therapy for just about everything—something Anita had learned early on. The two women sat in the hotel office, lighting only a small candle against the thick darkness. Somehow, in the cool of the south Indian winter, when the temperature dips as low as seventy degrees and a hand reaches for a shawl, the flame from the tall, thin candle seemed to give more than just light.

Anita explained her discovery of the woman, her symptoms, and the harrowing trip to the hospital. "The doctor doesn't know what it is, but she thinks Marge will be all right, but she can't be sure."

"Ah." Meena followed this with a heartfelt sigh. "What good is a reassurance if once given it is taken away?"

"Do we have information about who to contact? Did she give us that when she checked in?"

Meena shrugged. "I shall look." She made no move to get up and search out the registration form. "It is a shock, all this terrible business, and so late in the night. Such a bad time for things."

"But good for weddings," Anita said, reaching for the cup.

"Oh, Anita. Must you be so irreverent?"

"A bizarre thought, Auntie, that's all. But haven't you ever wondered about that?" She was tired, physically and emotionally, and that meant she was beginning to babble, saying nothing worth hearing. "This is such a dangerous time of the day, or night, rather, but also the best time for a wedding—just before dawn." She sipped her tea and lowered the cup. "But in America, it's the opposite. Wasn't it F. Scott Fitzgerald who said in the dark night of the soul, it's always three-fifteen in the morning?"

"Oh, Anita, I don't understand you."

"I'm sorry, Auntie. It's anxiety—I'm feeling really rattled."

Meena pulled her bathrobe tight around her. She had responded to Anita's telephone call by throwing herself into activity—rushing to find Marge's passport, rifling through her luggage to locate medications, checking the safety deposit box for any useful information she might have lodged there, scanning her journal and address books for names of relatives and friends who should be notified in case the crisis ended in tragedy. She had all but worn herself out, and was now slumping into exhaustion. The tangle of feelings was beginning to unravel, and Meena's composure with it. "If only it had happened earlier in the evening—we would have reached her sooner."

Anita gave her aunt a warm smile, then paused, with her hand hovering over the teapot. They were on their second pot, going over everything that had happened, everything they had done, anything they might have left undone.

"What? Anita, you are looking at me as though you have seen something unexpected. Did you forget something important?"

"You're right, Auntie. If it had happened earlier in the evening, she would surely have called someone sooner." Anita rested her hand on the still-warm pot, letting her fingers caress the rotund sides and enjoy the heat seeping into her skin.

"It is what always happens, isn't it?" Meena shook her head. "Do you remember the woman who had such terrible stomach pain some years ago? She was too embarrassed to speak to anyone about it until she fell on the ground in front of the taxi stand."

"That was appendicitis, though."

"It was the same reluctance to speak up. Are they ashamed of sickness, these foreigners?"

"I don't think it's the same thing, Auntie."

"Not appendicitis?" Meena leaned back in her chair and sighed. "That is disappointing." Suddenly she lurched forward. "Where did she eat last night? Oh no, not here. I'm sure it wasn't here. Oh, Shivayashivoo!"

Anita reached across the table and patted Meena's arm. "It's all right, Auntie. She didn't eat here last night, I'm sure of it. I ran into her and Jean outside the Bamboo Village Restaurant. You know, that new resort with the little huts for rooms? They were leaving just as Anand and I were arriving."

"Oh, that is such a relief."

"Yes." Anita paused as she frowned into her teacup. "Auntie, I thought Jean and Marge had checked in together as friends."

"Friends! Like twins they have been, consulting each other over every aspect of their vacation. Did they not spend an hour yesterday morning, an entire hour, reviewing the best route to Suchindram Temple, and should they go today or tomorrow? An hour! And there is only one route! Yes, they are indeed close."

"Yes, and they had dinner together last night. But Marge didn't go to Jean last night. You don't think Jean is also . . ." Anita stood up. "I'll be right back." Meena folded her arms on the table and lay her head down.

"I want to cry, Anita. I want to cry."

"Don't give in just yet, Auntie," Anita said as she trotted out of the office.

Anita slipped the master key into the lock of Room 5 and swung open the door. This too was a room with twin beds pushed together in the center of the room, with windows facing the ocean and a small balcony outside a center door. Anita flicked the light switch, but she didn't really need it. Dawn was at hand—the most dangerous time of day in Hinduism—and she often understood why. Transition, time for those who need the night to hide away from the daylight, time for change which brings both good and bad, time for wariness.

Anita stared at the neatly made beds—neither one looked like it had been used, not even for an afternoon nap the day before. She went at once to the armoire, opened the doors, and glanced over the carefully hung clothing, the toiletries set out on the lower shelf, the cardboard box taped shut. She closed the doors and turned to the luggage sitting on its side next to the armoire. When she felt how light it was, she lost hope of finding anything inside, but opened it anyway, laying it out on the bed. The only items in the pockets were an extra washcloth, a few loose paper clips, some hard candy in cellophane wrapping, and a collapsible tripod. She didn't know if she should be relieved or disappointed. Would it be better to find something, anything, to point her in a specific direction, or was it just as well for her to stumble along the narrow unlighted path she now trod? Well, she had no choice. She had nothing to go on now but her eyes and her instincts. Jean's room was a model of tourist efficiency and irreproachability.

The curtains on the open windows trembled in the early morning breeze. Anita opened the narrow doors and stepped out onto the small balcony, leaned on the parapet, and looked down on the sandy dining terrace. A waiter looked up at the sound of her hello, and waved, a look of surprise on his face.

"Has anyone come in for an early breakfast?" Anita asked.

He shook his head. "No one is coming anywhere." He shrugged and returned to his work. A bright, red-checked tablecloth unfurled with a swift wave of his arm and snap of his hand, and floated into place on a table for four. He moved to the next table and repeated the maneuver and soon the terrace began to feel alive with color and activity. Breakfast on the terrace didn't begin until 8:00 A.M. for guests staying at other hotels, but things would be busy at 7:00 in the upstairs dining room, which only served Hotel Delite guests.

Anita let her glance drift to the rocky headland to the north, where the lighthouse stood in quiet and stalwart isolation. A man in an orange lungi was making his way across the rocks, jumping from boulder to boulder, until he reached the outermost rock above the waves. He settled down, crossing his legs, and began to meditate as the sun rose and golden light began to reach into the crevices. Along the small crescent beach to Anita's right two foreigners in bathing suits worked their way down the steep slope, dropped towels onto the sand, and ran into the waves, splashing and laughing, lifting gobs of water to pour over their heads. It all seemed so ordinary, just an ordinary beginning to an ordinary day.

"Jean isn't in her room," Anita said, returning to the office. The news had the expected effect on Meena. Whatever her emotional state had been before, she was once again ready for action.

"Not there?" She stood up and took a step toward Anita. "Not there?"

"Not there." Anita sat down. "I have to think."

"We have to find her. We must search." Meena looked around her, as though the missing woman might be hiding in that very room. "I will call the staff. We will mount a search."

"Before you alarm the entire resort, hold on just a minute."

"But this is serious!"

"Yes, it is. But listen to me first, Auntie. Last night Anand and I ran into Jean and Marge at the Bamboo Village Restaurant. They were leaving and we were just arriving."

"Yes, yes, you were telling me this." Meena stood over her

niece, looking more and more anxious. "But we must be looking now. Come, come, let us go."

"Just wait. Listen to me." Anita stood and held her aunt by her shoulders. "We ran into them again at the Kali Temple." Anita frowned. "It was late, all the activity was almost over. When Anand and I left—"

"Anand went with you to the Kali Temple?" Meena peered into Anita's eyes, but she was focusing on something else. "Yes, he did this? But is he not wearing cotton pants?"

"What?" Anita screwed up her face at the question. "Cotton pants? Well, yes, I guess so. Why do you care what he was wearing?"

"I am only asking and observing. I am your aunt. I am interested in these things." She stepped back and waved her hands dismissively. "And were Jean and Marge still there at that hour?"

"Yes, they were there, watching the last part of the puja." She paused. "There was something about it, something I can't quite recall."

"And afterward? You are speaking to them?" Meena peered at her.

"That's what I was trying to remember. We didn't speak. But I think when they left they went up the lane to Lighthouse Road. I don't know where they went after that, if they went anywhere or they came back here." She frowned again. "Ravi was on the desk last night, wasn't he?"

"Ah, oh, ah, I think so."

"What do you mean you think so?" Anita said, turning to face her squarely. "You know where he is every second of every minute of every hour of every day that you're paying for. He'd rather jump off a fisherman's boat and face sharks than fudge his hours with you." She headed for the door. "I have to call him. He'll remember when they returned to the hotel."

"But, Anita, it is so early! Let the poor fellow sleep." Meena pressed her hands against her chest, pleading with her niece.

"Since when did you ever care about Ravi's sleep?" Anita gave her aunt a crooked smile. "All right, if you insist." She paused to regard her aunt another moment, then said, "I'm going to check out the beach, just in case Jean got up early to watch the sun rise or take an early morning swim." She raised her hand as Meena began to object. "I know, I know. It's absurd, but I don't want to expect the worst just yet. She might have gone out early."

"Indeed. And Anand might be a Nayar." Meena fell back into her chair, slumping over her now cool tea. She missed Anita's quizzical smile.

Anita made her way down the stone steps to the courtyard in back. To her left the dhobi was readying his stone stall for the day's washing, stringing line and laying out soaps. He gave a slight jerk of his head by way of acknowledgment, but barely interrupted the rhythm in his work. Anita followed the path through the compound, the tufted ground glowing in the early morning sun. The gate was unlocked now, ready for guests eager for an early morning swim, but when Anita stepped onto the rocks she saw no one else on the beach.

It would be some hours before the village women showed up with their baskets of fruit and long, broad knives, ready to offer up a hefty bowl of sliced mango, banana, papaya, pineapple, and more. The fruit was fresh—picked that morning—the bowls large, the price cheap, and the result served directly to the customer on the beach while he or she lounged in the sun or beneath a striped umbrella. But none of that would prevent some from complaining about the price or the odd piece that wasn't quite ripe or perhaps too ripe. The complaints and counter replies sang in the background of Anita's work, and she had never taken any of it seriously. But at this hour the beach was quiet, not even a fisherman down for an early morning bathroom visit. Anita walked slowly across the beach, looking for footprints in the sand, a towel or shawl left behind, perhaps a beer bottle abandoned after a late-night rendezvous, though Jean seemed the least likeliest of ladies to have a fling complete with midnight trysts while on vacation.

Anita crossed the beach, then returned along the sand toward the stone wall, climbed the few steps to the lane, and once again looked for some sign that Jean had passed by. She followed the lane back toward Hotel Delite, all the way to the still-locked main gate. The guard noted her appearance, but remained at his post, smoking a cigarette near the parapet overlooking the rocks. There was nothing of significance that she could see. She turned and followed the lane in the opposite direction, passing the gate to the new hotel on the rise to the left, and moving on to the little wooden gateway that once led up the hill to an old estate now long gone. Anita climbed from rock to rock, noting the growing piles of trash along the path.

Tourists weren't expected to come this way, so no one had undertaken to keep it clean and tidy. No, this was the lane for villagers coming to work, for bored and frustrated young men with motorcycles and too much cash in their pockets to escape for a long drink of whisky, for fruit sellers tired at the end of a long day in the sun trying to make a little money from foreigners who had enough to buy all the fruit in the hotel but haggled over a small bowl freshly made for them. Anita passed little piles of blackened trash left to smolder here and there, a cache of empty and broken whisky bottles, the occasional torn lungi abandoned in the scrub.

Jean wouldn't come this way, certainly not at night. She had no reason to. The path led to the paved road, which, to the right, ended at the Muslim village, with its new, shining white mosque, and to the left, ran into Lighthouse Road. Across from her the dirt path continued, down a slope, across a marsh, and up a slope into the Christian village, its new church sitting high on the opposite hill. Anita couldn't believe Jean would come this way. Surely she would notice at the little gate, before the rocky path grew steep, that this area was uncared for, past hotel grounds with well-tended gardens.

Anita turned around and made her way back along the lane, scanning both sides of the path as she went. To her left, farther along the coast, was a wire-mesh fence surrounding a new house in the traditional Kerala bungalow style. A goat feeding along the fence stopped and looked up at her, chewing and staring. Anita began to smile. Then looked again. Caught in the fencing was a fragment of fabric; the other end was churning in the goat's mouth. She drifted closer to the goat, trying to keep him calm and curious. But just as she reached out, to put her hand through the fence, to grab at the fabric, he balked and bolted, tearing most of the cloth from the fence—but not all. Anita clapped her hands and chased him away. She didn't want him returning while she examined the fence.

Caught in the fencing was a length of aqua fabric, cotton knit, about five inches long. Anita knelt and fingered the fabric, tugged gently at it. Jean had been wearing an aqua sweater last night, when Anita saw her leaving the Bamboo Village Restaurant. Anita rose and began to rummage through the scrub as she made her way along the fence. No one came here—that was obvious—it was unkempt, unclaimed. She felt briars catch and tug at her pants, felt thorns scrape her ankles and toes, but she continued on until she was a few feet from the cliff, and felt the ground soften beneath her feet. Here is where the ground began to hang over the edge, no longer supported by cliff rocks.

Anita grasped the fence and leaned over the edge to get as much of a view as she could. The drop was a sheer one, down onto rocks that were covered by ocean twice a day. She exhaled sharply, relieved at the sight of smooth sand—and no body anywhere. She moved away from the cliff and glanced back at the fence.

"Oh, damn. I can't believe she wandered out here last night." Anita stepped back and looked around. "I hope she hadn't been drinking." She scanned the ground looking for bottles and didn't know if she should be relieved at not finding any.

Chapter Six

Meena's voice floated out to Anita along the hotel hallway. Her aunt was performing the important function of making sure her guests were happy, and on this morning that meant keeping them blissfully unaware of what had transpired the night before. Meena told stories about her first visit to Ponmudi, the maharajah's hill station that is now a resort, or the best way to enjoy the backwaters around Kochi, or the best restaurant for Chinese food. She gave advice on where to find the best souvenirs made in Kerala, and even promised to bring in a supplier to show off special goods.

"She must be more worried than I realized," Anita thought as she turned into the office. She rummaged in the desk for a large envelope, slipped in the fragment of aqua cloth, and folded over the flap, holding it shut with a paper clip.

"I shall prepare a place for breakfast?" Moonu leaned in the doorway with a tray tucked under his arm. His job was to make sure everyone in the upstairs dining room was well taken care of, but that sometimes meant he had less to do than the waiters working on the terrace. On some days, he might spend half the lunch hour leaning against the front desk gossiping with the manager or dhobi or anyone else who happened to pass by.

"I don't think I should be in the dining room right now. I look too exhausted. Someone's liable to become suspicious."

"Tea, Missi?"

"I've just had two pots, thank you, Moonu," Anita said, falling into the chair, "but I think I'm ready for breakfast." She rubbed her eyes. "Actually, I'd like to go back to bed, but I don't dare. Too much is going on."

"Coffee?" Moonu was nothing if not determined. He didn't blink an eye at the news that Anita, at this early hour, had already had two pots of tea and was ready for a nap. He came from a fishing family and exhibited the patience and stillness that Anita sometimes thought had to be a prerequisite to survive in that business.

"When is Ravi due in?"

"Soon. Fresh mango juice?"

"I have to see him as soon as he gets in. An omelet, please, and toast and juice."

"No tea? No coffee?"

"All right. Tea. I'm going to need it, I think." Anita laid the envelope on the desk, and dropped her hands onto her lap. She didn't want to think about what this might mean—one tourist falling sick with some kind of stomach ailment, at the very least, and her traveling companion disappearing at night along a stretch of cliff where the fall is steep, the ground unsafe, and tourists are not expected to go. Anita thought about the smashed liquor bottles she had skirted along the path, the general air of neglect that was usually the sign to visitors to turn back. But Jean had not turned back. Or had she?

Had Jean been led there, taken a look at her surroundings, changed her mind, and hurried back along the path, leaving her sweater behind? Anita rubbed her forehead, trying to remember just how the sweater had appeared last night. Had Jean been wearing it? Was it opened or buttoned up? Had she tossed it over her shoulders? Were the sleeves tied together in a loose knot, or hanging free? Had she been wearing it at the temple? Had someone just taken the sweater from her when she was absorbed in the puja? Had someone else taken it, thought better of the theft, and thrown it to the goat, not wanting to be caught with it? Had Jean just left it somewhere for a stranger to find and use during the cool of the evening, before abandoning it like other used garments, to be burned some day when someone got tired of the debris out there?

"Omelet with cheese. Cook insists cheese is good for the thinking, and you are thinking today of many things." Moonu brushed aside a stack of papers and set a plate in front of her. "He is telling me this. And toast. And juice." He arranged her breakfast on the cluttered desk, stepped back, and gave a jerky bow before leaving the office.

"Meena must have let something slip with the cook," Anita thought as she picked up her fork. The omelet, light and puffy, stuffed with cheese and softened tomato wedges, smelled wonderful—she'd have to get him to tell her the spices in it. She discovered at her first bite that she was ravenous.

By ten o'clock Anita had napped, showered, had a brief conversation with the local constable about a possibly missing tourist, and returned to the beach. The constable's general air of calm made her wonder if she was overreacting, and she vowed to give Jean time to return from her overnight adventure without embarrassment. The tourists would be out in force soon, she knew, and she smiled at the few early birds slathering on tanning lotion or arranging lounge chairs beneath brightly colored umbrellas. Anita lifted her camera, fiddled with the settings as she strolled to the far end of the beach.

Tides were shallow in this part of India, so close to the equator, barely showing any change in height to the uninitiated eye. But there were some differences between high and low tides, just enough to cover over a piece of clothing or small object left behind. Or maybe enough to wash off blood from a rock.

Anita capped her camera lens and lifted it above her head as she moved toward the waves, letting them wash past her, swirling around her ankles, rolling up her legs like a pair of heavy socks. She moved deeper into the waves, following a line of outcroppings until the waves rocked back and forth against her thighs. These rocks would have been all but covered last night, as she tried to recall when the tide was high. She waded among the rocks, putting each foot in carefully, extending her leg in the water to test for the signs of an undertow.

When Aunt Meena and her husband had first opened Hotel Delite, they had sought the advice of other hoteliers, who were glad to offer them the benefit of their experience, including the long list of warnings about guests who didn't speak enough English to understand the bill, guests who responded to the lack of a specific service with "Well, can you get it?", and other surprises of catering to a transient population. Meena returned from these visits with a headache. When she was on her own, after her husband died, she confessed to her niece one day, "Anita, every day I watch from my window the women going into the water."

Anita began to smile. "And you wonder if you should run down to the water's edge with a modest robe for them. Yes?"

Meena blushed, then shook her head. "That is a matter I do not understand, yes. But no, it is something else." She leaned toward Anita, making sure no one else could hear her in the hotel empty during the monsoon. "I worry they cannot swim."

"But, Auntie, they're the only ones here who *can* swim." Anita sighed and kissed her aunt on the cheek as she left. A month later she realized just how serious were her aunt's worries. A parcel arrived at the hotel. Anita opened it and lifted out a stack of small laminated signs. At the top was the title: Ocean Swimming Safety. After this came rules for swimming in the resort waters, ending with the instruction to relax, do not panic, you will be saved. Anita liked that last admonition—it seemed to fit with all those who came to Kerala expecting to discover the secrets of the mysterious east, which would then lead to miraculous insight and world peace. But alas, the instructions were far more practical than that. Secretly, Anita was impressed with how sensible they were.

1. The most common circumstance of drowning is drinking and swimming. You are admonished.

2. Beware backwash. Waves drive water in surges to the shore. Some of this returns seaward in surges. Weak swimmers in hip-deep water can be swept off their feet and carried 20 to 30 meters into deep water.

3. Rips. Water driven shoreward by waves can return in narrow, fast-flowing streams. Sometimes the stream digs a trench in the sand, so persons walking in hip-deep water are suddenly in chest-deep water, with no weight on their feet. One or more rips exist at all times at the resort beaches. If you are taken out seaward by a rip, do not swim against the current. Swim parallel to the beach for 50 meters, then swim shoreward. Alternatively, relax, tread water, and the current will bring you back in.

In case of difficulty, remember: Panic kills. RELAX. Tread water. Wave one arm!

Call "Help!" loud.

Relax! Do not panic! You will be saved!

The signs were hung on the main door of every room, and the old signs advertising price, check-out times, and other practical information were thrown away.

But Meena was wise to worry, Anita later learned. Inspired one early morning to have the whole beach to herself, she made her way down to the waves long before anyone else was up and about. The sun was lightening the sand and rocks, a slight breeze was moving haltingly across the water onto the land; in the distance a radio played, announcing the opening of a temple for puja. She ran along the beach and into the water, diving into an oncoming wave, surfacing, diving again. As she walked to the shore, rubbing the water from her face, and slicking back her soaked hair, she felt the retreating waves grab at her. Surprised, she turned. There, racing toward her, was a wave that must have been three stories tall. Alarmed that it might crash directly down on her, she dove into it, hoping to pass through part of it. Instead, the wave picked her up and carried her, dashing her onto the sand, rolling her again and again as it crashed and spread up the beach. She stretched out her legs and dug her heels into the sand, keeping herself from being sucked out again. A twist of the receding wave shoved her against a rock. She got to her feet, her knees shaky and wobbly. Her hand went automatically to her arm, where her fingers turned red from a deep gash. To her dismay she had been tossed half the length of the beach, landing among the sharp outcroppings and rocks. She had been tossed among stones that might have cut her to shreds or knocked her unconscious. She steadied herself against the nearest one, its sharp surface scratching her palm, then stumbled up to the dry sand and fell onto her side, grateful to be alive, only slightly injured, on dry land. It was an experience she never forgot, no matter how many times she told herself it was a rogue wave, like being hit by lightning.

"I shall sleep well tonight." Meena clapped her hands against her cheeks with pleasure at the sight of the last sign on ocean swimming being hung in place. Anita rested the hammer against her shoulder.

"Especially since we have no guests this time of year," she said.

But we have plenty of guests now, Anita thought, as she moved her leg through the water searching for some sign of the missing Jean. She continued to wade forward, trying to discern something in the area to tell her if Jean had been here the night before. When she surprised a fisherman engaged in his early morning business among the boulders farther on, she gave up and returned to the hotel. There was nothing, not a hint Jean had been anywhere on the rocks below the cliff.

Anita managed to get her photography gallery open for business by noon, but without enthusiasm. She pulled up the corrugated shutter, barely noticed the young Peeru when he slipped past her and began dragging the easels into place, absentmindedly handed him the key to the storage closet, and found herself wandering listlessly around the small space.

"Lunch, Memsahib?" Peeru stood in front of her, straight as an arrow. Anita let her gaze fall down upon him, barely hearing what he said. "Lunch?"

"Oh, sure, lunch. Yes, go ahead." Her arms akimbo, she continued to pace the gallery. When she turned back, on her route to the other end, Peeru was still there, looking uncertainly at her and then at the lane.

"Oh, sorry, Peeru." Anita turned to look for her pocketbook, and rummaged in the closet for it. She emerged with a wad of cash, which she handed to Peeru. With a big smile and a quick waggle of his head, he turned, jumping down onto the lane and skipping away. But Anita didn't notice; she had turned to the bulletin board covered with postcards. She stopped in front of it, arms crossed, brow furrowed.

Had she seen what she thought she had seen when Marge had looked through her gallery the day before, or was she now rewriting the moment to help explain the inexplicable events of the last twenty-four hours, or possibly twelve hours? Did Marge notice something on the bulletin board, or did she see something in one of the photographs? No, Marge had paid almost no close attention to the photos, just browsing and glancing from one to the other, the way people do when they want to know what something is like but lack the curiosity to study it well. No, it wasn't the photos that grabbed her attention, it was the bulletin board.

"Chinnappa?" Anita peeked into the tailor's shop next door. A series of grunts emerged from the dimly lit interior. Anita entered and cleared a chair to sit on in the back, opposite an old man with half a dozen straight pins held between clenched lips. He waggled his head in greeting, winked at her, and went on stitching a metal clasp enclosure on a pair of slacks. "I have a question for you, Chinnappa."

The old man lifted an eyebrow and shook his head. He might have been smiling if he hadn't had to hold onto the pins so tightly.

"Did you notice a large American woman coming into my gallery yesterday afternoon?" Anita described Marge and what she was wearing. The man looked away, his expression growing vague while he pondered the question. He nodded absently while he finished stitching. The task completed, he pulled the straight pins from his mouth and stuck them into a large pin cushion.

"Yes, I am noticing this one because she is much larger than the others." He held up the pants for a close inspection, turning them in his hands, and peering at the seams and clasps. "But they are all so large. It is because these Americans are eating meat even as children, isn't it?"

"Well, over many generations, yes, I suppose so." Anita hadn't really thought about it. After all, in some parts of North India, Indian men were just as tall as American men. "But, yes, Marge is a large woman—large bones."

"Yes, I am noticing her. Did she take something from you?"

"No, no, not at all. But she seemed to notice something on the bulletin board, something that upset her. And frankly, Chinnappa, I can't see anything there that is the least bit unusual."

"Ah, then it must be something usual." He stood up and shook out the pants, neatly folding them and setting them aside. Peeru appeared suddenly, holding out a tray of closed containers; Anita sent him back to the gallery to begin his lunch, promising to join him in a moment.

"He will eat it all before you get there," Chinnappa said.

"Good. That means he's hungry."

"And you are not?"

"Not really."

"He takes advantage."

"He's a child who needs to eat. And he earns whatever I give him." She raised her hand to stop the impending flow of invectives against the boy. "It's the bulletin board I'm worried about now. Marge must have seen something there, and I have to figure out what it is."

"A simple task." He gave her a big smile, revealing numerous gaps between the remaining teeth.

"I'm glad you think so." Anita stood up, deciding she was hungry after all.

"Easier than other tasks. This one sits still, pinned to a board. It will not change no matter how long you take to figure it out."

"That's one way of looking at it, except that Marge may still be in danger, and I have no idea where Jean is, and the answer could be on the bulletin board."

"Ah, motivation, purpose. Now you will have the goals like your American cousins." Chinnappa gave her a wicked little wink, and pulled an unfinished blouse off a rack and spread it out on a worktable. "Like that man. Such determination. What your American cousins admire, isn't it?"

Anita turned back to face Chinnappa. His tone of voice had changed from teasing to warning, though his eyes were fixed on his tailoring work. "What man?" Her voice was soft, just in case someone was near enough to hear.

"Ah," Chinnappa said, smoothing out the fabric with large hands rippling with age. "The one who hides behind the stairs to the bookseller, reading a newspaper, the same page, over and over. Since early morning he has been here, on this part of the lane, or lingering farther down. Such persistence. You should be flattered."

"Flattered? By a stalker? Do you know who he is?"

Chinnappa shook his head and proceeded to fix straight pins between his lips.

Anita set out her lunch, and then, suddenly, jumped onto the lane and walked straight to the stairway, ready to challenge the man lingering there. But no one was concealed behind the stairs. She scanned the lane, walked a few feet in either direction, but saw no one who fit Chinnappa's description. She returned to the gallery, waved to Chinnappa, gave him a shrug in response to his raised eyebrows, and turned her thoughts to the bulletin board.

The board was an ordinary piece of cork banded with gold-embroidered, deep blue silk fabric, about two inches wide, folded neatly at each corner. The cork surface was covered with postcards from all over the world, in various sizes and languages, though mostly English. Anita hardly knew where to begin—she had put them up because they were fun, and reminded her of the inspiring links between ordinary people around the world. We are all connected, the postcards seemed to say, even if we don't know each other's names or families. Somehow, we are all connected. And somewhere in here, among the fifty or so postcards and notes, was something that connected to Marge in a frightening, disturbing way.

Anita leaned in close to the board, scanning the notes, some in graceful looping script, some in neat block letters, others in crabbed or chunky letters. Most were readable, a few illegible. Many wrote to Anita to tell her about the rest of their trip, to tell her how much they enjoyed meeting her, to show her a picture of their hometown, to thank her for a small act of kindness, to ask a question, to pass along a note to a friend who would be passing through, as though Anita were a postal station.

Anita tried to recall where Marge had been standing—then stepped back and tried to recreate her pose. She had been looking at this section, Anita recalled, the northeast corner possibly. Or perhaps it was the center portion, where the postcards from England and the States overlapped with one from Indonesia. She remembered the family—diplomats—who had so loved the way some tourists chatted with the women selling fruit that they went around getting tourists to pose with the fruit sellers, ignoring the temples and palaces nearby. The Spanish woman couldn't believe anyone would go to sea in a boat that was no more than four logs tied together ("But they're so portable!") that she tried to buy one and ship it home until she found out how heavy the wood was and how much it would cost. Then there was the American student who was stunned by the reality of Asia after studying it for years; the real thing overwhelmed her, and she wanted Anita to know and be kind to her friend when she passed through on her way back from Thailand.

"It's in here somewhere." Anita stepped back and frowned.

"Something is wrong?" Peeru was immediately at her side.

"Nothing's wrong exactly, Peeru. I just can't see what is in front of me."

"Ah." He nodded. "Yes, this is so. You are using your eyes, but you see through the camera."

Anita opened her mouth to comment, but instead said, "You're right. I do see through a lens." She turned to the closet, searched till she found what she wanted, and came back to the board. Focusing a small digital camera, she took several shots of the bulletin board.

"Now you are seeing?"

"Not yet, but I will." She slipped out the memory card and put the camera away. "Now, let's take down the postcards and put up some newer ones. I want to spend some time with these."

Peeru jumped to the task, and soon Anita had an envelope full of postcards and Peeru was arranging another set on the board.

CHAPTER SEVEN

"I thought you weren't coming back to this area until later in the week," Anita said. She and Anand were sitting in a café one story above the beach walk, almost close enough to lean over the railing and pat the strollers on the head. Both had a tall glass of coffee in front of them while tourists in bathing suits, sarongs, and long, loose, flowing cotton blouses dined on a variety of fare—both European and Asian. So far she had watched three Australian girls argue loudly with a fruitseller, a dog steal a plate of food on the beach, a tourist start down a narrow lane between stores and be turned back—lost, Anita surmised—a vendor chase a sarong caught by the breeze, and a chagrined Candy emerge from the narrow lane, also lost and confused, judging by the look on her face. Anita leaned back and propped her feet up on the table cross piece, her knees bumping the tabletop underneath.

"A side trip." Anand smiled and lifted his glass to his lips. "I stopped at the hotel, thinking you might still be there."

"Oops! And how was Auntie Meena?" Anita was surprised at her reaction—she was cringing. She gave herself a good shake, pushed herself up in her chair. She simply could not understand Meena's reaction to Anand—he was everything she wanted in a husband for Anita: Indian, educated, single, good caste, good family, good job. This was the kind of man that should have Meena drooling while Anita said no, no, not yet.

But instead of one of those adrenalin-gushing arguments over

Anita's future and choice of men, Meena looked like she was going to burst into tears whenever Anand's name came up. It didn't make sense. Anita didn't want to marry the man; she just wanted to enjoy his company and have a good time. After all, if life were a bit different, she'd probably be a full-time party girl. She loved to laugh and have a good time and then go her own way. But instead of having a good time, she was starting to fret about what was wrong with her aunt. Worse, it was starting to have an effect on Anita. She found herself avoiding the topic of Anand and their time together, hiding his notes and letters, urging Ravi and the others not to mention having seen Anand. "I'm acting like an alcoholic hiding liquor," Anita thought to herself one morning. "This is stupid," she thought then, but there didn't seem to be anything she could do about it. Though she vowed to stop this absurd behavior, Meena didn't seem to be willing to cooperate.

"She wasn't there; at least that's what Ravi said." Anand lowered his glass.

"I get the feeling you didn't believe him."

"Who else wears a sari and sits in the office?"

"Oh." Anita looked out over the beach. "She didn't come out?"

Anand shook his head.

Anita looked through the railing to the strollers below. "I don't get it, Anand. But I'm sorry, I really am. She's behaving abominably."

Anand leaned closer to her, and said, in a voice so soft it might have been a whisper if she hadn't been able to hear the strong throaty timbre that made her knees wobble, "We'll win her over. My mother is especially charming."

Anita felt a little gasp deep in her windpipe. This was getting out of hand. If Anita took Meena to meet Anand's mother, her aunt might get even worse. "Do you think that's a good idea?"

75

"It can't hurt." Anand waved to the waiter for the check.

"You don't know Auntie Meena." Anita slid down in her chair, wondering where this was all going.

"And I have no idea where Jean has gone," Anita said as they arrived back at her gallery. "But that's only one of my questions."

"Why don't you just ask people what you want to know?"

Anita let out a peal of laughter. "Because they lie, Anand."

"I thought they lied only about money."

"Maybe in your world. Actually, what do they lie about in the temples you work with?"

"Money."

"That's depressing."

"What else is there?" He patted Peeru on the shoulder when the child stood and saluted. "Anything stolen while we were gone?" he asked the boy.

"Oh, no." The boy stiffened his shoulders and gave Anand an uncompromising look.

"Don't be mean, Anand. Of course, he didn't have any trouble, did you, Peeru?"

"None at all."

"You see?" She turned to Anand.

"I sent the strange man away."

"What strange man?" Both Anita and Anand spoke at once.

"The man reading the newspaper. He said he was a friend of yours. Chinnappa said he was a bad egg. I sent him away." Peeru looked from one to the other, and when neither responded he began to look less resolute. "Yes? He was a friend?"

"Doesn't sound like it." Anita walked over to Chinnappa's shop and leaned in. "The same one who was here this morning?" Nodding while fitting a pair of slacks to a man speaking in German, the tailor tugged and pinned and pulled and shifted.

"Not a friend, Peeru."

"Who is this?" Anand turned to Anita, who gave him a quick rundown of the tailor's report. "I don't like the sound of this."

"It's nothing. Just an ordinary thief trying to get clever. I'll let the constable know." Anita stepped into the gallery, hoping she sounded more confident than she felt. She was used to the beggars of all stripes waiting outside shops or restaurants until the generous customer emerged, but being targeted by someone not a beggar—that was different. Creepy. It made her hyper alert—sizing up strangers as she passed along the lanes, keeping an eye out for anything unusual, even while she told herself she was overreacting. It was probably just someone who wanted to approach her about showing his photography in her gallery, someone who didn't know how to get into business at the resort. She turned to Peeru, to escape her own discomfort.

"The board is complete, Memsahib." Peeru pointed to his handiwork, taking a place modestly next to the easel and framing the board with his arms.

"Good work."

Anita explained to Anand why she had changed the postcards.

"Maybe she had a stomachache," Anand said. "And it had nothing to do with postcards."

"You should go into business with Chinnappa," Anita said, giving him a friendly glare.

Anita settled into her lounge chair and began flipping through the postcards and notes. Some were from the States or Europe, several from Australia and New Zealand, a few from Southeast Asia, and one from Tokyo. They all said about the same thing—we loved that part of India and someday we might be back, but don't count on it. That last sentiment was stronger or weaker depending on when the note was written, soon after departure or long after arriving home and sinking into the known life.

Relatively few people returned, Anita knew, unless India captured them in unexpected ways. Emily was a case in point. There was a very good chance that she would return often, if the ecstatic experience took, like a vaccination. Otherwise, she would return to her old life, get teased by her friends about "going native" while on vacation, and though faintly embarrassed would try to put the whole thing behind her, at least publicly. Anita guessed that however far Emily went from India, however quickly she returned to her old life, something of her experience in front of the Kali shrine would remain deep within her. She had that look, a look Anita recognized even though she didn't see it often.

It occurred to Anita that she hadn't seen Emily that morning; perhaps she should make sure she was all right. After all, an ecstatic experience for a staid Westerner could easily go awry, or at least they had occasionally in the past.

"Trouble, Memsahib?" Peeru stood in front of her with a worried frown and arms rigidly at his side.

"No, only more of the same," Anita said. "I'm just thinking about our hotel guest who has gone missing. Poor Jean. Now she's proving the truth of something she said yesterday. And I still don't know where she is or if anything has happened to her."

"Ah." Peeru waggled his head.

"I think I'll go take a walk, say hello to some of the other shopkeepers." Anita pushed herself out of her chair, put the postcards and notes into a neat stack, wrapped an elastic around them, and stuffed them into her purse. "Guard the place for me, okay?" He waggled his head yes. "You know where the cash register is?"

"Of course he knows. And you are a fool to tell him."

"Thank you, Chinnappa." Anita waved to the old man as she left the gallery.

Anita didn't really want to spend the next hour or so talking to the other shopkeepers, but she found walking around helped her think. She didn't know if it was because it stimulated the blood flow to her brain, rattled her thoughts, or put her next to people or things that jogged her imagination and gave her ideas. Whatever the reason, however it worked, she liked to walk when she had something on her mind. Sometimes she didn't walk farther than her suite of rooms, where she leaned against the porch parapet and tapped her foot, or down to the terrace where she sat at a table in the middle of the afternoon and let the waves batter her brain until something fell out.

Images of Emily standing at the window facing out to sea, a stunned but slightly beatific expression on her face, flitted across Anita's mind, alternating with imagines of Jean and her self-satisfied smile as she talked about her plans for visiting Burma. She was brave, Anita thought, to undertake such an arduous task, or perhaps foolish. It was hard to tell. But she was risking a lot—or would be if we ever find her, Anita thought. If she's lying sick somewhere, she may spend her vacation in a hospital bed.

A tailor was laying out fabric for a tourist to consider, a foreign woman in a bathing suit and sarong was studying the glass-enclosed shelves of a small pharmacy and notions shop, just large enough for the owner and his cash box inside, and then for his swinging shelves at closing time. She tapped on the window and asked for the small tube of hair conditioner. The salesman emerged to unlock the window.

Farther along was a framed gateway leading into a new hotel, its grounds dotted with small red-painted café tables and chairs, and after that another stretch of shops, and then the computer café. The broad glass doors were folded open, inviting passersby to sit down at the white laminated tables and computers. At its height, the café could probably accommodate ten customers, plus the manager, a young man in light beige slacks and a white jersey sitting at a desk peering at his own computer screen. Anita stepped into the café, and the manager immediately stood.

"This one," he said, pointing to a computer desk set against the back wall.

"I'm not here to use the computer." She spoke softly, so as not to draw the attention of the two other individuals in the shop—a middle-aged man in the far corner staring at a screen while he talked on a cell in German, and a college-age Asian, probably Indian, typing rapidly and only occasionally glancing up at the screen.

With that reply, the manager looked Anita up and down. "What do you want?"

"Someone I know, a friend, came in here yesterday." Anita described her briefly.

"Friend or hotel guest?"

"Oh, okay, hotel guest." Anita gave him a closer look but didn't recognize him, though he obviously recognized her. "She seems to have fallen ill. She didn't look well when she left my gallery, which is where she asked about the computer café, so I sent her here. I'm wondering if she made it here."

"Yes, she did."

"And if there's any way I can find out what she did?" Anita was not uncomfortable with silence, a trait she was especially glad of as she waited for the young man to consider the merits of her request. He studied her, glanced over at his two customers, and then back at Anita. He lowered his eyes, waggled his head, and sat down at his desk. He pushed aside the keyboard, and drew a large ledger toward him, turning the pages back to yesterday. Anita tried a quick count of the number of people who came in and out in a day, using the computer for sometimes as short as five minutes, or as long as several hours. She followed his finger as he scanned down the page looking for the one he thought was Marge.

"Here. This is the one, yes?"

Anita looked at the time given for her log-in. No one else had logged in for an hour before and half an hour afterward. "Was she the only one here then?"

The man looked at the bottom of the preceding page. "No, one other person here, one who is coming regularly. That one." He nodded to the man speaking in German on his cell.

"Okay. Which computer did she use?"

"This one." He walked her over to a computer in a row facing the German but farther down. Marge would have been closer to the wall than the door. "Do you want time?"

"Yes. Log me in. Thanks." Anita sat down and looked at the blank desktop, its few icons coming with mild warnings: Do not click here without permission. Not for use of customers. She wondered how the manager could stop a wayward customer but decided not to try to find out. If nothing else, Marge would have gone online, Anita decided, thinking that a safe bet over using the computer to type a letter or make notes. She logged on, pulled down the history, and worked down to the day before.

The computer had hosted a variety of users, it seemed, with many of them checking sports scores, researching travel destinations, logging onto email sites. It was impossible to know which ones might have been Marge's choices. And if she had been checking and sending email, then Anita was just wearing out her fingertips for nothing. She began a methodical trek through the list. When she was less than halfway through, stuck momentarily in the land of cheap washing machines delivered to your home before the ink is dry on the sales receipt, the German user snapped shut his cell and leaned back in his chair.

From the sound of his clicking and pausing, Anita surmised he was logging off. She leaned over to introduce herself, and quickly explained she was trying to track down information that might help Marge, now lying in a hospital.

"I was hoping to find out how to contact her family," Anita said, not for the first time wondering at the smoothness with which she slid into lying. It made things so much easier. "We don't have telephone or email information for her," she explained.

"Ah, yes, I can see that would be difficult." He gave her a cold look, and spoke as though he were reciting. But when the computer gave a final ping and he waved to the manager, telling him he was finished, he turned to Anita with a friendly smile. "It is so very complicated here, doing business at such long distance."

"So you're only partly on vacation."

"Alas, I fear this is so. But about your friend? Yes, she looked very unwell. Did she fall ill at lunch?"

"We don't know. It might be she had something when she got here—she only arrived that night, well, early in the morning, and she might have been emailing her doctor or someone who knew about what she had. We just don't know."

"Ah, yes, but I think not." He leaned toward her and spoke softly, turning his head slightly as though that would prevent the manager from overhearing.

"I asked her if she was unwell, did she want a doctor? It can be hard for a woman traveling alone to speak of such matters to strange men." He nodded toward the manager, but Anita got his drift. What foreign woman would want to take her medical problems to an Indian man? She'd have trouble in a pharmacy with that attitude, but Anita didn't tell him that. "I offered to assist her."

"What did she say?"

"She said she was not unwell. I thought perhaps she was again, ah, being modest, but no, she is insistent. She tells me she has had a shock. She and her friend must return home as soon as possible."

"Oh, something happened in the States?"

"That I cannot say. She is only saying she has had a shock and it is not wise for her and her friend to remain here. They must return home. She has just learned this unfortunate news." He picked up his cell and slipped it into his pants pocket as he stood up. "Unfortunate. She was quite distressed over it, whatever it was." He wished her a good afternoon and walked over to the manager to pay his bill.

CHAPTER EIGHT

Anita returned to the gallery, and for the rest of the afternoon she stared at the postcards and notes, arranging them according to the location of the sender, then according to the dates, then according to nationality, according to gender, enthusiasms, destinations, subject matter of the postcards, postage stamps. She tried every conceivable arrangement, forcing herself to see each one in a dozen different ways, but at the end of the afternoon, she had no better understanding of what Marge had seen than at the outset.

Maybe I'm deluded, she thought. Maybe I should throw them away and just go to the police about both Jean and Marge. But she knew the response she'd get—official, careful, slightly suspicious, and slow. No, there wasn't time for that. And she was convinced that the answer to Marge's sudden distress was in the postcards, and that meant digging deeper.

Anita left Peeru again in charge of the shop and headed back to the computer café, setting up near the entrance so she could watch the tourists and other people wandering by. Wherever the answer appeared, she wanted to be able to see it. Then she went through each postcard, googling the name of each sender, each recipient (if not her), each location and sender, and other permutations. Some names brought a few dozen sites, others nothing, and a rare few brought thousands of matches. Hotel Delite and Anita's gallery had attracted a diverse crowd, all right, including some well-known art collectors. Anita allowed herself several moments of smug satisfaction at the thought of her photography finding a home amid the greats, or at least other framed work worth spending money on.

She was barely through the first third of the stack of postcards when she stopped to stare at the article on the screen. She checked it against the postcard sitting on the top of the pile, resting her index finger on the name. This could be a mistake—but it wasn't. One Jake Lanier had sent Hotel Delite a postcard asking to reserve a room for the two weeks after Christmas. Although the postcard was undated, it was almost exactly a year old; Anita remembered the incident because Jake Lanier was a no-show—and that was extremely rare. Not only that, but he had offered to pay half in advance. Meena had taken the reservation and held it long after the expected arrival time, but Jake never showed up, never called, never emailed. The hotel cancelled the reservation late on the second day, when other prospective guests were clamoring for a room during the height of the busy season. Jake was never heard from again.

It was easy for Anita to see why. Anita quickly read through the short article, barely a notice of the incident. An American, Jake Lanier, had been arrested in Thailand for drug-related activities. Anita searched for more information, but found little—this kind of news item was notoriously, frustratingly vague. A small notice dated several weeks later stated that an American was being held in confinement while authorities decided what charges to file. Embassy officials were visiting the young man. His family accused authorities of neglect and even torture in an interview in the States before they left to visit him in prison.

Anita scanned the remaining articles but they offered nothing more and began to veer off into articles about a Jake who sold vegetables door to door and a list of members of the Lanier family in Wisconsin. Anita set aside the postcard and returned to the pile.

Anita closed up the gallery later in the afternoon and headed back to Hotel Delite. She had more research to do and she might as well focus on that and forget trying to run a gallery and figure out a missing guest at the same time. She sent Peeru off with orders about tomorrow, bade Chinnappa a good evening, and turned along the path leading to the back of the hotels, following it into the quiet of the palm-covered lane and guesthouses emptied out of beach-loving visitors. The noises from the beach grew fainter and fainter until Anita could hear the scuffing of her sandals on the sandy concrete slabs. She climbed the few steps to the lane veering up the hill, waved to an old friend lounging on his private veranda atop his hotel. At the next turn she stopped to buy a bottled lime drink, waking the girl behind the counter from her afternoon nap. The air was cooler in here.

"Has she been found?" the girl asked.

"How did you hear about that?"

The girl shrugged. *Who didn't know,* she seemed to say. And that was just what Anita had hoped to avoid—a burning trail of gossip about the missing foreigner—but that was probably impossible in this tiny community. The tourists were many, but the workers were few. And they all knew each other.

"Not yet, but we should know something soon. She can't just disappear."

"I have heard stories," the girl said.

"Yes, so have I. Tell me what you've heard."

The girl lowered her eyes, began to demure, then looked around to see who might be within earshot, gave a little grin, and said, "She is smuggling. I don't know what," she quickly added. "And also she is paid by a government." The girl watched

Anita for a reaction that would tell which part of the story was true.

Anita walked on, marveling at the grapevine, and wondering if she was spending too much time on Marge's distress at the bulletin board and not enough on locating Jean. After all, there might be no connection at all between the two incidents and either one of them and Marge's sudden illness. Anita glanced at her watch, and realized how late it was—almost six o'clock. She had meant to call Anand and invite him to dinner—there was a restaurant she wanted to investigate. Anita wound her way up the lane, looking up at the steepening hillside when she reached the outer temple compound. Sitting on the stone wall at the top of the stairs leading down into the compound was Emily.

"It's going to be a lovely evening," Anita said, approaching her. She turned and looked down into the compound, where the priests were preparing for the evening puja. Emily showed little sign of having heard Anita speak, and she moved closer and sat next to her on the step. "Are your friends coming this evening?"

Emily turned her head and gave Anita a pitying smile. "After last night?" She shook her head.

"What happened last night?"

"Kali!" Emily leaned forward, waiting to see if Anita understood.

Anita looked down at the temple, where priests were moving in and out of the small office and supply rooms, arranging things for the puja. "I guess I missed it. What happened?"

"Kali and me."

"Oh, of course." Anita nodded. Yes, the woman had felt called. "I see. But aren't your friends coming to see the temple? The tourists always say the puja is one of the high points of their visit. It's such an unusual experience, they say."

Again the pitying look. "Not after me. They think I've gone

nuts. One of them said, 'As long as you don't talk about it, we'll get through this trip. Just don't talk about it.' "

"That doesn't sound very promising."

"And it's only the beginning of our tour."

"So, will you be traveling alone now?"

"Sort of. But Candy was telling me about her plans. She's thinking of traveling up the coast and then across to the other coast and down again, and back up to Trivandrum. I might go with her."

"And just leave your friends?"

Emily shrugged. "They'll be happier and I'll be happier. Besides, Candy knows a lot about temples and stuff. She's ready to move on, she said. Oh," Emily said, sitting up straighter and turning to Anita, "she said something happened to Marge and Jean was missing and it didn't sound like Marge was coming back. Is that true?"

"Well, Marge is in hospital. That's true, but she's getting excellent medical care—from doctors who have had distinguished careers in Europe and the States." Shivayashivoo, Anita thought, I'm beginning to sound as defensive as Auntie Meena. It must be bothering me more than I realized. "We're expecting her to be released soon—the hotel's been keeping in touch with the hospital."

Emily leaned toward her, lowering her voice. "Is there any chance I could use her room—just until she's released, I mean? I know, it's ridiculous. It's just that I'm not sure I can sleep out in the hall again."

"You slept in the hall last night?"

Emily nodded. "They were all so mad at me for talking about Kali that they said I should sleep on the sofa in the sitting room."

"So, you slept on the sofa downstairs in the parlor area?"

"No. Upstairs. I started to sleep downstairs but it just felt so odd and empty, and lumpy—is that real horsehair?" Anita sighed and nodded as Emily continued. "Besides, I was worried the guard would come in and send me back upstairs—he was asleep in his chair by the door—so I went back upstairs and slept on a rolled-up mattress—one of those cotton mats—on the floor. I just spread it out and lay down." She quickly added when she saw the expression on Anita's face. "I saw it in the laundry room."

"But I didn't see you there, Emily. I came to Marge's room around two or three because the guard was worried; he thought she was very ill. No one was in the hallway when I went up to her room."

"I sneaked back into the room. I guess Candy heard me thrashing around trying to get to sleep, and came out to see what was going on. She told me to go back into my room and stop being such a wimp. She said they had no business putting me out of my room." Emily laughed. "She was right. So I did."

"Do you remember what time this was?" Anita tried not to show her surprise as she went on questioning Emily. Here was someone who could be a witness to whatever had happened—if something had in fact happened.

"Maybe one o'clock."

"Did you see or hear anything while you were out there in the hall? Anything out of the ordinary?"

Emily shook her head. "I was so tired and wrought up. I was mad at my friends, and mad at myself for letting them push me out, and mad at myself for caring. I've just had this incredible experience and everyone's acting like I'm some kind of freak. Well, except for you and Candy. Even Mrs. Nayar thinks something is wrong. She asked me if I wanted to see a doctor this morning."

Anita clamped her lips shut and stifled a laugh. "She's the

motherly type. It doesn't mean anything."

Anita found Auntie Meena sitting alone in the office, her head resting in her hand as she stared at the ledger, not seeing the individual columns of figures running down the page, just staring as though she alone could see the dark and gloomy message hidden therein.

"The numbers don't grow by staring at them, no matter how much you try to frighten them." Anita touched her aunt gently on the shoulder and swirled the ledger toward her, reading quickly to the bottom.

"Holy Moley, Auntie, what're you spending money on?"

"Nothing! Nothing!" Meena grabbed the ledger and slammed the cover down. "Do you think I do not know how to run a hotel? Have I not done this for years and years since my worthless, beloved, feckless—;"

"That poor man you married wouldn't recognize himself in your lamentations, Auntie. And you could at least be consistent. Is he worthless or devoted? Hardworking or feckless? Which mood are you in today?"

"You mock me." Meena threw up her hands, then dropped them onto the ledger. "And I only want what is best for you."

"I thought we were talking about the expenses, which seem to have gone up considerably in the last month." Anita reached out to take the ledger from her aunt, but Meena wrapped her arms around it and held it to her chest.

"We are not talking about expenses. Such mundane matters." She put the ledger back on the table, folded her arms over it, and lay down her head on it. "It is the suffering of this life. It is too much for a frail woman such as I. Too much. And so much more painful when you mock me. I am your aunt, your mother's younger sister, devoted daughter and granddaughter and great-granddaughter. Can you not lift my sorrow?"

Anita sat down opposite her aunt and took her hand. Could this be the same woman who even counted coins? The only woman who mistrusted the scales at government banks? Could this be the woman who rounded up every price, even if the amount was a tiny paisa? Was this the woman who pondered every menu at the vegetable market, remaking the cook's plans morning after morning according to the price of vegetables that day? "Auntie, what is going on?"

"Nothing is going on."

"Auntie, am I blind? Tell me." She stroked her aunt's hand.

"This man. It is always a man, isn't it?"

"What man?"

"Anand."

"Oh, for the love of Nandi's hump."

"He is not the man for you, Anita. I know. Trust me. I know these things." She grasped Anita's hands in her own and pressed them to her breast, pleading with her niece.

"Auntie, he is my friend. We just enjoy each other's company. That's all."

Meena looked as gloomy as if Anita had said she was returning to America to marry an American. "Can't you find another friend?"

"Not at the moment. We have bigger problems, Auntie."

"There is nothing bigger than this."

"Marge and Jean."

"Oh. That problem." She sighed and released Anita's hands. "Yes, that is a problem. I have called the hospital. Marge will live. She is coming back to consciousness. They will want to be paid," she added.

"I'm sure she has health insurance."

"Not the doctors. The priest. I have given much today to ensure her safe recovery. Well, promised much."

Anita shook her head. She knew what that meant—a miscellany of prayers in various temples conducted by a myriad of priests who all expected additional compensation appropriate for their success. "Okay. Any news about Jean?"

"I am calling the police hourly. Nothing. They are most solicitous—they have even sent inquiries to Varkala."

"Auntie, she did not run off to Varkala in the middle of the night." Anita leaned back in her chair. When she let herself think about this, she knew how bad it really was. Foreign women tourists did not go missing overnight and then reappear. Wherever Jean was, she was not going to simply walk back into the hotel. "I think we should plan for the worst."

"That's what Kumar said to me." Meena looked up at her niece. "The priest at the temple at the crossroads. He said I should not hope." Her eyes began to well up with tears, not for the first time surprising Anita with how deeply Meena cared about her guests once they were here in the hotel. "He is knowing. He has that skill."

"Meena, do you remember a man named Jake Lanier?" Anita set a cup of tea in front of her aunt, gave her back a gentle rub, and urged her to have a biscuit with her tea.

Anita handed her the postcard. Meena read it and gasped. "Where did this come from? Oh, no, we cannot accommodate. Booked, we are fully booked!"

Anita took the postcard from her. "That's what I thought you might say," Anita said, studying the card. "But you can relax. This is from last year."

"Not just coming?" Meena sighed, and picked up her teacup. "Who is this person?" She sniffed at the tea, judging its aroma before sipping with a skeptical look on her face. Anita imagined she was weighing its cost against her satisfaction with it.

"Jake Lanier. He made a reservation about a year ago, maybe more, and he never showed up. He was a guest here some time before that, liked it so much that he wanted to come back, so he made a reservation far in advance. Do you remember him at all?"

"Why would I remember a guest who never showed up?"

"This is important, Auntie. Think back. You really liked him because he tipped well even though he didn't seem to have a lot of money." Anita reached for a biscuit. "He made a point of tipping all of the waiters, the dhobi, even the cook the night before he left because he was leaving at one or two in the morning. He went into the kitchen to find the cook, remember?"

"Oh." Aunt Meena began to smile, a warm glow suffusing her face. "Ah, he bought one of your photographs. Ah, yes, I recall. A wonderful man. I am reserving the best room for him." Her face fell. "Why is he not coming? He has never explained this." She put down her teacup and grew sad. "How could he be so generous and then so inconsiderate?"

"I think I just found out. He was arrested for drugs in Thailand."

Meena gasped. "Shivayashivoo! Drugs? We are lucky! He is arrested before he can get here. We don't want such people here in this hotel. Think of the scandal!" Meena clasped a hand over her mouth, her eyes wide with dismay. "He has done a terrible thing. Think of his family!"

"Yes, they must have been pretty miserable." Anita shook her head. "And you liked him. Do you remember? He was thoughtful and generous, not at all the kind to get arrested."

Meena mulled this over while Anita pulled out her notes on the news item she had read.

"But the news story doesn't say what happened to him."

"Ah, that is simple to learn. I will ask my friends at the consulate in Chennai. They will find out for me." She reached for a scrap of paper and a pen and copied the name from Anita's notes. "I will email them later tonight."

"You can do it now, Auntie. It's not like it's cheaper at night."

"Of course it is. Don't you know anything? You are so profligate." Meena rose and marched out of the office, the ledger tucked under her arm.

CHAPTER NINE

Anita made her way down through the hotel and out to the yard between the hotel and the beach. The dhobi was finishing up his work for the day, folding and wrapping in newspaper the perfectly washed and ironed slacks and blouses of the guests. Brij was a young man about her age and had inherited his job from his father, who had joined the hotel when he was a young man and the hotel was more of a house rented out to visitors. Anita wandered over to the first concrete washing stall, where the clean clothes were waiting to be collected and delivered, and sat down on a rock.

She settled herself on the stone and counted the number of people still on the beach. Some liked to come late, after the heat of the day, and enjoy the relative peacefulness of the late afternoon. If they timed it correctly, they might have most of the beach to themselves. At five o'clock, guests could be having a late tea on the terrace or asking for an early supper, leaving the cooling sand to the latecomers. The sun would set soon, and already it felt like the end of the day. Brij continued his work while Anita watched a couple of foreigners enter the yard through the gateway from the beach and follow the path to the hotel stairs.

"They are not staying here, are they?" Brij asked.

Anita shook her head. "Some of them come through the compound instead of going farther down the lane to the public stairs." Anita turned back to the piles of laundry, noticing that none included sheets or towels. "One of our guests found your sleeping mat in the laundry room and used it last night."

Brij lifted up a shirt to fold and held it in midair, letting it flap in the light breeze. "My mat?"

"She said she found it in the laundry room."

"Not my mat." Brij gave the shirt a shake, snapping out a tangle of sleeves, and lay it down on a clean sheet to fold. "I am not napping in the hotel during the day. I have a mat here, in the shade." He nodded to the far corner of the yard, where a bicycle and a bundle lay against the moldy gray compound wall. Sticking out of the bundle was a straw mat faded to a soft pink, its reds and mauves and yellows blending into pastel tones.

"Oh. I assumed it was yours, that after you delivered the first part of the laundry you had taken to having a nap or something upstairs. I don't know why I thought that." Anita leaned forward. "Whose else could it be?"

"The guard?"

Anita shook her head. "He sleeps in the chair by the registration desk, and he keeps a mat beneath the desk for when he thinks he can stretch out for a while."

"The cook?"

Again Anita shook her head. And she continued to shake her head as Brij went through the list of employees. "So whose is it?"

"What does it matter? If no one is complaining that someone has stolen his mat, then it is there for you to keep. Perhaps someone will need it and there it will be. This is convenient, isn't it?"

"But it must belong to someone, Brij. After all, would Auntie Meena allow things that don't belong to her or the hotel to litter her property?"

"Then it must be hers, yes?"

"What would Auntie Meena be doing with a mat in the

laundry room?"

Brij didn't have an answer, and Anita didn't try to invent one. Instead, she went back into the hotel, up to the second floor, and into the laundry room. The laundry was a small room diagonally to the left of the stairs, just beyond Room 4. Just large enough to hold piles of dirty laundry and cleaning materials, including ironing boards in case a guest requested one; the room was used only to store and retrieve items.

Anita began rummaging through the piles of laundry until she came upon a tightly rolled cotton mat, the kind used by South Indian villagers on their own beds, preferably in fives or sixes. One mat was liable to wear out in a matter of months if not sooner, its cotton batting flattened or crushed to the edges, but half a dozen made for a pleasant night's sleep. Anita unrolled the mat and pinched it along the sides. This was a new mat, still stiff and tight, and not a single stain on it. Why would anyone leave a brand new mat rolled up in the laundry room?

Anita found Ravi hunched over the desk in the hotel office. He glanced up at her, then, to Anita's surprise, seemed to blanch and tighten his shoulders even more as he turned away. Anita pulled out a chair and sat down.

"You're not going to ignore me, Ravi." Anita tapped her index finger on his hand. "I know for a fact that Auntie Meena has gone across the lane for a few minutes, so you needn't worry about her rushing in demanding that you work harder, harder and not waste time." Ravi groaned. "What is it, Ravi?" Anita leaned closer to him, worried now that something was seriously wrong.

"What is it? What is it?" Ravi looked at her with deep, dark pockets beneath his bloodshot eyes and pale skin.

"Ravi! You're unwell. You shouldn't be here." He looked awful—she couldn't recall when she had ever seen him look so bad. Usually cheerful, insouciant, though painfully afraid of Aunt Meena, Ravi was a rock for the hotel. He never lost track of a registration or a detail about a guest; he could soothe the most ruffled feathers among vendors and guests after Meena had swept through like a typhoon, and he did it all without complaining about Meena. Anita secretly thought he adored her, the replacement for the mother he barely knew as a child.

"I am well, just in need of sleep."

"That's obvious, Ravi. In fact, you look awful." She stood up. "I want you to go home and get some rest, and leave Auntie Meena to me." Ravi gasped.

"No, no, not that. I am fine. It is my evening on the desk. Do not worry about this at all. I am fine." He pushed himself up and stumbled to the registration desk, leaving Anita to watch in amazement. He settled himself on a stool and promptly lay his head down on his folded arms on the counter. She let him nap for a few minutes before pulling over another stool and settling in beside him. After a while he sat up and looked at her; he seemed even worse, Anita thought.

"You're going to have to tell me what this is all about."

"I am so tired, Anita. Your aunt will kill me if I don't work tonight."

"What about last night?"

"Huh?"

"You were on the desk last night, and I wanted to ask you about one of the guests, but Meena put me off. I wondered about it at the time, but I had a lot of other things on my mind also, so I forgot about it. I figured I'd catch up with you soon enough. So, Ravi, what about last night? And why was Auntie so averse to my questioning you?"

"I am sure I don't know." Ravi let his head swing away so he was gazing out the open doorway. Up the lane a few autorick-shaw drivers lounged along the wall, waiting for a fare. He turned back, staring at her.

"When did Marge and Jean come in last night?"

"Ah . . ."

Anita didn't know what to make of Ravi's expression. He suddenly looked frightened, blinked furiously, and turned away again. "You were on the desk, weren't you?"

"Am I not hired to attend the desk in the evenings as well as certain days?"

"You're prevaricating, Ravi."

"I do not lie!" He pulled up his shoulders and tried to glare at her, but his uncertainty undermined him.

"Tell me the truth, Ravi. Did you see Jean and Marge come in last night?" She leaned closer. What was wrong with him? He was like a brother to her—he never lied to her. He might not like being caught between her and Meena, but he was always on her side, in his own way. But today, something was wrong. "Ravi, tell me." She spoke gently, touched by his distress.

"I can't. I just can't." He all but whispered.

Anita and Anand climbed Lighthouse Road toward the temple lane, but before they got there, Anita stopped and said, "This is where we're going." She nodded to a dirt driveway leading the short distance to a small house. In front, under a sparkling white canopy hung with brightly appliquéd and embroidered festival hangings, four small tables were arranged. Electric lanterns cast warm shadows in the early evening darkness, the light bouncing off the bright red molded plastic chairs. Anand gave Anita a questioning look as she nudged him toward the house.

"It's new." Anita walked slowly, to give herself time to explain. "This is the owner's home, and his wife is known as a great cook, so he talked her into trying this out. He's only open for dinner right now, but perhaps he will add lunch later, if the restaurant does well in the evenings."

Anand looked around him, checking out the rows of potted plants along the driveway as they approached.

"That's not a problem, is it?" It just occurred to her that he usually picked the restaurants, and she had no idea if he did so because of dietary restrictions. Maybe Auntie Meena was right about this little detail. Anita felt her heart sink. Would he suddenly balk at eating food prepared by someone not of his caste? Did he really care about such things? "Anand?"

"Our shadow might get hungry, but perhaps he can pilfer a few bananas." Anand shrugged. Anita slowed her step and turned her head to look over her shoulder.

"Shadow?"

"Didn't you tell me you've seen him before? You thought he was sizing up your gallery, but it turns out he was looking for me."

"I don't understand."

"He shows up outside my office." He smiled. "It is no matter. I am used to that sort of thing—the company I work for is on the cutting edge of just about everything right now, and our competitors are trying all sorts of ways of getting information, eavesdropping is only one of them. I don't worry about it—or him." He motioned to the lane and Anita felt an immediate easing of tension she hadn't been aware of.

"I wish you'd told me earlier—I was beginning to wonder what that guy wanted."

"Secrets, IT secrets." Anand shook his head, then nodded to a row of plants. "You should ask the owner if he does these orchids himself. That is a very impressive crab claws over there."

Anita looked in the direction he indicated, to see a row of potted orchids on a three-tiered stand. The crab claws stood at one end, its row of bright red and orange and green flowers hanging long over the lower tier. "I'll ask him." She sighed with relief that Anand was open to the new restaurant and put the comment about the man shadowing them aside. "The owner's name is Moosa."

The tables were widely separated, so Anita and Anand were not uncomfortable being seated in the table next to the only other guests, a trio of blond women speaking a language Anita didn't recognize and chatting and laughing with abandon. Moosa left them with one-page menus handwritten in red ink on plain white paper and hurried into the house to bring bottled water. Anita ordered shrimp with coconut milk and coconut rice.

"And I'll have a thali," Anand said as Moosa retrieved the menus. He departed with a modest bow and a warm smile, obviously pleased with his customers' orders. "The thali," Anand said, turning to Anita, "will tell me how good a cook his wife really is." A moment later a short, stout woman in a red-flowered sari, with a wooden ladle in her hand, peered out the door, then withdrew.

"That must be Moosa's wife." Anita nodded toward the doorway.

"Good. I'm hungry." Anand took a deep breath and leaned back in his chair. "You must ask about the orchids."

"You said that."

He grinned, then let his gaze wander around the compound. "Few things in life bring such rewards as orchids. My father has exhibited his at the Flower Show year after year, for no other purpose than to share their beauty with others." He pointed to a cluster of pots at the base of a palm tree. "Those, they could win a prize. I must tell my father. He never wins anything because he refuses to complete the paperwork for the contest, but he applies to exhibit every year."

"Why doesn't he enter them in any of the contests?"

"Many reasons, I think. I don't know for certain, but I am

thinking he hides many reasons beneath his modest demeanor." Anand smiled, then shifted in his seat so his shoulder was almost brushing hers. Indian restaurants had recently adopted the Western practice of seating two diners at adjacent sides of the square tables, so they looked out upon the dining room, instead of seating diners so they were facing each other.

"You can't stop there, Anand." She was intrigued; he rarely said much about his family, which didn't bother Anita. She rarely said much about hers.

"My father's friend enters and wins often, but also he is complaining more and more that we are becoming a most competitive culture for no good purpose. We compete now for the sake of competing."

"That's human nature."

"And for that reason it is to be allowed to run unchecked?" He pushed his chair back and stood up. "Come, let us look more closely at these flowers." Anita followed him, and they strolled along the plants for several minutes, admiring and wondering, Anand identifying and explaining the peculiarities of several of them. "My father will be jealous," he said as they returned to their table.

Moosa appeared in front of them just as Anita was explaining about Ravi's poor condition. The restaurateur slapped a banana leaf in front of Anand, and another in front of Anita. "Yes?" he said. Both Anita and Anand agreed that they'd rather eat in the traditional manner and settled back for the rest of their meal. Moosa returned with a large bowl of rice, and delivered a substantial serving on each leaf. A moment later he was back with Anita's shrimp curry.

"And here's mine." Anand pulled himself up in his chair and watched Moosa closely as he ladled out several dishes from his tray—avial with its tasty drumsticks, beet thoren, cabbage thoren, mango pickle, okra in warm and spicy yogurt, spicy potato curry, banana chips, and two pappadum. Before he could return to the kitchen, however, Anand called for more rice, waiting somewhat impatiently for Moosa to serve it. He began to taste each item, alternating the vegetable dishes with a little rice mixed with plain yogurt. While he was checking out each item, Moosa added a small banana to the leaf and stepped back.

"You are liking?"

Anand leaned back in his chair, nodded a few times to Moosa, and settled in to dine, resting on his left arm. "And how is yours?"

"Mild, and very tasty. I think she uses nutmeg instead of cloves." Anita happily licked her fingers as she surveyed her leaf. "There's something else in here I don't recognize—at least I don't think I do, something I wouldn't ordinarily put in a shrimp curry."

"You can put anything into a shrimp curry."

"Even mustard seeds?"

Anand laughed. "Why not?"

"I wasn't sure you'd like this." Anita spooned out more curry onto the rice and began to swirl the two together.

"I always like good food."

"Maybe if we're really complimentary, he'll let me poke around in the back of the house."

"I should have known." Anand gave Anita a smile and waited. When she refused to meet his eye, he went on. "What do you think is hidden back there?"

"I don't know if anything is hidden back there, as you put it. But I saw someone come down a lane from there, and it got me wondering what else was there. I couldn't tell if the person I saw was a foreigner or an Indian in a sari, but something made me notice her, and it got me wondering."

When both were finished, a young boy appeared, folded up

the leaves, and slid them off the table. Anita and Anand walked to the nearby water spigot and washed their hands. A moment later Moosa appeared with two bowls of payasam, and two glasses of water with a short stick of patumukam in each.

"Ah," said Anand, reaching for the glass as soon as Moosa put it down. He raised it in a salute to Moosa and drank. When he was finished, he said, "Far too few even bother these days."

"I think you will like the payasam." Moosa departed with a broad smile.

"Do you think our bill just went up?" Anand winked at Anita. "Worth it."

Anita picked up her spoon and tried the payasam, its thick, milky texture dotted with raisins and cashews. "Well, I'm happy." Anand mumbled agreement, his mouth full. When she was finished she said, "I don't think I've ever seen this side of you, Anand."

He laughed. "I've been hiding my true self. I'm at heart an epicure, really, a hedonist."

"I got that. Tonight." She left some of her payasam uneaten, her thoughts now on Anand. He had always been so reserved and self-disciplined; as much as she enjoyed his company, she realized that she hadn't seen him quite this loose and unguarded before. It surprised her. It even made her feel a little unsteady. And that, she decided, might be a good thing. He was now, as far as she could tell, less predictable than she had thought—a man of depths hitherto concealed from her. And that, of course, made her curious.

When Moosa appeared with the bill, Anand took it, gave it a quick glance, and slapped it face down on the table. He pulled out his wallet and said, "Moosa, my companion is greatly curious about this area. She wants to wander around your yard, but I assure you, sir, she is not intent on stealing your recipes." He slid six one-hundred-rupee notes across the table to him. "But I wish she were."

Moosa led Anita and Anand to the back of the house and left his new guests, a party of four, under the attentive eye of his son, the young boy who had taken Anita and Anand's banana leaves. "It is a poor place, my wife's family home, but we are happy here. I am no longer the fishing man—I have a small shop just there." He nodded to Lighthouse Road. "And now I have a restaurant."

Moosa stopped and turned back to the house, for a moment lost in a reverie of pleasure at the thought of his new endeavor. "Yes, I have a restaurant." He sighed, then turned back to his guests. "Come."

He led them into the backyard, where a pair of chickens scratched in the dirt, a young girl knelt on the back veranda scrubbing pots, and a dog slept under a tree. The woman presumed to be his wife appeared in the doorway, a wooden ladle still in her hand, gave them a quizzical look, frowned, and quickly returned to her kitchen.

"I didn't realize there was so much back here," Anita said, moving to the narrow lane bordering the property.

"Ah, not so much. Just a few neighbors. Not so much."

Anita glanced at Anand, who turned to Moosa and expressed his interest in the orchids out front. It was exactly the right move—Moosa was voluble about his hobby, so much so that he completely missed Anita's drifting out of the yard and onto the narrow dirt path. She nodded to a family sitting out on their veranda and passed on, knowing they were watching her. Ahead she heard a sewing machine running, and saw a man at work in the front room of his house. Propped up against the front step was a sign—Nuisance Works. Below this were the words: All Problems Solved.

"Would that life were so easy," Anita said to herself, and passed on to the third house, the same size as the first two but without the chairs and activity out front.

At the end of the lane was a compound wall enclosing one of the new guesthouses built into the side of the hill. Anita pulled herself up just enough to peek over, and thought she recognized the back of Golden Palms Guesthouse. She dropped back down to the ground, turned, and followed the lane to the other end, where it led out into the open, facing the newly excavated land at the back of the temple grounds. This was where she had seen the woman emerging, pulling her pallu over her head. Anita looked across to where she had been standing yesterday morning, camera in hand. Yes, she thought, I was clearly visible. Anyone standing here would have recognized me there, a woman with a camera. She turned back to collect Anand.

"Did you find what you were looking for?" Anand asked as they strolled along Lighthouse Road.

"I'm not sure."

"What's out there?"

"A few families live out back on a tiny lane—just three houses. It runs up to the back of Golden Palms Guesthouse, and then in the other direction it comes out at the temple."

"Hmm."

"There was one thing, a sign at a house. I didn't recognize it. What is a Nuisance Works—All Problems Solved?"

Anand laughed. "I don't know, but I hope you find out that it is a place where all people can go. It sounds very necessary in this world."

CHAPTER TEN

Anita sat stock-still at the desk in the hotel office, listening to the fading whine of Anand's mini as it made its way up Lighthouse Road and into the night. She should have gone straight to her rooms over the garage, but instead the guard, Sanj, asked if he could run back to his house to check on his wife and their new baby. Anita said yes, mostly because she felt so unsettled she wanted to sit for a while and sort herself out.

She could not have said what was bothering her so much, but she couldn't shake this heaviness in her chest, as though her body were anticipating a great sorrow. Or perhaps it was the unspoken threat of the man Anand called his shadow, that slight, dark, wily-looking fellow she had first seen across the gallery, beneath the stairs to the bookshop. But she hadn't been the first one to see him, she now remembered. He kept popping up, and others noticed him more often than she did. But no one knew who he was. Was that what was distressing her, seeping into her mood like a pest in a forest, eating up all that was healthy?

Anita turned off the overhead light and switched on a single lamp on the desk set against the wall. This was where Auntie Meena filed her bills and other important papers, unless they went into the safe or a dead file. Sitting on top was the ledger she had been reading when Anita had come into the room and found her with it.

She picked up the ledger and set it on the table, pulled up the heavy cover and lay it flat on the surface, then turned the pages until she came to the current week's expenses. She read down the column, noting the usual expenditures for fresh produce, the charges for the special delivery when the regular van broke down and couldn't bring the fish, the fees to the workers, a fee to a villager to repair a portion of the fence butted by a meddling goat, a fee to a villager for commissioned work. Anita's index finger came to rest on a single line. The man was expensive, whoever he was. She followed her finger down the column. There he was again, and again he was expensive. She scanned to the bottom line—it was much higher than that of the previous week—and as far as she could tell by a cursory reading, the only significant difference was the commissioned worker.

But what was he doing? She would have to get the truth out of Auntie Meena. If this were one of her extravagant plans for enticing new customers, the hotel could go bust before it paid off. Anita thought back to the plan to offer guests what she announced, without warning, as the holy diet of the sannyasis—nuts and raw root vegetables. The hotel had emptied out overnight. And then there was the week that she had brought in a gaggle of priests to exorcise the hotel after a guest had been arrested for drunken behavior. The chanting through the night had enraged the remaining guests, who left the following morning, suddenly no longer interested in traditional India, only in getting a good night's sleep. She hoped this new extravagance wasn't more of the same. She closed the ledger.

Funny that Anita didn't feel tired exactly, just despondent. One guest had come close to death, and another was missing and probably already dead. It sickened her. What on earth had happened to Jean and Marge? Could two accidents, each so deadly in its own way, be a coincidence?

Of course not. She knew that. She folded her arms on the ledger, lay down her head, and closed her eyes. Something was eating away at her and she just couldn't figure it out.

"Hi!" The voice came again, repeating the greeting, a little louder the second time.

Anita opened her eyes. She straightened up when she heard the voice again.

"I didn't mean to wake you up."

"That's all right, Emily. I'm not really asleep. I'm just waiting for the guard to come back."

"Can I come in?"

Anita nodded, and Emily lifted the counter top and joined her in the office.

"I was lonely." Emily rustled in quietly in bare feet, her sari barely brushing the floor.

"It's late. I thought everyone was asleep." Anita leaned back in her chair and thwarted a yawn with pursed lips.

"Almost. I'm waiting for my roommates to get to sleep before I go back in. I don't want to get into any kind of hassle about you know what."

Anita nodded. She felt sorry for Emily, who obviously meant well but was having a rotten time with her traveling companions. "You tie that sari well, Emily. Westerners usually get it very wrong in the beginning. They walk out of the sari shop with everything just so, but the next day they have a hard time recreating it. I used to get called up to the guests' rooms regularly whenever we had a tour here, to help the women tie their saris on the second day."

Emily glanced down at the sari folds across her chest, then tugged the fabric a little higher over her shoulder. "Candy showed me how to do it."

"That was nice of her."

"She understands completely about Kali." Emily nodded gently, her eyes growing vacant, as though she had drifted off to a private world. Then suddenly she looked alert. "She's the one who suggested I talk to the priest about getting instruction, learning about Kali."

"Good idea." Anita didn't know if this was or was not a good idea, but it seemed a safe enough comment.

"There won't be anyone to turn to when I go home."

"There are lots of people in Philadelphia—you're not so far away from there, if I recall. Didn't you say you were from King of Prussia?"

"Oh, yes, that's true. But I was thinking about things more personal. Here I can just walk out my door and talk to anyone about the things that happen to me here—Kali, the astrologer, the palm reader, the one who interprets dreams."

"You can get that in Philadelphia too, especially down near Penn's Landing, near First Street."

"Maybe. But Indians probably interpret dreams differently than people at home."

"So maybe your dreams here are Indian-style dreams and in the States they're American-style dreams." Or maybe they're just dreams, Anita thought. She was coming to believe that not everything had meaning; it could be exhausting to find meaning in every coincidence, every snatch of conversation, every twinkle of a star.

Emily peered at her, her eyes growing bleary at the late hour. "You think so?"

"Could be." Anita had no idea what she should say. The whole thing seemed a bit odd to her. If Kali called someone, she called someone, and you lived your life accordingly, following her with meditation, worship, and vows. What else was there?

"I don't know. The dream interpreter was so comforting."

"I hope you didn't pay him a lot," Anita said automatically. As soon as she said it she realized how tired she was.

Emily smiled. "You're cynical, aren't you?" She shook her

head. "No, I didn't. He was so wonderful. I told him my dream, and he said it was about being removed from the polluting life of the westerner and welcomed into the world of Kali." She sighed. "It was a wonderful dream."

"It sounds like a good enough interpretation."

"I was in a dark place, thick and heavy and black. And then I started to float upward, but it wasn't easy—it was like being pulled through mud. And then I saw green shoots emerging from the ocean and finding soil on the rocks and growing there into a great plant." Emily began to elaborate on her dream, filling in details that may or may not have been part of the original dream. She warmed to her story and Anita listened in silence. When she was finished, Anita leaned forward.

"When was this?"

"Last night."

"When you were sleeping on the mat outside your bedroom?"

"No, not then. I think it was earlier, when I was downstairs, on the old settee, waiting for the others to go to sleep."

"By the window."

"Right. By the window. It was so beautiful that night. I've never slept in the open air like that. My family never went camping. And we have screens on our windows at home. It was so fabulous—all that air flowing around me. I almost brought my mat down there to sleep." Emily paused, aware that Anita seemed less approving. "Probably not a good idea, huh?"

"I think your dream is very interesting," Anita said.

Anita stood on the boulder waiting for the man ahead of her to lower his kerosene lantern, to better light her path. As soon as she had managed to send Emily on her way, Anita called Sanj on his cell phone and had him bring back a couple of fishermen with lanterns to help her search the rocky headland where the lighthouse stood. The guard didn't ask why, and Anita wondered

111

if he and the other guards in the resort had been waiting for the body of the missing tourist to be found in just such a spot.

Although the lighthouse compound itself was closed, anyone could approach the rocks along the shore. This part of the coast attracted lanky European men in worn lungis eager to meditate with the sun rising over the hills, American women seeking a private spot for a cup of coffee, swimmers looking for a quiet beach for an early morning dip. Fishermen used to having the space for their early morning toilets had moved farther south, to less inhabited areas. Dawn was some hours away, but the line of searchers moved erratically over the boulders.

The fisherman dangled the red-iron lantern over the black holes, and Anita jumped along after him. If she looked back, she knew she'd see Sanj up on the back wall of the parking area, cell phone in hand, ready to make the call Anita had warned him about.

"I think we should look along the shore here and all the way around," Anita said to the first fisherman. He nodded, and began to jump from boulder to boulder closer to the water.

The waves were quiet at this hour of the night. It was well after midnight, and although the tourist hotels were mostly quiet, guests and workers asleep and lights dimmed, Anita knew that many of the villagers were awake and at work. Out on the horizon were hundreds of lights, not those of a small town on the opposite shore, but dozens of fishing boats swinging their lanterns to attract fish to their nets. The two who had not gone to sea this night were older men content to let their sons and sons-in-law take over the family boat. These were the men she saw mostly during the day, scouring the rocks in the small inlet in front of the hotel for colonies of mussels, which they harvested with long knives like machetes, leaving their catch in rock pools while they cleared each section. She had seen them that morning working for several hours, before they tied up their bundles of mussels and carried them off, to be sold by wives and mothers and daughters at the fish market near the crossroads to the Catholic village nearby.

Neither fisherman asked her why she wanted to search the rocks at this hour of the night. They were content to supply the service requested, knowing they'd be well paid. Anita wondered if anyone along the shore would notice. Would the lighthouse guard peer out and, alarmed at their behavior, show up with a shout and a threat if they didn't move. Or, more likely, would she turn around to find the guard following her, his curiosity aroused.

The first fisherman pointed to something among the rocks close to the waves. Anita stretched and jumped and stepped boulder to boulder until she reached him. She knelt down and looked where he pointed—a white towel in a plastic bag held in place by an iron rod plunged in between the rocks. She stood and shook her head.

"It belongs to one of the foreigners who comes out here to meditate in the morning. I've seen him with this bag." I've wondered where he kept his things, she added to herself, since he seems to come across the rocks empty-handed.

The fisherman moved on. Anita followed, watching the shadows of the kerosene lantern slide and shift across the shore. As they reached the farthest point with nothing to show for their efforts except a few bits of refuse, some broken liquor bottles, and a scraped knee, Anita began to wonder if she'd been wrong about Emily's dream. Perhaps the dream was just a metaphor for her plunge into a new life, perhaps it was just a dream. But Anita didn't think so. It was the bit about the green sticking out of the ocean that got to her.

"Here. It is here." The fisherman spoke softly, leaning over the deep crevice between two boulders, waving his arm to Anita

113

to come along, but not turning to her, not taking his eyes off his discovery.

This must be it, Anita thought. He is concerned, circling the spot to get a better purchase.

The second fisherman hurried ahead, his lantern bobbing on its stick behind him. When he reached the spot, he peered at it, turned, and waved to Anita to stay back.

It must be bad, she thought. She knew both had seen crew members fall to their deaths in the ocean, to be eaten by sharks. There wasn't much left on earth that could surprise or frighten them. The lighthouse guard materialized behind her, just as she had expected, and hurried ahead, his soft rubber chappals molding to the boulders. He glanced down, then stood and raised his arms as he tried to shield Anita from the sight.

"It is a body," he said with an ominous frown.

"I suspected as much." Anita slipped past him.

Yes, it was as she suspected. Emily's dream was an incorporation of reality. She had seen something late last night, a fragment of a vision of Jean floating in the water toward the rocks, finally snagged among them, her green kerchief prominent in the moonlight. Even now, Anita thought, it seemed to glow, the only human element in this mass of decomposing flesh. She turned away from what was left of Jean's battered and disintegrating face and shoulders. She wouldn't have recognized the figure without the clothing, and she wouldn't have wanted to study the body any longer than the mere seconds necessary to identify it as human.

The others also turned away for a moment, the expression of compassion that one of their own should end this way; then they turned back and crouched as Anita worked her way back up the boulders and waved to Sanj, who waved back, then lowered his head over the cell in his hand. Behind her the fishermen and the lighthouse guard discussed how the police would extricate the body from its resting place, what damage might be done if they moved her this way or that, or perhaps an approach by sea might be best. Anita listened to their earnest planning, and felt a small hole in the universe close, erasing the life that had once been Jean.

For the first time Anita began to wonder deeply about Jean and who she was. She had shown so little of herself at the hotel, or perhaps she hadn't had enough time to share who she was other than her awkward bragging at breakfast on her first morning. But however it was, she was little known to them, and the one who knew her best, Marge, was still in hospital, recovering slowly.

Sanj waved, nodded to her, and turned away, walking out of sight.

The police would be here shortly, Anita knew. And they would have to decide how the body landed here, and what they would do, if anything, about it. But that didn't mean that she couldn't do something herself.

CHAPTER ELEVEN

Auntie Meena took the news of the discovery of Jean's body the way she took all news that might affect Hotel Delite—with a stoicism that bordered on the neurotic, ready to fend off any threat that might endanger her hotel, family, and guests. And that was any threat, no matter how minor, trivial, or invented. It meant, however, that she was fully alert, ready to manage every contingency. And that meant that she entered the dining room that morning with a broad smile and reassurance leaking from every pore.

"You see why our hearts are so solicitous for our guests," she said, leaning over the breakfast table. Emily kept her eyes fixed on Meena, whereas her friends and traveling companions barely glanced up from their appam and vegetable stew. They hadn't known Jean. A new guest was dining on cereal with buffalo milk, sort of inhaling the flakes and avoiding the milk on the spoon; she paid no attention to Meena, while her husband leaned back in his chair, sipped his coffee, and seemed to be evaluating Meena's performance.

"I read the sign on the back of the door, about undertows." Emily matched Meena emotion for emotion.

"Yes, this is so important, so important. We want only a safe visit for our guests, so you may return many times, many, many times." Meena gave Emily an especially endearing smile. "You must not be concerned. We keep our beaches very safe. You are swimming in the protected areas under the watchful eyes of the

116

guards, and you are safe. Perfectly safe." She flicked her fingers in a rush of relief.

"Good morning, Meena." Candy marched into the dining room, patted Meena on the arm, and slid into a seat. It must have startled Meena to be addressed so familiarly, but she didn't blanch.

"She's telling us about Jean," Emily said. "Poor Jean, they found her last night—in the rocks over there."

"Oh, I heard!" Candy's eyes popped open, and she spun around to look up at Meena. "Who found her? Fishermen?"

"Yes, fishermen found her." Meena looked away and began to shift her shoulders as though she were turning to leave. Poor Meena, Anita thought, she hates to lie, but she simply will not tell anyone that I found a body out there. Anita buried her head in her newspaper.

"What were they doing out there so late?" Emily asked.

"Fishing," Candy replied.

"We are having special breakfast breads today," Meena said. "Perhaps you have tried some of these. I think you are having them as pastries in your own countries."

"Count me in," the man at the opposite end of the table called out. Meena smiled at him, and went in search of Moonu. Great trick, thought Anita. Ply them with pastries and they'll forget their questions about Jean.

"I thought you handled it very well, Auntie," Anita later told Meena, after breakfast was over and the guests had cleared out. The two women were sitting at the small table under the window, a nearly empty pot of tea between them, their dishes cleared away. Moonu was wiping down the dining table and replacing the bamboo mats on the sideboard. He hummed a monotonous tune to himself as he went about his duties. Anita watched him, wondering if he sang better, would he be more graceful. She had never noticed before how lumpy his movements were, but at least he was careful. He wasn't known for breaking things, dropping trays, or mixing up orders. All in all, the hotel was lucky to have him—an honest, easygoing, careful employee, but tuneless.

"Why do they not read the sign?" Meena slumped in her chair. "Why do we strive to instruct and have such things happen?"

"I don't think it had anything to do with the sign, Auntie."

"Of course it does." Meena waved away Anita's comment. "And now all will know such a tragedy is tied to my hotel!"

"No one accuses you, I can assure you of that." And Anita was confident she was right.

Anita had been asked to unofficially identify the body, which she did to the best of her ability, pointing repeatedly to the green kerchief and the torn clothing. The police had examined the location with care, studied the shoreline south of the headland, discussed tides with the fishermen, and taken down the name of Hotel Delite, but little else.

The removal of the body had drawn the large crowd Anita had expected and proven to be the must-see event of the morning. It took the police all the time the fishermen had predicted to extricate the body—all the body—from its lodging place, and remove it from the rocky coast. They had resorted to a boat borrowed from the local fishermen on the next beach over, and motored away to the applause of the watching tourists.

Anita took the key for Jean's room off its hook and climbed the stairs to the second floor. She had been given Room 7, diagonally across from Marge's room and Emily's shared room. Anita unlocked the door and entered, closing it behind her. She had given the maidservant, Pama, instructions to plan on cleaning out the room for a late-afternoon arrival. Meena could in good conscience stop turning people away now that she knew Jean's fate.

But that didn't mean that Anita could close the door on Jean's disappearance. How did she get to that spot in the rocks? Is that where she would have landed if she fell in from the cliff farther down the shore, where Anita had found the scrap torn from her sweater? Would the police be able to tell if she had been injured before she entered the water? Anita doubted it. The image of Jean flashed into her mind again—the flesh decomposing, the body twisted beyond recognition. Her stomach seized, and she felt a deep sorrow for this woman who had meant to do so much good for a little village in Burma. She might have acted foolishly, even recklessly, but she was determined to act generously.

Anita threw the heavy key onto the bedside table and scanned the room. The windows were open, the door to the small balcony shut but not latched. The bed was made, and seemed untouched. Nothing had changed since her first quick look earlier. Anita walked over to the armoire and opened it. Jean was neat—slacks hung on hangers, blouses were folded in tidy piles on the shelf, toiletries were arranged in a traveling case. On the desk was an unopened bottle of mineral water, two small bananas with a couple of flies working on them, small chits for a restaurant meal and snacks, a paperback novel by Mishra Pankaj, a guidebook to Thailand, and a few Indian coins.

"This could be anyone's room," Anita said to herself. She tried the bathroom, but there too the items were generic, nothing personal, nothing indicative of a particular life. She turned to the suitcases, and pulled the smaller one onto the bed. The sound of the zipper momentarily filled the quiet between the crashing of the waves on the rocks below. Anita flipped open the top and began searching through the pockets—nothing significant, just a few pieces of hard candy, a pair of stockings, a few sanitary wipes in individual packets, a pen that had leaked ink, a few U.S. coins, and a packet of tissues. Anita closed it up and tried the second one, smaller and lighter.

This seemed to be Jean's traveling office, with a pad of paper, numerous pens and pencils, an envelope of U.S., Indian, and Thai stamps of various denominations, an appointment calendar with nothing in it for the current month, and a personal address book. Anita pulled out the remaining pockets, and came up with a thick manila envelope larger than a number ten business envelope. She looked in—letters with Thai addresses. Anita settled herself on the bed and began to read.

The first was a blue airmail letter, addressed to Jean in the States in a mature hand trained in a different script, but the letter's interior seemed to be written by a child just learning English. It thanked her for her help a year ago and promised that she was studying hard and doing well and would recite all that she had learned over the last year. The writer ended with the endearments of a grateful and dutiful child.

The next letter, though apparently not written by a child, was similar in tone and content, thanking Jean for the connections that brought him his new job, where, he assured her, he was flourishing and quite happy. Anita checked the addresses. They seemed to come from the same province, but beyond that she had no idea where they were from.

Anita went on through the letters, reading each one with its rigorous review of Jean's generosity, the recipient's success, and the gratitude of the entire family so wonderfully affected by her kindness. Jean was invited to school visits, home visits, tours of the temple, special festivals, special rites and holidays; she was offered a room to stay in, a free maidservant, a chef, food from the local tea shop, newly woven fabric and a tailor to make her clothes, and more. Anita opened and scanned half a dozen of these.

But one letter was different. This one came from an old woman who spoke of her kindness to her husband, who had now died. And since he had not been able to benefit from her medical care, perhaps she would consider looking at her granddaughter, who was languishing and had faced death many times. The illness was a muddle of words Anita couldn't make sense of, but the cry from the heart came through. And whatever Jean was bringing with her, the old woman wrote, was sure to be the answer to her prayers. She had healed others; she could heal her granddaughter.

Anita folded up the letters and slipped them back into their envelope. No wonder Jean had been so proud of her journey, so eager to share, even to brag. These letters were heady stuff— abject devotion from villagers who hadn't expected to have such good fortune, and it all just fell into their laps. For all her brusqueness, Jean must have flourished in an environment where she was truly needed and appreciated.

The last envelope was closed, but easily opened. Anita opened the flap and let the contents slide into her lap—a key, a business card, an address book with only four addresses in it, a receipt for a money exchange business, and a wad of Thai money, clean, crisp bills Jean most likely received when she exchanged money in New York before leaving for India. Anita studied the names— they were numbered one, two, three, or four, but listed alphabetically, not numerically, throughout the small book. Two names seemed to be European-American, and two seemed to be Thai.

"Another puzzle. First Marge, then Jean, and now this." Anita replaced the items in the envelope, closed up the small suitcase, and picked up the key, taking the suitcase with her. She would leave the rest for Pama, the maidservant, to pack and put away until they could decide what to do with it.

"And one last puzzle," Anita said as she turned the key in the lock. "Jean's purse."

Anita checked her watch, and decided not to call Anandabudhi Hospital just yet. She wanted to make sure she had all available information about Jean before she spoke with Marge and broke the bad news; she also wanted to find out everything she could about Marge's condition before saying anything. There was no telling how the woman would react.

How would I feel if I were traveling in a strange country and my good friend turned up dead and I almost died myself? Anita tried to imagine this scenario, thinking about traveling in places she knew nothing about—Latvia, Finland, Argentina, perhaps Fiji—and wondering how long it would take to feel balanced again. She slipped a key into the safe deposit box Jean had rented on arrival and slid out the metal drawer.

When Auntie Meena had first installed the safety deposit boxes, no one but the user had a key. But then a customer lost his key and couldn't get at his passport to prove his identity to the police after a traffic mishap. With the image of an angry Hungarian being released from a local jail fresh in her mind, Meena had duplicates made of every key and kept them in the hotel safe. Until now, Anita had never had reason to use one of them. As far as she knew, Jean's key was lost forever.

Anita tipped the box forward, and a number of items slid toward her. Anita turned the box over and its contents fell onto the desk. She poked among the clutter—a plane ticket; a passport; an envelope with U.S. dollars, clean, crisp bills; and a hand-drawn map. Anita pulled this out, opened it, and spread it on the desk. The names written in Roman letters were clearly Southeast Asian, probably Thai, but Anita couldn't have said where these places were. But she could guess.

"So this is where she was going," Anita said to herself.

"Who?" Ravi appeared in the doorway, leaning in and doing an abbreviated pushup by holding onto the jambs on either side. He bounced in and out, in and out, with a broad grin. "Who's going on a trip? You?"

"No, not me. I'm thinking this is about Jean's trip to Burma or Thailand." She slid the map across the table so he could see. He leaned in farther.

"Hmmp." He wrinkled his nose, as though the paper had a smell. "Are you recovered?"

"What? Oh, yes. I guess. You know, I've never seen anyone in such a condition before. It makes me feel like I understand how someone becomes a Buddhist. When you look down on something and you can't even recognize that this was someone you know, it feels like there's no substance to life at all. I wasn't ready to see how easily the human body will disintegrate." She looked down at her own body, at the light blue embroidered salwar khameez. She took a deep breath and looked up. "The police are trying to figure out how it happened."

"Ah." Ravi smiled sadly and continued his gentle bouncing.

"We don't know enough about them to figure this out." Anita folded up the map and returned it to the box. "They arrive and then the next thing you know, one is gone and the other is dying."

"Ah," Ravi said, nodding. "Karma."

"No, Ravi, it's not karma. It's ordinary human evil."

"Yes, karma." He leaned against the jamb and gave her a stern look.

"Okay, skip that. Do you remember what happened their first night? They went out to dinner, remember?"

Ravi began to look uncomfortable, pushing away from the doorjamb and looking around him. "They are coming so early in the morning."

"Yes, but that night, Jean and Marge went out to dinner—

Anand and I saw them—and then they went to the Kali temple"

"Everyone went to the Kali temple—is it not their festival time?"

"But then what, Ravi? I know you didn't actually see them, but I have to find out what happened when they left the temple."

Ravi turned away as Anita pelted him with a series of questions, looking this way and that as though some exciting activity was getting ready to overwhelm him. Beyond him, Anita saw two guests pass the registration desk, towels over their shoulders, hats covering their heads; they dropped their key on the desk and gave a languid wave. Ravi dived for the key, wishing them a wonderful day in God's Own Country.

"Ravi?" Anita followed him out to the desk. "What's going on?"

"Nothing is going on. I am preparing for my duties." He lay out a ledger, flipped it open, pulled out a stool, and hopped up on it. With great seriousness, he studied the pages before him— they were a mosaic of different-colored blocks signaling who was staying where and the sort of room they had and for how long—it was Ravi's and Meena's own private code for managing the hotel. Anita lay her arm across the pages. "What?" Ravi gave a good imitation of someone feeling indignant.

"What did Jean and Marge do after the puja? Did they come back to the hotel?"

"Am I expected to know all these things?"

"Expected to? No. Likely to? Yes. Aren't you the one who figured out who was pilfering towels and cutlery just by reciting the times a certain guest came and went? And who knew we should even be paying attention? Of course you know when Jean and Marge returned to the hotel. Don't you?"

Ravi made a face a Kathakali master would have been proud of.

"Oh, Ravi. When you admitted to not being at the desk, I

thought you meant you first went off for a minute. Weren't you here at all?" Anita sighed, and sagged against the counter. "Oh, Ravi, just when I really needed you. You know, if Meena finds out you weren't here . . ." She leaned closer to him. "Who covered for you?"

"Ah, well, a relative."

"You let a relative cover for you—here? Don't you realize what Meena would have done if she'd found out?"

Ravi nodded vigorously, looking greatly relieved. "But it is past now. And you will not speak of this again to anyone, right?"

"You are a reckless man, Ravi. Reckless."

"Yes, Missi." He smiled, tapped his fingertips lightly against his lips, and returned to his study of the ledger.

"In that case, I need to ask your relative when Jean and Marge returned. Who was here?"

"Who?"

"Ravi, you looked awful. Are you frightened? Who did you get to stand in for you?"

"I shall ask him. Do not concern yourself. I shall ask him when these women are returning and shall present this information to you. You shall be informed shortly." With that he hunched over his pages and turned his face away. "Now I really must study this. We are having tour of Norwegians coming soon."

CHAPTER TWELVE

At a little after eleven o'clock in the morning Anita arrived at Anandabudhi Hospital and asked to see Marge's doctor. She settled herself on the banquette lining the windowed wall and prepared to wait. The line of patients and family members grew, and the seats filled up, but with the air conditioning purring along, no one was complaining except the sickest patients. A tall Indian in an elegant pair of slacks, silk shirt, and Italian leather shoes inspected a seat, then lowered himself onto the vinyl, nodding shyly to the holy man sitting next to him, his long, matted locks wound around and around his head like a giant wasp's nest.

After a half hour wait, a young woman in the green uniform sari appeared before Anita, wiggled her fingers in a signal that Anita was to follow her, and headed down the long hallway. Anita followed her down into a large space, down a corridor, and around a corner to a hallway lined with offices with wide wooden doors. The guide motioned Anita to take a seat on a narrow bench, and she did; she was soon alone. Other patients and guides passed along the hall she had just left, and she was alone in this corridor, staring at the door ahead, waiting for it to open and the doctor to emerge. Eventually it did.

"You are Shreemati Nayar?" The doctor waved her into the office. She was a young woman in her late thirties, perhaps, wearing the obligatory Kerala gold earrings, but no bracelets and Western-style makeup. When she spoke, Anita thought she

126

detected an American accent beneath the Malayalam.

"Ah," Dr. Premod murmured after Anita explained her mission. "Yes, we think it was something she ate. We do not yet have toxicology results in hand, but we expect to identify the cause." She leaned over the open file on her desk, then looked up. "There was some trouble for others also. Some similar malady, though not as severe for the other tourists."

"I hadn't heard that." The thought flashed into Anita's mind that the entire incident was just a matter of poorly cooked food. "Were these people who dined at the new Bamboo Village Restaurant?"

Dr. Premod frowned, and began to shuffle papers. "No, no, they were dining at a guesthouse—Savitra's Rest. It is on the road into Kovalam, I am told."

"That's a different place."

"Perhaps the staff are shopping at the same market and purchasing the same contaminated goods." The doctor smiled and opened another folder.

"Will the toxicology report take long? I'd like to see it." Anita wasn't ready to dismiss Marge's crisis as merely accidental food poisoning, not after what had happened to Jean.

"A matter of days, I am thinking." The doctor leaned over the file. "She is much recovered now and eager to be discharged. Does she have family with her?"

Anita explained about Jean, and the doctor looked worried.

"She is not yet ready to be on her own. Can you make arrangements for her to convalesce at the hotel? She will need a nurse standing by. She wants to leave today, but I think tomorrow is better."

"I'm sure we can do something." Anita pulled out her cell phone and began to imagine different scenarios and who she'd have to call. "Would it be all right if I spoke with Marge now? I have a couple of questions that are confusing me, and the answers might help the police figure out what happened."

Dr. Premod began to squirm in her chair, paused, then with a shake of her head and a shrug, agreed. Anita was taken once again on a long walk through corridors and hallways, until she came to a wing of private rooms.

Dr. Premod waved Anita into a small but tidy room and nodded to a figure sleeping in the dim light. Marge lay dozing in a wood-framed bed, the cotton sheet pulled up over her chest, a smooth expanse of white, as though anytime she moved or wiggled, a nurse came by to correct the disarray. Anita was glad of the moment before Dr. Premod called out to the patient—it was just enough time for Anita to cover the shock of Marge's appearance.

Anita was used to seeing men and women ruined by drugs in northern Indian cities flopping around the cheaper tourist sites in the south, the child beggar carrying a younger sibling whose head bobbed dangerously on a shriveled neck, the beggar whose illnesses far outstripped the meager diet he commanded. But Marge was an American who had arrived only days before in robust health, and now, today, she looked frail and drawn, all resources depleted, her skin waxy and pale. It reminded Anita of a body waiting for the undertaker—it was hard to see any life in Marge.

"Good of the hotel to make the arrangements," the doctor said as Marge began to focus on the two women. She produced a surprisingly warm smile, and a sparkle enlivened her dull eyes.

"I'm ready to leave as soon as you'll let me."

"Ah, well, tomorrow I am thinking." The doctor stepped back and swept her arm out. "And here is Miss Nayar from your hotel inquiring after you. Shall I leave you together for a few minutes?" Marge nodded yes, to Anita's relief, and the doctor left the room.

Anita pulled a chair out from the wall and sat down facing Marge. She had been given a private room, small but painted pale yellow with a comfortable reading chair against the far wall, but Anita could see that Marge did not want to remain here; the patient was ready to leave even if she wasn't yet advised to.

"Good of you to come." No longer the cautious uptight woman Anita had first met at breakfast, the American nurse seemed frighteningly fragile, as though she had imploded, collapsed within, the poison sucking in her once robust body. Her voice occasionally broke into its earlier timber, but mostly rasped as she struggled to get the words out.

"I was hoping Jean would stop by. I'm not sure what day it is, so I don't know if she's still here or not."

Anita winced. This wasn't going to be easy at all, she thought. Jean sounds so driven that she'd leave without saying goodbye to her traveling companion, and Marge sounds like she'd be upset if that happened.

"What's wrong?" Marge asked.

"I do have some bad news. It's about Jean. She seems to have fallen off a cliff over the ocean and been swept away. They found her body this morning." Anita watched Marge for her reaction, ready to jump up and summon an attendant and the doctor, but Marge surprised her. A wave of sadness seemed to wash over her as she turned her face away, pressing her eyes shut, then staring up at the ceiling; her breathing accelerated and a pink flush came into her cheeks. Marge was trying not to cry. "I'm very sorry."

Marge shook her head. "Thank you, but it's all right. We were colleagues. I've known her for years, through one job or another. I just think it's sad that it had to happen here and at this time."

Anita couldn't comment—this was an unexpected reaction,

more pragmatic than personal—a desperate attempt to control her feelings.

Marge took a ragged breath and turned again to Anita. "She was so looking forward to her return to Burma—it meant everything to her. You must have noticed how proud she was of what she was planning."

"I did wonder that she spoke so freely about it."

"Indiscreetly, you mean."

Anita smiled.

"It was all she talked about at home too, the few times I saw her there outside of work situations. And even in some work situations. The time she spent collecting equipment, raising funds, making contact with anyone who might be able to help her over there." Marge let her eyes fall shut, and Anita fell to imagining the number of people who would be surprised and saddened to hear about all these plans coming to nothing. But who would tell the villagers?

"Marge, I know this is unpleasant, but I'm wondering if you remember anything that could help us."

"What do you mean help you?" Marge struggled to pull herself upright in bed and only succeeded in making her face red. "It wasn't just an accident, was it?" Marge glared at her. "I knew it. I knew it. I told her to stop talking all the time about it. I told her we should leave. And . . ."

Marge began to cough and choke; Anita jumped up but Marge's hand shot out and grabbed hers.

"I'm all right. Really, I am."

Anita sat down again as Marge relaxed her grip. "Tell me about that evening, Marge. My friend and I saw you leaving the Bamboo Village Restaurant just as we were arriving. And then we saw you at the temple. Did you go straight back to the hotel?" Marge nodded. "Do you remember the time?"

"It was after ten, maybe ten-thirty. I know because I commented on it to Meena. I mentioned what a long day she had, and how glad she must be that it was almost over, working from breakfast up to such a late hour. Actually, I was shocked she was up so late, but she said the guard was just about to take over. I saw him, at least I think it was the guard, hanging around the parlor near the open windows, in a red plaid lungi and a white T-shirt. I would have thought he was someone who should be sent away for annoying the guests, but Meena seemed to trust him."

"That's Sanj," Anita said. And a finer man you'll never meet, she added to herself. "And that was the end of the evening for you? You went up to your rooms?"

"I did. I'd begun to feel sick, well, tired, heavy. I'm not sure what Jean did." Marge's voice began to fade, as though the horror of the events was at last overtaking her. "I didn't pay any attention to her."

"I don't want to tire you," Anita said. "Could I ask you one more question?"

"Sure." Marge lay back now, her head sinking into the pile of pillows, her skin fading to the color of khadi cloth. "But I really don't know anything more about what she did that night."

"It's not about that night. It's about my gallery down near the beach."

"Your gallery? What do you mean?" Marge managed a puzzled look, though her eyes were growing dull again.

"Yes, you came in earlier that day and you were looking at the photographs, but then you stopped to look at the bulletin board where I pin all the postcards and notes I get from people who have been to Kovalam and visited my gallery. You were reading them and something there seemed to upset you." Anita didn't have to ask Marge if she remembered; her expression said it all.

Her hands began to twist the starched sheet into little cones and she seemed to struggle with what she would say. In the end she pressed out the wrinkles in the sheet as she spoke, softly, choosing her words carefully. "Yes, I was upset. I told Jean about it, but she just dismissed me. She wasn't worried at all. She kept saying, it was all in the past, all in the past. I'd made a mistake."

"What was all in the past?"

"The trouble she ran into last year." Marge turned her head away and stared at the ceiling.

"I can see this is hard for you, Marge, but this could be important. It might have something to do with Jean's accident."

Marge's eyes gazed at Anita, without shock or fear or surprise. "It wasn't really an accident, was it?"

"No, I don't think so. And if you don't think it was either, you have to tell me why."

"I knew it, I knew it. I told her to be careful, but she wouldn't listen. She kept saying nothing's going to happen this time. I've taken care of everything."

"Nothing's going to happen this year?" Anita leaned closer, feeling she was about to get at something real, something more than the hints and suggestions that had been suckering her along without adding up to enough to tell her anything real.

"I didn't believe her, not really. That's why I couldn't bring myself to go with her." She squeezed her eyes shut. "She really made me feel like I was some sort of coward, but I just couldn't do it."

"What about last year?"

Marge kept her eyes shut, her breathing growing labored, as though it was easier to talk without looking at anyone. "It was awful."

"You were there?"

"Oh, no, not me. But I got all the frantic phone calls, then the irate ones, then the last ones telling me not to talk to anyone or believe anyone." She sighed and tried to get more comfortable in her bed, struggling against the emotion she had called up, the memories of something that had gone terribly wrong.

"Tell me about last year." Anita urged her on with a soft voice and an almost physical need to get the story out of her.

"You really don't know, do you?" Marge gave her a pitying look. "It's not all that dramatic, except for Jean. It did upset her."

"It had to be something big if it upset Jean."

Marge laughed, but without goodwill, a sort of wretched gurgling emerging from her throat. It occurred to Anita that Marge was bitter—about what she couldn't say, but definitely bitter. "There's not much to tell," Marge began. "She sent supplies ahead of her—medical stuff—and it was stolen. Black marketer got hold of it, and she said it just went to show that you couldn't trust anyone, and she wouldn't make the same mistake twice."

Anita repeated the last part. "So, she was refusing to be frightened off, no matter what."

"I don't know about that," Marge said, relaxing into the pillows. "But she seemed to feel the trouble was behind her."

"Medical supplies."

Marge nodded, a bleak look spreading across her weary face. "They even tried to force Jean to give up more supplies—kind of blackmailing her—but she didn't have anything you couldn't buy right there in Bangkok. They didn't believe her at first—that was the scary part—they kept threatening her." She closed her eyes and calmed her ragged breath. "But you didn't know Jean. She stood her ground and they left her alone after a while."

Anita leaned back in her chair and considered this. Asia was practically a boom town for medical care—where she was sitting at that very moment was certainly an example of that. Foreigners came to India for the best care at one third or less of the cost in the United States. India had a huge manufacturing segment that produced everything an advanced hospital needed. Would black marketers really be so interested in the meager supplies of an American nurse going into the Burmese jungle? "Why was she so sure it was black marketers that took her supplies?"

"She saw some of the equipment for sale in a local market— she recognized some of it."

"What did my bulletin board have to do with this?"

"There was a postcard from a man Jean thought was behind it all."

"So, was it the postcard from Jake Lanier?" Anita asked. "Is that who you were trying to trace on the Internet?"

Marge stared at her, her pale face pinched and spotty. "How did you know about that?"

"I went down to the Internet café to see if I could trace your usage. The owner put me on the same computer and I checked out the sites you had visited."

"You're pretty nosy. You do this all the time?" Marge gave her a look of complete distaste.

"There was a chance, Marge, a very good chance, that you might not have lived to have this conversation with me, so, yes, I do this when I feel I have to." Anita stopped telling herself the woman was sick and glared right back. "You were very sick, Marge, and Jean is dead. And both incidents are tied to my aunt's hotel. I mean to figure them out."

Marge let her eyes fall shut and seemed to drift off into a private world. "All right. Sorry, I'm just feeling, oh, I don't know. Yes, I wanted to find out if he was still out here, this Lanier person, but I couldn't find anything, just that news piece about him being held for questioning for drugs or something." Marge coughed. "Jean said the postcard had to be over a year old and he probably wasn't anywhere near here. I didn't realize it was so old. I thought he was going to show up while we were right there in the hotel."

"Seeing that postcard really spooked you," Anita said, trying to gauge if Marge was telling her everything.

Fear flashed across Marge's pale face. "Well, Jean said he threatened to turn her into the authorities."

And you were afraid, Anita said to herself, that this time you could be in danger too; you could end up in a prison in India. "No wonder you were spooked."

"Jean insisted she had everything covered and it wouldn't happen again. There was nothing to worry about."

Anita opened her mouth to point out the obvious—that anything could happen with this kind of venture—but didn't bother. It was too late anyway.

"You think it's nonsense, don't you? I can see it in your expression. But the black market is worth millions, and Jean made it so easy for them. She barely knew the people she was working with. And god knows, she was never discreet." Marge turned away and didn't try to hide her weariness. "Jean was asking for trouble, the way she talked. She had so much money with her, and all that equipment she kept talking about. It's not cheap, you know. And plenty left over for travel? She couldn't stop talking about it."

"Last time also? Did she talk about her plans last time she went?"

"Even worse. She all but named the village. She had been told not to, and not to name anyone she was working with. It was worth their lives if she did."

"But the rest of it she didn't hold back on," Anita said, half to herself.

"She was so proud of what she was doing." Marge's face softened, and Anita began to wonder again about the nurse at the breakfast table—which one was the real Marge? "And she really was doing an awful lot of good."

"Was she known on some sort of circuit? Some inner circle of nurses and doctors doing work sub rosa?"

Marge laughed, a sound more of coughing and an interrupted giggle. "No, not Jean. She spent her whole career in private clinics and hospitals training other nurses to manage anything that came along. She loved her work, and I don't think before this she ever left the United States."

"What happened?"

"She got to know a nurse whose family was from Burma, and she used to talk about how hard life was, without medical care, the way the military burned the farmers' crops to force them away from the border and into the interior, the way soldiers came into their villages and took the men and the boys."

"And it got to her." Anita nodded, having no trouble imagining the horror stories.

"Not that stuff. You would think it would—it gave me goosebumps listening to her—but Jean was pretty inured to any complaints she thought were about political issues. No, it was a photograph of a village clinic. The nurse showed Jean a photograph of her family with the newest baby in front of the local clinic where her mother had been a midwife. And Jean was so shocked by the conditions, she went around sputtering for days. She kept saying to everyone, 'And they do surgery there! Surgery!' " Marge began to cough from exhaustion and excitement.

"I'm tiring you out."

"It's all right." She took a deep breath and exhaled. "I'm okay."

"And that's the village she was going to visit?"

Marge nodded. "She has—had—a list of contacts and a map, so she could get in and out without anyone in the government knowing. She made arrangements for her equipment and supplies—much better, she said, than last time."

"I think I found the list of contacts; I did find the map."

"I feel so sorry for the villagers. Jean made it sound like they lived for her return. That's probably an exaggeration, but still. What will happen to them now?"

Anita shook her head. "I don't know. We'll try to get word to them if we can. But, in a case like this, they'll just have to decide on their own why she isn't coming. The foreign newspapers aren't likely to carry a report of her death, at least not one that the villagers would recognize."

"That's so sad." Marge closed her eyes again, and this time turned her face to the wall.

At the door, Anita paused. "Could I ask you one last question? It's about what made you sick." Anita waited while Marge turned back, her face pale and blotchy, clearly that of a woman still sick, tired, barely able to manage the moment.

"I don't know what it was. Dr. Premod hasn't told me. I can't seem to remember to ask when she comes in. Does it matter?"

"It might. I think it does." Anita took a step closer. "You were leaving the Bamboo Village Restaurant when Anand and I were arriving. You didn't notice us. But do you remember what you had?"

Marge looked blank for several minutes, and Anita thought she'd fallen asleep. Maybe it was a stupid question, she thought; after all, I can barely remember what I had, and I haven't had any shocks or sickness since then.

"I had a vegetable curry that seemed pretty sweet—lots of coconut milk. And plain rice. And Jean had the Goa fish curry." Marge smiled, a thin smile that seemed forced. "She liked to tell everyone how much she liked Indian food, so she always ordered hot food. She seemed to think Indian food had to be hot to be spicy. I don't think she really liked it that much. She drank an awful lot of water with her meal."

"Did you try it?"

Marge shook her head. "Not me. I learned my lesson years ago."

"This was Jean's second trip to India. And your first?"

"That's right." Marge watched Anita.

"Okay. Samosas?"

"Oh, yeah, the mixed platter of starters. They were good."

"Was that it? You didn't eat anything else after that?"

"I had some fruit later, and, oh, yeah, the prasadam at the Kali Temple." She gave a sigh and closed her eyes. "The fruit here is so cheap but so good."

CHAPTER THIRTEEN

Anita stepped out into the harsh sun—it was nearly noon—and crossed the tiled entry yard, deep in her own thoughts and oblivious to the autorickshaw wallahs clamoring for her business. She came to at the sound of a horn, and smiled at her driver, who had pulled up a foot in front of her. On the way back to the hotel, she had plenty of time to think about Marge's story. About Jean's pride in her efforts, the loss of her supplies the first time around, the involvement of a supposed tourist who had passed through Kovalam and his subsequent arrest, the coded information on how to pass in and out of Burma, and the innocence of Jean and Marge's last evening together.

After Anita paid her driver, she headed straight into the hotel, past the registration desk, and on into Auntie Meena's office, closing the door behind her. Anita dropped her purse on the table, pulled out a chair, and sat down facing her aunt.

"Eh? You have become your mother overnight?" Meena's eyes widened as she took in her niece's behavior. "But it is my hotel."

"First, you were on the desk the night Marge got sick and Jean disappeared. Not Ravi."

"Ah . . ."

"Don't bother with the lying. I know it's true. But we'll come back to that."

"I am your aunt! Your mother's younger sister! Is this not my hotel?"

139

"Tell me what Jean did after Marge went upstairs. Did you see her go anywhere else? Talk to anyone?"

"Oh, is that what this is about." Auntie Meena leaned back in her chair with a visible sigh of relief. "Only I mean you are sounding like you are giving the ultimatum for leaving India, and what would I do?" She let her hand flutter across her chest and come to rest over her heart.

"Auntie Meena, this is important. I'm annoyed with you for lying to me, but I'm not going to leave India just because you're . . . well, whatever you're doing." Anita sighed. "I have to know about that night."

"Oh, yes, so I see. It's just that you are worked up. All right." Meena brushed her hair away from her face and settled herself into her chair. "There is so much to do these days. I am sending Ravi on an errand, one I cannot undertake myself at such an hour. So, I am sitting at the registration desk as the late arrivals appear. Then I am closing up, and handing over to the guard, Sanj. So reliable, Sanj. And such a good nature."

"Jean and Marge, Auntie. Marge said they returned at around ten or ten-thirty. Do you remember? Marge said Sanj was hanging around in the parlor waiting to close up."

"Quite probably. Let me think, Anita. You are so angry with me that I find it hard to think. I do not like anger—it is unsettling, yes?" Meena gave Anita a pleading smile, then hurriedly added, after seeing Anita's expression, "All right, all right."

"Think, Auntie."

"Yes, it was close to ten-thirty. I asked Sanj to be here by ten-fifteen because I was so weary. He was here on time, ready to take over, and I was just saying good night to the two American ladies. One of them is feeling unwell—she is looking somewhat unwell. Marge? Yes, Marge. She intends to go straight to bed, she says, and so she takes the stairs up to her room. I hear the door opening and closing. She has gone to her room, I am thinking. But the other one, Jean, isn't it? She is going into the parlor because the night is beautiful and she is gazing out the window. And that is all I know. I am retiring with exhaustion." She lifted her hands, palms upward, and gave a shrug.

Anita studied her aunt for another minute, then rose and pulled open the hotel safe. She drew out a metal box, opened it with a key from her own keychain, and fingered the many keys therein.

"What are you doing?"

"I'm going to look through the safety deposit boxes. Someone here must know Jean from Thailand, and I want to check their passports and anything else they've put inside for safe keeping."

"Are we allowed to do this?" Meena tipped her head to one side.

"I'm doing it." Anita pulled out a set of keys from the box, walked over to the case of boxes, and unlocked several at once. She pulled one drawer out and glanced through its contents—a return plane ticket, passport, extra cash, some jewelry, credit cards. She went on through several more drawers, finding the same items in almost every one. At the fifth drawer, she stood for some time going through the items.

"What are you finding?"

"Emily passed through Thailand. It's in her passport."

"Let me see." Meena joined Anita, and took Emily's passport from her. "Yes, you are right. But she has not mentioned this."

"No, she hasn't."

"It is only for a week. How can this matter?"

"I don't know, Auntie. But her being called by Kali could be a cover for something else."

"Ah, this is not good. To use Kali as a shield." Meena clucked disapproval.

"Marge said that other than her restaurant meal, the only other foodstuff she ate was prasadam from the temple."

"Ah," Meena said, shaking her head, "she is not eating this, at least not all of it. Pama is finding it in her room and bringing it to the cook."

"You're sure about this?"

Meena nodded. She was sure.

"So that leaves only the food from the restaurant."

"But who else? Perhaps there is more in these boxes?"

"You mean, now that I'm snooping, I should finish the job, just so we won't miss anything."

"Anita, such talk." Meena pulled out the next drawer and peeked in. "Ah, this belongs to Candy." She opened the passport and scanned the pages. "Candace Arabedian. She too has been to Thailand in the past year. These foreigners have so much money. They are traveling everywhere, and yet they dress like paupers."

Anita crossed the sand to the beach promenade and stopped at the first fruit seller, a woman she had done business with frequently. She ordered a bowl of fruit and sat down on the stone walk to wait, her toes wiggling in the sand cooled by a tattered beach umbrella tilted over the woman. The woman chatted about her life and how hard business was this year—"The foreigners want to bargain, to bargain, to bargain. Don't they eat fruit in America?"—and how little help the constable was when someone pilfered from her meager supplies. Anita was on the verge of agreeing that life was pretty rotten when she was handed a bowl of fresh-cut fruit and a small spoon. Anita ate, and the woman hummed and chatted.

"More? You are having more?"

"This was plenty." Anita handed back the bowl and spoon.

"You eat like the hunger is in here, not here." The woman patted first her heart, then her stomach.

"It's both." Anita explained her unsuccessful efforts to figure out what happened to Jean and Marge. "Marge will live, but Jean is gone."

"Yes, we are all hearing about the body," the fruit seller said.

"She went off two nights ago, and we don't know why. We don't know where she went, though I have an idea, and I'm at a dead end."

This was the toughest one. Yes, Jean had been indiscreet, a bit hard to take with her talk about her special work in Burma, her dismissal of anyone else when she was caught up in her own chatter, but there was nothing that Anita could see that explained why someone would want to harm her. Anita shared it all with the fruit seller.

"Hate or fear. One of those. What else is there?" The fruit seller began to clean the bowl, and dropped the spoon into a small red bucket of soapy water.

"Greed, lust, envy," Anita said.

The woman shook her head. "No, no, isn't so. The animal heart is not so complicated. Greed is hatred of those who are richer than you are, who have what you want; lust and envy are the same."

"Hate or fear." Anita repeated the words as though she had never heard them before. She had been wondering in the back of her mind why Jean and Marge had been targeted, thinking that as soon as she found out who, she would understand why. But perhaps the why was simpler than she'd thought. Perhaps it was simply a matter of someone hating—or fearing—one or both of the women.

Anita thanked the fruit seller, and clambered back up onto the walkway, heading for her gallery. She had been neglecting her work over the last several days, and this might be just the time to sit still inside the gallery, let the tourists pick at her artwork, and let her own thoughts drift about the questions surrounding the death of Jean and the attack on Marge.

Anita turned into her lane, nodding at the young man lounging outside the doorway to the gift shop on the corner; his front window, narrow and shiny clean, was filled with miniature figurines—elephants, palm trees bending over grass huts, figures of Nayar women with stylized hair not seen since the 1800s, fishing boats, and more.

"They will have to name these lanes some day," she said to herself. "There are too many of them now for foreigners to be able to tell them apart without names and signs. 'Go three buildings past the Bakery, to the lane at the corner of the suitcase store.' No, formal names will have to be chosen."

She was thinking of how sensible a proposition this was as she headed toward her gallery. Three women in bathing suits and wraparound skirts passed her, a man with his finger marking his place in a thick paperback book stepped aside to let them pass, and a child selling handmade wooden figurines from a basket atop his head twirled one way then another in a vain attempt to interest one of the foreigners into buying. In this whirl of colors and bodies Anita barely noticed the dark eyes watching her. And then she recognized him—understood who he was. She knew him. He knew she recognized him—she could see it in his eyes, a tiny flicker of acknowledgment.

He slipped behind a middle-aged couple and ran down the lane, weaving around foreigners and Indians alike. Anita bolted after him. He was thin, wiry, fast—but Anita was angry and determined. She bumped into foreigners and didn't bother to apologize, Indians quickly jumped out of her way. The man turned into a narrow alleyway, bricks rising in waist-high walls on either side; Anita raced after him, just catching a glimpse of his red lungi disappearing around the far corner. She turned, darted through a crowd, and found herself in the dirt yard of a private home turned into a guesthouse. A man sat reading on the veranda. He glanced at her, then pointed to the dirt path leading through a bare plot.

She jumped through the gate and ran, again catching sight of the man as he turned a corner. She followed him through another yard. He jumped the narrow canal, and raced on past the beggar sitting on the walkway, jumped over a dog sleeping in the middle of the lane. Anita raced after him; in the distance she heard the sound of a motorcycle starting up. She rounded the corner just in time to see him guiding his bike through a yard, swerving around a well, scattering chickens, then climbing a hill up to the road.

Anita bent over, bracing her hands on her knees while she tried to catch her breath. Exhausted from both the heat and the exertion, she sucked in great gobs of air, then started back to the gallery. A beggar woman smiled at her and lifted her open palm. Her breath still ragged, Anita stopped and rummaged in the purse still slung across her chest for some small bills.

"Bad man!" the old woman said.

"You know him?" Anita was nonplussed. She hadn't expected someone so averse to being spoken to or identified to let himself be known to anyone in the resort.

"A bad man." The old woman took the money and touched the notes to her closed eyes. She tucked the money into her choli. "Very bad man."

"Who is he?"

"Black marketer." She began to look woeful again. Anita pulled out more rupees. "He is worker for much bigger man. Buying and selling." She again touched the notes to her eyes, and secreted them. "Mostly selling, very little buying. Mostly stealing and selling."

"Stealing from tourists?"

"Anyone, but especially tourists. Jewelry, tickets, passports.

All sorts of goods."

Anita gazed down at this wizened creature in a thread-bare sari, her bare feet dangling over the weed-choked canal, her tin box battered and rusty, and holding little more than a samosa, perhaps some paper to prove her identity. How did she know so much? Behind Anita the resort unfolded in a maze of lanes and hotels and tailors and restaurants that constituted the fastest growing tourist attraction in this part of the world. She glanced again at the beggar woman. For her, sitting here and watching the Indian workers and foreign tourists walk by must be like watching a movie. She has nothing to do but watch and hope someone, anyone, will take the least used path and spare her a few coins.

"How does he operate?"

The woman frowned at the expression. "How does he manage his motorcycle?"

"No, I mean, how does he know who has something to steal? I live here. What would I have?"

"Yes, this is true." She paused to study the canal, which would soon be choked by so many lotuses that it was unsalvageable. The old rice paddies that edged the beach were only a memory now. Anita pulled out more rupees. "But they are knowing these things. Guards at the airport, drivers to hotels, sweepers in banks. Do they not have eyes and ears? And if a woman from a hotel dies, her property remains at the hotel, isn't it?"

"So that's why I am of interest to a black marketer." Anita felt a chill go through her. Were there others? How long had they been watching her? "What else do you know?"

"I am a poor woman."

"But getting richer by the minute." Anita handed over more rupees. The old woman smiled, completed her ritual with the money. "Tell me what you know."

"He is a bad man, but he is only one. He follows many paths

and sees many things. But I am a poor woman. How much can I know?" She turned her seeking gaze to a couple wandering along the walkway, and opened her mouth to wail. "Maaaa!" she cried in the plaintive wail of the Indian beggar.

Anita left her to it.

Anita pulled up the metal shutter and opened her gallery to a stifling hot day inside and out. She could feel herself getting angry—she didn't like the feeling of being hunted and chased. No, she wouldn't take that. Next time she'd catch him.

Peeru emerged from the end of the lane, skipping toward her as though the sound of the metal shutter was a whistle calling him from his hiding place. "You are so very late, madam, so late!" He stood before her, his arms rigid at his sides, a worried expression on his face. "And you are running past me, running and running. What trouble is this?"

"No trouble, Peeru, no trouble." She opened the storage room, and began the work of setting up. "When this is done, we'll have a meal."

Peeru gave his enthusiastic assent, and soon all was ready for anyone foolish enough to be out in the noonday sun, which meant just about all the tourists at the resort. Anita sent Peeru off for a meal for two, knowing she'd eat far less than half, and stepped into the tailor's shop next door.

"Chinnappa," Anita said with a smile and greeting.

"Ah, you are rested now after so much excitement?" The old man pulled the remaining straight pins from his mouth, stuck them into a pin cushion at the end of the table, and motioned her to a seat. "You have sent that worthless boy for food?"

"I know, I know, he'll steal me blind someday."

Chinnappa grunted and pulled his chair up to the sewing machine. "Who is this madman you are chasing?"

"Didn't you recognize him? You told me he's been hanging

147

around for the last couple of days."

"Ah, that one." Chinnappa snorted and pulled two pieces of fabric into alignment with the needle of the sewing machine. His feet began to work the treadle, and a low purr complemented by a high-pitched whirring sound filled the shop. He finished stitching, and pulled the fabric close to his eyes, to inspect his handiwork.

"I got some information from someone else who has seen him around." Anita repeated some of what the old beggar woman had told her.

"And does this American woman have such valuable property with her?"

"Not that I can see." Anita leaned forward and waved to the bookstore owner as he came out to the upper veranda to watch people pass by. "She sends it on ahead, from what I understand. I've checked everything she has in the hotel, and there's nothing remotely important enough for someone to want. As far as I can tell, everything must be waiting for her somewhere in Thailand."

"Then why do you worry?" Chinnappa repositioned the pattern and began stitching the other sleeve. Anita waited for the noise to die down.

"This man looks like someone who could do me harm, that's why."

Chinnappa gave her a stern look. "This is your true feeling?"

"Yes, it is."

"Then I too shall worry." With that, he snapped the thread with his teeth and pulled the blouse from the sewing machine.

CHAPTER FOURTEEN

At five o'clock, Anita sent Peeru off to buy a few items for the gallery and then closed up, hanging a sign on the front handle promising to return by eight that evening. She wasn't sure she would actually return, but it at least covered things for her. People were less apt to ask nagging questions about closing early if they thought she was opening later for evening sales.

Anita scanned the lane, but found no sign of the man she had chased earlier that afternoon. She had asked the bookseller and some others nearby, but they had paid little attention to him, since he showed no signs of purchasing anything. Resigned to having lost him, perhaps for good, Anita turned her mind to other questions. First on her list was learning more about the homes on the hill behind the temple, where she had wandered briefly after dinner with Anand the night before. She hurried down the lane and up the hill past the temple, onto the dirt path leading around the temple compound and into the small enclave.

Small neighborhoods such as this one usually reflected an expanding family trying to remain close as more successful families or businesses closed in around them. Anita climbed up under the trees onto the path, and uncapped her lens. By now most of the resort residents were used to her, and let her and her camera blend into the scenery; she was counting on that this time too.

After a few minutes Anita arrived at the house with the sign

Nuisance Works: All Problems Solved. Anand was right—this was a great idea for a business, whatever it was. In the courtyard was an old hibiscus tree, its blood-red flowers so thick on the branches that it seemed more shrub than tree. This seemed a good excuse to stop and hang about for a while. She sighted her camera and began taking photographs. She had all but let herself fall into the compound before a curious woman appeared in the doorway, a towel in her hands. Anita offered her apologies, profuse compliments on the gorgeous tree, and a timid query about getting a different angle on the tree. The woman seemed to think it over, then with a warm smile invited her into the compound.

Anita was right. The three houses clustered together along the dirt path belonged to members of a single family, and they did feel crowded from all sides. Holding their own against encroachment had taxed their ingenuity and financial resources.

"Our paddy fields are long gone," the woman said, motioning Anita to a chair while she herself sat on the cement steps. "Such change. But we are having television now! But so much money."

Anita commiserated but secretly wished all televisions in India would implode. And what about work, she asked. What sort of work did the families do now, now that the farming was literally impossible?

"A good thing it is too," the woman continued. "Weren't the farmers in the hills killing themselves because crops were so bad and Government offered no help?"

"Ah, well, but now you do something else?"

"Ah, what else is there to a paddy farmer? Always we are missing our work."

Anita capitulated. "But don't you have a sign somewhere along this lane? I thought I saw a sign that said Nuisance Works, or something like that."

The woman began to laugh and flapped a dismissive hand at

Anita. "It is only a sign. What do we know?"

"But what did you do? What did the sign mean?"

"Ah, it was to alleviate the discomfort of the many insects foreigners dislike."

"Bug spray?"

"Not spray. Salve. We are making a very fine cream for the body, and bugs are avoiding. Good fragrance also. But foreigners are very particular." She seemed to have learned this the hard way, ending her explanation with a heavy sigh, and leaning her head on her hand.

"Can I get some of this cream?"

"Yes, yes, you will get. You are happy with this." She jumped up and waved her hand in a small circle. "We are having many supplies ready for purchase." She walked to the low compound wall separating her house from the next one. With a sharp call, she brought a child to the front door of the second house; the child then disappeared, calling for her mother. The woman who appeared at the door looked harried, but listened, and the two women negotiated arrangements for the cream to be made up and entubed, as the other woman said. "Come, you will see. Very professional process."

The first woman led her across to the second house. Once again Anita was waved to a chair in the courtyard while her first hostess entered the house and began calling out to everyone. She returned with a thin white tube banded in red with the company name on it, which she then opened and squeezed—a thin line of yellow cream emerged into Anita's palm.

"Superior nuisance works," the second woman said. "You are liking?"

Anita sniffed at the cream in her palm. She couldn't quite get at the smell, but there seemed to be something familiar about it. "And the yellow is turmeric?"

"Yes, turmeric. Very healthy."

151

"Are you selling much of this?"

"Not so much. Shops are not wanting."

"Does it work?"

"Very good cream."

"I saw a friend in here recently. She told me about it."

The two women looked at each other, but both shook their heads. "No one is buying," the first one said, and the other repeated. "Looking and sniffing, like you, but not buying."

"Maybe I got it wrong."

"Very good cream," the second one said. "You are using and telling others. We will sell to shops, yes."

"Sure, I'll give it a try."

Anita capped the tube and slipped it into her purse. "How much?" Anita paid, and turned to go. She hadn't learned much—after all, there was only so much damage a tube of insect repellent could cause—and was ready to give up. "Who is in the next house? Another relative?"

"Our youngest sister," the first one answered. "See there." They pointed to a young woman with a large basket on her head coming toward them. Catching sight of her sisters, she stopped by the wall, ready to chat for a minute. After giving Anita a suspicious glance, she began to lament the state of her life with her sisters. That and the price of cashews and channa dhal seemed to have ruined her day.

"You are going to temple this evening?" the youngest asked. She lowered the basket to rest on the compound wall. Inside Anita could see bags of provisions—rice, dhal, cashews, okra, mangos, and more; she just barely kept herself from rummaging in the basket to get a look at the rest of the items in there.

"I may stop by," Anita said, putting her off.

"Ah, you will not come." The young woman looked crestfallen.

"Does it matter?"

"Foreigners are not generous. They see the coins and one rupee notes in the donation catch and give so little themselves. What is one rupee to a man who flies from another country? Not even ten rupees do they give."

"Does the temple need money so badly?"

She shrugged, but looked uncomfortable with what she had said. "We are poor people. This temple festival gives pleasure to many. Should they not thank us?"

"Yes, I suppose they should." Anita smiled. "Is that for the prasadam?" Anita nodded at the basket.

"Now during the festival I am helping."

But if not enough people come and make a donation, Anita added to herself, you might not get paid. "I'll be sure to stop by tonight."

"And you will use the cream this evening and tell everyone it is very good." The second sister nudged her way past the oldest one.

"I'll try to remember to do that." Anita began to search in her pocket for a tissue for her hand.

"They will trust you."

"They don't know me," Anita said. "They have no reason to trust me."

The older one said, "If you use, they will trust. Foreigners are very particular."

"Yes, I suppose they are."

"Please, what is organic?" the second one asked. "Is this a special ingredient in States?"

Anita managed to get back to Hotel Delite without anyone stopping her and asking about restaurants, trips into the hills, the location of the nearest holy man, or where to get the best massage. And to her great relief, Ravi was at his expected post, seated on a stool behind the registration desk.

"What is this?" Anita shoved her open palm at Ravi, who jerked back, startled and confused. "Smell it."

"This is a trick, isn't it?"

"It's not a trick. Just smell it."

"Is that the yellow of turmeric?"

"Yes. But smell it. What does it smell like?"

"Don't you know?"

"I can't tell for sure. I can just almost get it, and then it slips away. I can't quite identify it. You can because you always smell what something is right away."

Ravi gave her a skeptical look, then glanced at her palm. "Where did you get this?"

"Oh, just smell it, Ravi."

"But it could be bad for me."

Anita drew her palm to within an inch from her nose and gave a strong sniff, inhaling deeply. "Okay? Now smell it and tell me what it is." She stretched out her hand.

Ravi leaned forward, glancing up at Anita every other second as though he expected some trick. He sniffed at several inches, moved closer, sniffed again. "Hmmm. I do know what this is." He leaned back and began to think, twisting his lips into different configurations. "I do know this." He jumped down from his stool and slipped under the counter. "Cook!" he called out as he walked back to the kitchen.

The cook leaned out of the kitchen doorway, a wooden spoon in one hand and a dish cloth in the other. He didn't bother speaking to either Ravi or Anita, used as he was to their habit of breaking into the middle of his work at any time to quiz him about something irrelevant to the meal being prepared.

"Do you know what this smell is?" Anita stuck out her hand again.

"Not in my kitchen!" He turned around and went back to his stove. Anita followed him, but just as she set foot across the threshold he turned and yelled at her. "Not in my kitchen."

Anita jumped back into the hallway. "But what is it?"

"You don't know what this is?" His nostrils flared, his face flushed. "You are not a child."

"But I really don't know. That's why I'm asking. I know I should know it, but I just can't quite get it. What is it?" She was beginning to worry, scared by the cook's reaction.

"Go wash your hands at once." The cook began to look worried. "You know the stuff!" He named a common brand.

"That insecticide?" Anita studied the red-banded white tube while she wiped her hands with a paper towel, then tossed it into a wastebasket behind the registration desk.

"What is it?" Ravi stared at the tube lying on the counter as though it were a living creature that might start moving about.

"That is the product created by Nuisance Works, to appeal to foreign tourists." Anita picked up the tube and turned it over. "It must be mostly that stuff no one uses anymore, but I think it's a mix of insecticides in a cream base with turmeric and other spices to make it smell nice and look good."

"You are using this?" Ravi asked.

"No, not me. And apparently no one else is either. The women who make it say they haven't sold any, and they haven't been able to persuade the shopkeepers to carry it." Anita pulled up a stool and rested her elbow on the counter.

"Is this safe for people?" Ravi dared to poke the tube with an index finger.

"It might make them sick, but I doubt it would kill them." She picked up the tube, turned it over in her hands. "I'll take it into Anandabudhi Hospital and ask Dr. Premod, Marge's doctor, if this could be what made her sick."

"Ah, this is sad, isn't it?"

"Yes, it is." Anita leaned against the wall. The afternoon

breeze was like a ribbon of light through the hotel, in through the open parlor windows, and along to the desk and out the open broad front door. A half curtain on the single window in the registration area rustled as though someone had just walked by, giving the courtyard a feeling of barely suppressed energy. She should be feeling a quiet tingling thinking about the evening coming up. She and Anand were heading out again, to try another restaurant and catch up on their hours apart. But she felt none of that pleasant anticipation. Instead, she felt deflated, as though she had just suffered a great disappointment.

"I really thought I was on to something," Anita said.

Ravi gave her an affectionate if pitying smile tinged with relief, and climbed back onto his stool. "You will find the answer, I am sure. I have confidence in you."

"Thanks, Ravi. But I'm not feeling very confident. I was sure I saw a Western woman coming out of that lane where those three houses are."

"Perhaps you did."

"But it has no import even if I did. The families living there are all related, very poor, and one of them is trying to sell an impossible insect repellent and the youngest helps with the prasadam for the Kali temple. The cream will not kill and the prasadam is made under the eye of the priests."

"And of Kali, too, remember."

Anita smiled. "And under the eye of Kali, too. I will keep that in mind."

"She will be angry if her home has been abused."

"And we don't want to see Kali angry."

CHAPTER FIFTEEN

Anita found Anand waiting for her at the top of Maurya Hotel on Statue Road in Trivandrum. The minute she stepped off the marble-walled elevator and onto the roofed-over dining terrace, she felt like she'd left everything about her life behind for an entirely different world. This too was the world of tourists and overpriced meals, delicious though they may be, served by well-attired waiters standing behind a lavish buffet. But looking out over the parapet at the rest of the city below, its mix of red-tiled roofs turned black by monsoon mold, flat roofs on North Indian houses with laundry flapping from lines strung corner to corner, high rises popping up above palm trees, and the white Secretariat sparkling in the moonlight beyond, as she looked at all these familiar sights, she couldn't feel she belonged to one world or the other. She had entered into a world apart.

Flames from the small candles lighting each table shimmered on the cutlery and brightened the pink and yellow flowers in the glass vases. Anand, in his white slacks and light blue silk shirt, emerged from the crowd and came toward her. The room was filled with other diners, parties of two and seven and even twenty, but they seemed to shrink into an undistinguishable mass when Anita heard Anand's voice welcoming her.

He preceded her through the buffet line, commenting on the many dishes, but as Anita made her selections, and her plate began to fill up, she realized she was making her choices on the basis of color—bright red beetroot thoren, shimmering green okra avial, bright yellow potato curry dotted with black mustard seeds, golden-brown grilled fish steaks, bright orange-yellow mango pickle, shiny green chilies, and creamy white curd with tomatoes and cucumbers. I must be intoxicated with the colors, she thought as she held a spoon poised over the pineapple mango chutney.

"You all right?" Anand looked over his shoulder, one hand on a spoon ready to serve himself sag paneer.

"Don't you find food sometimes overwhelming in its beauty?" Anita sought his face, wondering that she felt so lost in the plethora of smells and colors. But when she saw his expression, her face began to burn so hot she couldn't look. She reached for more chutney, letting it pour softly onto her plate.

"When I think about it," she said, while they were eating, "it's no wonder food means so much to us here."

"Good food always means a lot to poor countries. Only rich countries can afford to eat badly—fast food, sugared everything." He used his fork to keep the curries separate, making almost separate colored mounds on his plate. Laughter burst over a nearby table and a number of beer bottles rose in the air in joyful punctuation.

"Meena sometimes comments on the tastes of our guests— the choices they make, what they choose and what they pass up." She continued to taste each item separately, trying to discern the ingredients to report back to the hotel cook.

"They make the same choices in the States," Anand said.

"How do you know that?" The question popped out of her mouth without warning, leaving Anita both embarrassed and newly shocked at how little she knew about him. How did he know how people behaved in the States? After all, she was the one who was half American.

"I know lots of things," he said with a smile that didn't reach his eyes, "and lots of people. Including some people at Anandabudhi Hospital. How is Marge doing? Do you know what happened yet?"

"Not really. Dr. Premod will let me know as soon as she's run some tests on the bug repellent."

"You're convinced this is what almost killed Marge?" Anand had already ordered more rice twice while Anita was still working on her vegetables. Adroit, she thought, the way he can change the subject.

"Not really, but I don't have anything else." She gave him a wry smile. "And yes that means I'm desperate." A waiter arrived to offer more water, leaving the bottle on the table; Anita waited for him to finish. "But I did have one success today, sort of."

Anand looked up, his right hand poised over his meal, waiting for Anita's great news.

"I found out, well, sort of, who that man is who's been following me around." She leaned forward. "He's a black marketer, and he's really been interested in Jean."

Anand looked skeptical. "And how do you know this?"

"A beggar woman told me—for a small sum dribbled out for each word." Anita shook her head at the memory; she didn't like paying people for information. "She said he's known as a black marketer, and works for someone else. He's part of a network."

"That fits with something else you told me, doesn't it?"

"That her equipment and supplies were stolen last year. Yes," Anita said, nodding. "They must be looking for whatever she brought with her this year."

"And did she?"

"Bring things with her this year?" Anita shrugged. "Not to the hotel that I can see." She paused. "I don't think he'll be back. At least, not the same one."

"Anita, what have you done?"

"I chased him. I almost caught him but he got away on a

motorcycle."

Anand cringed. "And what would you have done if you had caught him?"

"I don't know. That's probably why I didn't catch him." She laughed. "I knew I didn't have the strength to do anything with him if I did catch up with him."

Anand shook his head. "He might have turned on you, led you into a remote area—injured you."

Yes, thought Anita, he might have done all that and more, but he didn't. But she kept her thoughts to herself. The evening—with its clean, warm air, colors and smells—was too beautiful to spoil with an argument. Anand seemed to sense her mood, because he too paused, gave a half laugh. "This week is Kathakali," he said. "Something very sedate."

"You don't like this business about Jean and Marge, do you?"

Anand let his gaze rest on Anita's face, but she was too intent on his answer to be embarrassed. He frowned, thoughtfully, and raised his hand to call the waiter. The man arrived and cleared the table; he returned with a dessert menu.

"So we're not going to talk about it," Anita said when the waiter was gone.

"Black marketers invading Kovalam is more serious than even I understand," he said. "You have surprised me." He pushed the menu away from him and smiled. "But not for the first time."

He's rallying, Anita thought. We're not going to dive into a battle over what I do, whether he agrees or not.

"Just be careful," he added. "And soon we'll have a very ordinary evening—Kathakali at the temple."

"Just what I need." She glanced at the menu. "I'll ask the temple to reserve two chairs."

"For a donation, of course."

"For a donation."

"I've reserved five chairs."

Anita paused, surprise haunting her smile. "What does that mean?"

"It means I think it is time to address the Aunt Meena issue." Anand ordered coffee for them, to the surprise of the waiter. "He wants us to order drinks."

"It looks like most everyone here does." She turned in her chair. "Is that the band setting up?"

"It's the high-tech crowd showing up for some fun before going to work—they want to be on U.S. time." Anand waved to a couple of men crossing the floor to a large table of Indian men and women in various forms of dress—women in saris, salwars, slacks and overblouses, jeans, but all the men were wearing jeans and shirts, no lungis, Anita noticed. The men called hellos to Anand and their friends in the crowd.

"What about Auntie Meena?"

"I think it's time she met the family she is so worried about."

Anita could feel herself sinking into her chair. This evening was no longer a lark, an interlude of fun and warmth and cordiality with the entire world, not if Anand thought he was going to bring her aunt and his family together. All of a sudden, life had a disconcerting seriousness about it. She stretched her hand across the table, stopping several inches from his hand. "Anand, my Aunt Meena isn't as friendly as you think. She's very conservative." In fact, Anita thought, I'm not feeling very friendly myself either.

"I know. In fact, she is far more conservative than you know, but that is why I want her to meet my family. She must face the real world."

"And meeting your family—Nambudiri Brahmans all—is going to introduce her to the real world?" Anita frowned and pulled her napkin from her lap, folding it and pressing it against her lips before shaking it out, folding it again, and replacing it across her purple silk slacks. She always felt a little different in Western clothes, though she had grown up wearing them. They made her feel as though something was expected of her—some behavior or wisdom or sophistication—and she found herself walking differently, sometimes even speaking differently. But Anand's challenge to her stirred up a different emotion, one that she was surprised to feel. "Anand, I love my aunt. I annoy her, manipulate her, ignore her sometimes, but I don't ever want to do anything that could hurt her. You don't know how she feels about India and the way it is changing."

"Because she is not?"

"Something like that." How can I tell you, Anita thought, that she is not the only one who likes things the way they are? She knew where she and Anand were going—easily, gently, inevitably—but she didn't want that change set into a legal document. There was just something about official permanence that repelled her.

"We should be brave, Anita. It is for the best." He reached across the clean white linen tablecloth and rested his hand over hers. "You'll see."

The guard was already strolling the enclosed compound behind a locked gate when Anita and Anand arrived back at the hotel. The young couple watched his slim figure in navy slacks and light gray shirt with a dark cap pulled low over his eyes come in and out of view as they pulled up at the top of the short lane. Without a word, they climbed out of the car and walked along the wall toward the lighthouse, stopping midway to gaze out upon the ocean, its horizon bright with lights from the fishing fleet.

Anand leaned his elbows on the stone wall and looked down at the crescent-shaped beach. Anita leaned against the rough stone, her hands in her pockets. The waves breaking on the sand sent a rush of sound up the rocky hillside, but she could still hear the bursts of laughter coming from the end of the lane, near the beach. She walked a few feet farther on, to the bend, and saw a gaggle of four women coming up the steep walkway.

"It's that crew of women sharing the family room," Anita said to Anand as she turned to him. She took a day-old newspaper from a nearby shop doorway, spread it on the wall, and jumped up to sit on it. It was coolish now, at least for an Indian, and Anita found her thoughts turning to the light shawl she had left lying on her bed earlier in the evening. "I haven't had much to do with them—they're in and out all the time. Most people spend at least a little time hanging out in the parlor because of the view. Or they come over to the desk to chat with Ravi or Auntie Meena." She lowered her voice as the women drew closer. One of them was panting and laughing as she reached the top of the steep section; the other three seemed to be in better shape, and kept moving while the one slowed and finally came to a halt near Anita and Anand.

"I'm bushed," the woman said as her three friends continued on to the hotel. She propped her hands on her hips and took deep gulps of the warm night air. As her breathing eased, she moved to the stone wall. "That's where that woman was found, isn't it?"

Anand stood up and turned around to nod welcome. "A bit around the bend, I'm told." He looked to Anita for confirmation.

"You can't quite see the spot, but, yes, in that general area. You're Pam, aren't you?" Anita introduced herself and Anand.

"Really too bad." Pam leaned over the wall and peered into the darkness. "Do they really catch fish like that?" Anita assured her that they did, though the catch had been declining for some years.

"Yeah, at home too." She stepped away from the stone wall. "You work at the hotel, don't you?"

"My aunt owns it," Anita said. "I have an apartment over the garage."

"Way cool."

"Are you enjoying your visit?" Anand surprised Anita with his question, but he was settled on the stone wall himself and seemed ready to indulge the tourist with a short chat.

"The food is awesome," she began, "and the water is pretty good. Warm, though. I'm not used to it being so warm. And the elephant ride in the hills was awesome."

"I hope you're getting lots of pictures."

"Digital," she said, patting her shoulder bag. "I can get 250 shots on one disk."

"Yes, that's all the rage here too," Anand said, his arms resting across his chest.

"It's been perfect, except for Emily." She screwed up her face in a look of distaste.

"What's wrong with Emily?" Anand asked, before Anita could stop him. But then she was glad she didn't, thinking it would be good for him to get a close-up view of the foreign tourist everyone welcomed, no one understood, and most still catered to.

"She's been possessed by Kali. At least that's what she says. No, she says called. She's been called by Kali."

Anand glanced at Anita, who gave a brief nod, which the woman missed.

"She thinks Kali has called her to be a special devotee." This time her expression became one of annoyance and impatience as she rolled her eyes and shook her head. "I mean, get real. The temples are okay, I mean, no offense, but she's a Baptist, for god's sakes."

"It happens sometimes," Anita said. "It's not that unusual."

"It's weird," the woman said. "I mean, it's a great religion, don't get me wrong, but she's an American, she has a church at home she does things with. What's with this Kali business?" She threw up her hands and wrinkled her nose again. "Personally, I think it's all about her brother; I think she's been unstable since he died."

"I'm sorry to hear that," Anand said.

"Yeah, well, he had it coming, I guess. He got in trouble in Thailand—something to do with the black market, I guess." She waved off this tragedy with a flip of her hand. "She thinks he was murdered in prison and never got a fair trial. She's had a hard time accepting it." She took a deep breath and exhaled, her arms akimbo. "I shouldn't be hard on her—she's coping as well as she can. But Kali! I think she should go home and get into therapy."

"Yes, I can see it must be hard to travel with a friend who's undergone so much change all at once." Anita was ready to jump in with a thousand questions, but that would be too much for anyone. She leaned forward, her hands tucked under her thighs, trying not to show her eagerness.

"She's not my friend, exactly. Two of the others knew her from church, and I knew the others from work, and we all thought it would be fun to take this trip. Originally, there were six of us, and one had to cancel at the last minute, but we had already paid a lot, so we went ahead, just the five of us. It was probably an omen. We didn't know, at least I didn't know, about Emily." She paused and looked toward the hotel. "You know, her husband couldn't take it—he left her."

"Couldn't take what?"

"Her fixation on her brother. She spent all her time trying to get him out of prison, but no one would listen to her. She even went to Thailand, but they still wouldn't listen. Her senator said he'd look into it, but he warned her that drugs were serious business overseas." She sighed. "I shouldn't be so hard on her, but it does get to be a bit much to hear the same thing over and over and over."

"Whenever I talk to her, she seems quite calm, at peace," Anita said.

"Maybe. We're supposed to stop in Thailand for a couple of days before we go through Indonesia, and she's going to pick up his ashes. She arranged for the embassy to hold them, I guess. I think it's making her weird, this whole thing—traveling, going to temples, thinking about his ashes."

"Perhaps the love of Kali will help her find peace," Anand said.

Pam looked at him, as though not sure how to take his comment. "Yeah, sure." She stepped away, as though getting ready to leave. "I thought she was supposed to be bloodthirsty or something. She looks like a doll in that temple, all dressed up."

"It is the expression of one aspect of her personality," Anand said.

"So it's not really her. Just a picture of her."

"No, the image is Kali." Anand continued to smile, but the sparkle had gone out of his eyes.

"That's what I mean," the woman said as she shrugged her shoulders and headed for the hotel. "It's weird."

Several minutes passed before Anita and Anand spoke. The hotel guard opened and relocked the front gate, knocked loudly on the front door, to alert Sanj inside. Anita heard the heavy door open and close again, the muffled voices of guard and guest negotiating such a late arrival home. The fishing lanterns on the horizon bobbed and glimmered, and lights in the high-rise hotels disappeared a few at a time. Kovalam was a quiet place at night, with only a few workers moving about, a small city dominated by good middle-class virtues that left the natives only the nighttime to call the land their own.

"I think it is remarkable that you are as tolerant as you are," Anand said.

"I've learned to find most of it humorous." Anita watched his face. Perhaps it hadn't been wise to let him get such a close look at how some foreigners behaved. "I feel the need now to defend some of them—with the cliché of they're not all that bad."

Anand sighed. "I'm glad to hear it."

"I didn't know that about Emily. She never said a word to me."

"You've only seen her since she got here and had her experience with Kali."

"True. But I'm still sort of surprised she never said anything."

"Do you think her experience is genuine?"

"What do you mean, genuine?" Anita turned to him, surprised at the question. They had never spoken about the foreigners spread all over the country who come for spiritual discovery, renewal, and declare themselves sannyasis. Anita had seen them throughout her childhood, whenever her family traveled around India, but she never thought much about them. It wasn't until much later that she began to notice them, and wonder what they were up to. Didn't they know about religion in America? Didn't they know there were churches? Her parents never explained this, and she once again put it out of her mind. And then the next time she noticed the white sannyasis loping along the Mount Road in Madras, or hanging out at the Red Fort in Delhi, or carrying huge pots of rice for the devotees of Ammaji or another holy woman, they were part of the landscape and she simply accepted them. But once in a while, an inchoate question brushed through her thoughts, but she let it go. "Do I think she was really called by Kali?"

"Do you think she was called, and the call was there?"

"Oh, two different questions." Anita smiled. "Trick questions too."

Anand laughed.

"Yes, to both. But that doesn't mean that everyone who professes to be called is, or was, and that doesn't mean that everyone who is called hears the call. Or understands it."

Anand moved into the lane and reached for Anita's hand. Arm in arm, cloaked in the anonymity of darkness, they strolled back to the hotel. Anita lifted her head as if to catch the fragrance of flowers drifting on the air.

"I talked to Marge today about what she saw on my bulletin board and her Internet searches. She told me about a man who was arrested for drugs in Thailand, a man called Jake Lanier." Anita nodded to the guard as they approached, and let her hand rest on the gate. "But she insisted he was someone working with black marketers and he threatened to get Jean in trouble if she didn't turn over the rest of her supplies."

"Do you believe her?"

"I don't know. I just don't know."

Chapter Sixteen

At five-thirty the following morning, Anita unlocked the office and slipped inside. She unlatched the window and pushed it open. It was still mostly dark, with a thin strip of light across the horizon. Dotted across the quiet sea were fishing boats making their way home, their dingy white sails dipping and luffing in the still morning air.

Before Anita could finish her work, Meena pushed the door open and peeked in. "I heard something and came to investigate."

"You needn't have worried. Sanj is still out there."

"Asleep in his chair."

"It's just me, Auntie. He won't get up just for me."

Meena closed the door behind her. She was wearing a flowing, red silk bathrobe, and her thick black hair was loose, flying out around her suspicious face.

Anita smiled and said, "You look like Kali. A wild rage and menace." Anita lifted her hands and wiggled her fingers in an imitation of a person terrified.

"I feel like Kali. What are you doing here at this hour?"

"It's not so early."

"You are not a servant. Anita, what are you doing?"

"Rechecking the passports." She turned back to the row of safety deposit boxes and returned one drawer to its place and then another. "Last night, Anand and I got to talking with one of the women traveling with Emily, and she said that Emily's brother died in Thailand last year."

"Why does this matter?" Meena tugged her bathrobe tighter around her as she lowered herself into a chair.

"It matters, but I'm not sure how. Both Emily and Candy were in Thailand sometime during the past year. Candy was there for two months during the winter. Her visit would have overlapped with Jean's. But Emily was there six months ago, specifically to help her brother."

"You are not telling me why does this matter?"

"I'm sure it has something to do with Jean's death." Anita put the last box away and locked them all up.

"Let the police deal with this." Meena began to look plaintive.

"They think it's an accident, and that's the way they want it to stay. Better for business. But it wasn't an accident, I'm almost sure of it." Anita picked up a piece of paper on which she'd made some notes, flicking the paper up and down like a fan. "I know the solution is here. I just know it."

"Put that aside, Anita. Do not trouble yourself. The German tourists know nothing about this and they don't care about such things."

"Auntie, I cannot ignore what has happened. Even if you're not interested, I need to figure out the connections between everyone. Why would Marge get so upset about a postcard from Jake Lanier? I don't think she's telling me the truth. I'm going to have to get it from Emily or Candy." Anita folded up the sheet of paper.

"Anita! Listen to me." Meena's black hair shook and her eyes widened.

Startled by her aunt's passion, Anita sat down. "Of course, Auntie. What's wrong? Just tell me."

"Anita, I want to talk to you about something important. If fate has put us here with no guests clamoring for our attention, and no staff bumbling around—"

"The staff at Hotel Delite never bumbles, Auntie." Anita gave her a curious smile and waited.

"You know what I mean."

"Not really, but go ahead." It occurred to Anita that her aunt was aging, her cheeks growing slack, her jowels loosening. Running a hotel was tiring her out.

"It is about your future, Anita. I am worried." Meena avoided Anita's eye. "I must answer to your mother."

"My mother married a foreigner, remember?"

"We have other relatives, and they hold me accountable." A very un-Kali-like look of distress flashed in her eyes.

"Auntie, you have nothing to worry about. Look, there's a Kathakali performance tomorrow night at the Temple. Anand and I are going, and he's bringing his parents, and I'm inviting you. It's all arranged." There, she had done it—she was going to bring all the parental figures together.

"He has done this?"

Anita was shocked by the expression on Meena's face. "Auntie, are you all right?"

Meena burst into tears and fled from the room.

Moonu drifted around the main dining table, dropping bamboo mats into place, then swiveling each one this way or that until he was satisfied with its placement before moving on to the next one. Anita poured herself another cup of tea and let out a loud sigh.

"You are wanting something, Missi?" he asked.

"I am wanting the guests to hurry up and get down here."

"They are coming soon, very soon." Moonu didn't seem to believe it as he drifted to the next spot and dropped another placemat. When he had set out eight of these, he drifted over to the sideboard where glasses, napkins, cutlery, and other items were kept. He tipped his head to one side, then the other, and finally selected two glasses.

"You're not supposed to put your fingers in them. Take them to the kitchen and select two others, by grasping the base."

Moonu turned around and gave her a fretful pout. "So much work."

"Just do it. And hurry. I hear doors opening and closing."

This time it was Moonu's turn to heave a big sigh as he drifted off to the kitchen. He was soon back, however, walking a bit more sprightly as Meena followed him into the room, muttering that he should hurry before the guests see the table not yet ready.

"But it is never ready," Moonu said.

"But it should be." Meena sailed past him and came to Anita's table under the window. She threw herself into a chair and tugged at her red and black patterned sari. "This is a terrible thing, terrible, Anita."

"I know, Auntie, but I'll make it up to you."

"What are we talking about?" Meena said, with a suspicious look. "You never agree with me."

"Good morning, Emily, Pam," Anita said as she stood, greeting each of the party of five women traveling together. Anita ushered them to one end of the dining table and snagged Moonu before he could disappear back into the kitchen. "Moonu, what are we having this morning?" She smiled at the waiter, and with both hands grasping the back of a chair, leaned over the table.

"Ah, this morning," Moonu began, giving Anita a suspicious look, "this morning we are having idlies. This is a traditional breakfast with coconut chutney and tomato stew and perhaps we are having some yogurt with it." He kept looking at Anita to make sure his recital was acceptable. "It may be a bit dry for you," Anita added, "but the yogurt is just right."

Moonu was obviously disappointed when three of the five chose omelets and toast, and only two asked for idlies and curd. With a sigh of resignation, he wandered off to the kitchen, and Anita began a general conversation about their plans.

"We wanted to visit Kanyakumari—is that how you say it?—but someone told us it was all washed away by the tsunami a few years ago." Pam looked to Anita for confirmation, and she nodded and reported on the damage done that Christmas Day when an earthquake sent gigantic waves rolling across the ocean to break over unsuspecting villages and tourist resorts.

"It hasn't been restored yet, but soon," Anita promised, though she had no idea when that might be. The women discussed a number of other destinations, including a day trip to Varkala, to compare its beaches to those of Kovalam, a trip to a tea plantation, and a day on the beach.

"We're leaving soon, tomorrow night," Pam said. "I don't want to rush around and be in such a blur that I won't remember my last couple of days."

"I think I'll just go to the temple and meditate," Emily said. This produced a number of mutterings and rolling eyes.

"How about the Suchindram Temple, south of here? It has those granite pillars that sound like musical instruments." Anita hoped this suggestion would elicit some interest in the crew. "It's not far—a drive down, a nice meal in a local restaurant, a walk through a park with lovely songbirds, and a drive back. You can leave after a morning swim, and you'll be back in time for afternoon tea."

"Or another swim," one of the women said. Anita stepped back—her work was done. This woman would convince the rest. Anita listened to the rising voices behind her as she walked back to her table. Aunt Meena watched without comment, but kept such a fixed eye on her that Anita refused to look at her.

"Why have you done this?" Meena leaned forward and

whispered to her niece.

"Done what? I haven't done anything." Anita freshened her cup of tea, and picked up a cold piece of toast.

"I am watching you, Anita. You can't fool me. Everything must be out in the open."

"If you feel that way, then tell me about the new item in the hotel budget. You're spending enough extra that you should have another person on the staff." Anita had tried to put the irregular budget items out of her mind, but this seemed to be as good a time as any to bring them up—and distract her aunt.

"I have no irregular items." Meena drew herself up and stuck out her chin. "My books are always perfect, above question."

"That's very true, Auntie, but you still have an extra expense in there that's pushing the limits of your income." Anita sipped her tea and replaced the cup in its saucer. "Auntie, if there's a problem, you can tell me." She softened her voice, hoping to convince her aunt to confide in her.

"There is nothing, nothing." Meena stood abruptly; her fingertips tapped lightly on the table as she tried to find the words to address her niece.

"Tell me, Auntie."

"There is nothing. You will see, nothing." With that cryptic remark, she pushed her chair back and left the room.

If Anita judged correctly, the five women traveling together would break into two groups—four would head to Suchindram Temple, to listen to the resonating granite pillars, take photographs of elephants and bullocks being herded to market, and dine at a guesthouse dining room. And one, Emily, would remain at the resort.

"I have found them a reservation for luncheon at a small guesthouse on their return journey," Aunt Meena said when Anita appeared on the other side of the registration desk. "They are not particular, so they will enjoy the food. It is mild, always mild for the foreigners."

"As you say, Auntie." Anita patted her aunt's hand and followed Emily out the door. "You're not joining your friends this morning?" Anita asked her.

Emily paused to check the contents of her cotton bag, which was bulging with a very light cotton shawl, book, sunscreen, rolled-up cotton sunhat, large water bottle, towel, and iPod. She glanced up to give Anita a wry smile before returning to her search. "Oh, here it is." She extracted a small digital camera from the folds of the shawl and pulled it out. "Do you think the priest will let me take a picture of Kali?"

Anita felt herself wince. It surprised her. She didn't consider herself devout, though she was a devotee, nor was she a purist, though she felt the power of Devi pouring through her sometimes. But the idea of a Westerner photographing a murti made her uncomfortable. As she tried to open up her mind to a broader, more tolerant understanding, she heard herself thinking, This one feels called, this one is different. But that's only what she's told me, another part of her countered.

The argument began to bang around in her head while she watched Emily struggle with the neck cord, disentangling it from her fingers and draping it over her head. She was carrying too much, planning on doing too much in a single morning— visiting a temple, taking in the sun on the beach, reading her book, taking photographs, having lunch. She was a daylong event looking for a location.

"No one's supposed to photograph the image," Anita said, forcing herself to sound calm and matter-of-fact.

"That's what one of the priests said." She fingered the camera lying against her chest, its silver skin seeming pale in the sun. "But I want something to remember her by." She looked around her, as though there might be something nearby, something that

175

would fit her needs. "I don't mean it in a commercial way—the picture, I mean."

"No, of course not." Anita had to admit that she seemed sincere, genuinely in need of something of Kali to carry with her.

"Do you think if I ask him, he'll let me? It's for worship." She looked like a small child, like the Balabhadrakali herself, a soft sweetness around her mouth, an eagerness in her eyes, an innocence on her face. It would be hard to turn her away, Anita thought, she seems so sincere.

"Well, it can't hurt to ask." She capitulated, ignoring how she felt herself. "I'll walk up with you."

They turned onto Lighthouse Road, Anita waving away the autorickshaw drivers eager for an early fare, the sweepers cleaning the roadside before the shops were to open, the bearers hurrying down the hill with piles of coir carpets on their heads, or baskets laden with brightly painted wooden toys or other tourist items. A light breeze slipped up from the ocean, carrying just the hint of salt water, reminding Anita of how pleasant the area was away from the city and its high-rise buildings that were turning Trivandrum into an oven. The two women walked in silence, Anita nodding to friends and acquaintances, Emily lost in her own thoughts.

"You don't approve, do you?"

"Why do you say that?" Anita paused then walked on when Emily kept going.

"I can feel it. I don't mean that you disapprove the same way my friends do—did you notice that they don't even talk to me? They don't even acknowledge a question I ask or a comment I make. They just go on talking as if I wasn't even there."

Anita had noticed that, but it surprised her more that Emily took the behavior so hard. "They'll get used to the idea."

"No, they won't. And I don't care if they do."

Ah, the bravado, thought Anita. "It can take some people a long time to come around and get used to a new idea. Just give them time."

"And what about you? Will you get used to the idea?"

Anita had to admit it was a good question. They had reached the lane to the temple, where it was cool out of the sun, beneath the overhanging shrubs and gently swaying tree branches. Thick moss covered parts of the old stone wall, and the speaker for the evening music sat among weeds on the other side, wires dangling from the telephone and electric pole.

"You're not the first person who's felt called, or moved, or enthralled by a temple deity." She leaned against the wall, wondering how to explain her feelings. "I'm always glad to see someone respond to the Hinduism I know and love, but when you go home, I wonder how long it will last. Sometimes it lasts and sometimes it doesn't, and no one can predict."

"I suppose that's fair." Emily struggled to keep a pout from breaking onto her face. "I can't argue about how I feel."

"I'm not asking you to." Anita waited for Emily to do just that, but she didn't. She just shrugged and smiled. "Actually, I wanted to ask you about your brother."

"My brother?" Emily shook her head. "What do you know about my brother?" An expression that must have belonged to the old Emily crossed her face, one of pain and suspicion and strain, definitely strain.

"Pam told us about him, about his getting arrested in Thailand and what happened to him." There was no way to say delicately all the awful things that had befallen this young man, no matter how guilty he might have been. Just the mere mention must have triggered a flood of memories in Emily, and a cascade of emotions no one could assuage.

"He doesn't have anything to do with this." Emily gave Anita a fierce look and clenched her fists.

"No, I didn't think so. But I was wondering what he was doing in Thailand. He got himself into a terrible situation—it must have been horrible for you."

Emily suddenly looked frail, resting her arms on the wall and leaning over it, plucking at the tallest weeds clumped against the stones. All that fierce anger couldn't hold back the sorrow she felt. "It was horrible—a nightmare—I never knew I could feel such desperation and hopelessness. And despair. I don't think I ever understood what despair was before last year." Her eyes grew red and a sheet of tears began to wash her face. "I could do nothing, nothing for him. He was innocent, and no one would listen to me. They didn't even pretend to listen."

"Can you tell me about it?" Anita asked. She began to feel she was at last getting to the real Emily. "What was he doing there?"

"He wanted to work with refugees, or something. He was doing research in some rituals, in grad school, something about the way forms of Christianity are adapted to native practices in other parts of the world." She waved away the question. "I didn't really get it. He wasn't into telling me about his work, just that he loved what he was doing."

"Did he talk about any of the people he was working with, the people he was meeting?"

She shook her head. "We wrote, and a couple of times he called on his cell—it was really cheap—if he wanted me to send something he couldn't get there. Things like that."

"What about his letters?"

Again, she shook her head. "He asked me how our parents were—they like to travel and always send back great things from their trips—peculiar but great—and the weather, and maybe sometimes about the food if he had something really weird."

"Was he working alone? Was he living with other students?" Anita could feel herself growing frustrated. "There must be something that tells you how he got into trouble."

"You know, I thought it was all over, in the past. But it still hurts."

"I'm sorry."

"Why? What do you care?" She glanced down at the camera in her hands. "That was rude. I'm the one who should be sorry." She took a deep breath and looked up. "Yes, in answer to your question, I think he was living with someone for a while. But there wasn't anyone around when I got there, and no one came forward to help him, you know, to vouch for him." She turned toward Anita.

"That must have really hurt."

"Oh, yeah, for sure—all his so-called friends. This was a research project, you know? He managed to get one call out to the embassy after he was arrested and they contacted his department." She held Anita's eyes. "All they said was if he got into drug trouble, he was on his own. And no more personal appeals. It made no difference." She reached over the stone wall and plucked a slender stalk of grass, then tore it in half. "The message was he'd have to defend himself when he got back, prove he hadn't done anything." She paused, looking at the two strands of grass in her hands. "Can you imagine? He was in jail, desperate for help, and they were telling him that he'd have to prove he didn't do anything illegal so he could stay in the program. They were dumping him. The fuckers were just throwing him overboard. It made them look bad to have someone in their program get arrested."

"He was still being held at that point?"

Emily nodded. "They just left him there." Her tears were quiet ones now, tears of sorrow, not anger, of resignation as well as remembered love. "I went out there. I must have been out there for barely a week but that's all it took. I got the message. Everyone I talked to said I could do as much back home in the

States, so I came back. They were wrong. The next thing I knew he was dead."

"I'm surprised you were willing to travel through Asia again so soon after," Anita said. She'd been watching the deep emotions surfacing in Emily, wondering if she really was as stable as she appeared.

"My friends convinced me to come. They said it would be good for me, and they were right. It has been good for me—but not like they expected." A choked laugh escaped her. "Why do you want to know?"

CHAPTER SEVENTEEN

Anita didn't have an answer satisfactory to anyone else as to why she was digging so hard, but she was convinced that Jean and Marge and Emily's brother were intimately connected in ways still hidden from her. She couldn't have said exactly how, but she was sure they represented three sides of a triangle, and the deaths of two of them—and near death of a third—were connected.

The driver guided the Hotel Delite car through the narrow gates and on to Anandabudhi Hospital. Anita warned him to remain with the car, ready to drive up to collect Marge in a matter of minutes. At least, that was Anita's hope. Dr. Premod had assured Anita that Marge was ready to be discharged, and Anita had prepared a room and attendant for her back at the hotel.

"Yes, she is well enough for the hotel room," Dr. Premod said. She sat behind her desk, fully self-possessed despite Anita's close questioning. Relieved, Anita asked to collect Marge. "Come, she is waiting. Already she has her medicine and instructions in both Malayalam and English." She paused and added. "And she herself is a nurse, isn't she? Quite competent."

The doctor led Anita to a small anteroom near the ward where she had first seen Marge and first wondered if she'd survive whatever it was that had happened to her. Marge nodded and smiled at Anita's appearance and rose from her chair.

"Glad you're here. I'm ready to go." Marge's face paled for a moment, then color returned, and she took the arm of a young woman attendant. "Salt sea air sounds refreshing."

The attendant led Marge through the hallways and out to the main entrance. Anita and Dr. Premod dawdled behind, swapping niceties about the medical needs of foreign tourists, their penchant for getting into trouble in the most unlikely places, and Dr. Premod's overseas training.

"Oh, yes, you asked about what she might have ingested." Dr. Premod halted and pulled a folded sheet of paper from beneath several layers on her clipboard. "I have received a report from the toxicology department, and I have made a copy for you. It is curious, you will see."

Anita took the sheet, fumbled as she unfolded it in her eagerness, and scanned the list of items. Then she read it again. "I don't get it," she finally said to the doctor. "What does it mean?"

"I cannot say what it means, but it suggests that she ingested a multitude of ingredients for insect control." Dr. Premod tapped the corner of the sheet with her pink-painted fingernail. "None of these is likely to kill a normally healthy person. But together, and some even alone, can make someone quite ill with stomach complaint."

Anita folded the sheet of paper and slipped it into her purse. "That changes things—it changes them a lot."

"You see, you worried for nothing. A foolish accident it appears, and Miss Marge will return to her home having learned something about our medical care as well as our history and culture and beautiful land. Yes?"

"I am so glad to be back," Marge said, easing herself into a wooden-armed chair with deep cushions on the seat and back. She turned her head at the sound of a wave crashing on the rocks below, raised her hand against the curtain brushing against her head as a sharp breeze pushed in and sucked back out again.

Anita watched her as she ran her eyes over the rest of the room, as though making sure it was all still here, just the way she had left it, as though she had missed it hard during the last few days.

"We kept the room available for you," Anita said. "We were pretty sure you'd be back." It wasn't true, but it made Marge smile.

"Thank you." She pushed herself up in the chair. "I've never been on the other side of the medical encounter before. Don't get me wrong, Anita. They were all wonderful to me, but it was a little scary. I knew what they were doing all the time, but I've never felt so helpless. Knowledge isn't always a good thing, at least for me. I kept watching for someone to make a mistake. It was nerve-wracking."

Anita moved to the open door and called to the young woman outside. She introduced the nurse to Marge, and explained the arrangements. The nurse returned to her book and her chair in the hallway.

"Won't she be bored?" Marge asked.

"I hope so."

Marge laughed.

"The doctor was kind enough to reassure me that you hadn't actually taken anything lethal." Anita closed the door and moved to open another window. "Did she talk to you about it? Water?"

Marge took the glass of water and swallowed half of it. "I never appreciated good water until I got here. Just one more thing I've been taking for granted." She finished the glass and handed it back to Anita. "Dr. Premod told me this morning, when I was signing discharge papers. Did you know that I paid with my credit card? I have no idea if my insurance at work is going to cover this. What an experience." Marge leaned back, resting her head on the back of the chair.

"What did she tell you?"

"Just that I had ingested a lot of chemicals but nothing lethal." She closed her eyes for a moment. "Is it true that you could end up with potatoes soaked in kerosene or something like that when you shopped at the old ration shops?"

"Is that what you think happened? Something carelessly done in the restaurant?" Anita sat down on a wooden chair in front of a small desk. She had not considered the Bamboo Village Restaurant to be a suspect in this incident. The only other stomach ailments that night had all come from a small group of tourists that ate poorly cooked fish at a hotel at the other end of the resort. No one had had any kind of reaction like Marge's.

Marge shrugged and opened her eyes. "I have no idea. I'm just glad it's over."

"Could I ask you one more question?"

For a second Anita thought Marge was going to say no, but then she seemed to think better of it and nodded yes. "Go ahead."

"Tell me everything you had to eat that night."

"I have told you and the doctor so many times, and it never changes." Marge went through the dinner, her meal and Jean's. Then the piece of fruit outside the temple—a small banana she peeled herself. "I was nervous—that's why I was still eating after dinner."

"Even though Jean said there was nothing to worry about," Anita said.

"Look, I overreact sometimes. Jean knew that."

"I'm sorry. Go on. What else did you eat?"

"Just the prasadam that Candy and Emily gave me."

Anita leaned forward. "You told me about the prasadam Candy gave you, but when did Emily give you some?"

"Near the end. When we were leaving. I was going up the stairs—I guess I was at the top. Candy had left already—I could see her going on ahead on the lane. Emily showed me a banana leaf with prasadam on it, and she said it was supposed to be really good, not just holy, but really good. I took a piece."

"A piece? What was it?"

"A rice ball, sort of sweet. It was okay. I didn't think it was anything special."

"And you got that from Emily?"

She nodded. "I ate it on the way back."

"You ate a rice ball prasadam on the lane on the way back to the hotel." It wasn't a question—it was a recitation of the end of the evening. Anita frowned and shook her head. "I don't get it. Why would Emily give you a rice ball?"

"Maybe you should ask her." Marge seemed to speak without a hint of irony, and Anita realized that she was fast falling asleep. She wasn't yet nearly as strong as she professed to be. Anita left her alone, closing the door quietly behind her as she heard Marge begin to snore.

"She is well?" Meena was waiting at the bottom of the stairs as Anita descended, lost in her own thoughts. "Anita, is she well?"

"What? Oh, yes, Auntie, very well. The nurse is just what she needed. She's resting now, much more confident and feeling safe." Anita turned toward the registration desk.

"Then why this long face? What is concerning you?" Meena followed her, seemingly torn between conflicting emotions of fear for her guest and anger at what fate has wrought. She followed her niece into the office.

"Marge said she got a rice ball as prasadam from Emily." Anita fell into a chair.

"Ah! Emily is the one!" Meena frowned as she said this. "Are you certain of this? She seems such a nice girl and so devoted to Kali."

"I can only repeat what Marge said to me." She rubbed her hands along the edge of the table. "But I had prasadam and there was nothing wrong with it."

"I would like to have a rice ball prasadam—it has been some time since I have had such." Meena sighed and walked to a calendar hanging on the wall. "Let me see," she said as she began to read the tiny Malayalam print. "I think there is some event coming soon. Perhaps they will have such. Perhaps I should call first. Yes?"

"Auntie, you're absolutely right."

"Eh?" Meena turned at the curious statement of her niece. "But I am always wrong. You are showing me this—I say so and so died a natural death and you say, no, he was murdered—thrown into the river, knocked on the head, poisoned. You go on and on and on. And you are right." The last seemed to depress her, and she turned away, running her hand lightly over the calendar. "Perhaps I shall go to the Shree Padmanab-haswami Temple on my next trip into Trivandrum. There things are as they have always been. It is a great comfort."

Anita rose and gently wrapped her arms around her aunt. She hated to see her unhappy—she had had more than her share of unkind fate—but sometimes it couldn't be avoided. "I think sometimes, Auntie, that you and I live in parallel universes. It is perfectly all right for someone you know to die from falling into a river. This is the way you should see it. I, on the other hand, have to know why he fell into the river. You needn't pay any attention to me if it distresses you." She gave her aunt another squeeze, and headed for the door.

"Where are you going?"

"To find out why Emily lied to me."

CHAPTER EIGHTEEN

Anita waved away a swarm of gnats swirling in front of her face as she turned onto the platform high above the temple compound. There, below her, quiet in the midday heat and only partly sheltered by overhanging tree branches, sat the brightly painted temple to Balabhadrakali, its strings of tied fronds hanging listlessly in the heat. Anita scanned the temple grounds looking for some sign of activity. If Emily had come here, there was no sign of her now. The doors to the small offices to the left were closed. Around the corner came a sweeper woman with a reed broom in one hand and a basket of weeds and debris held against her hip with her other hand. Anita called out to her.

"Not now," the woman said. "All are gone. Evening they are coming." Not waiting to see if another question would follow, she walked over to the gate, dropped her basket, and began sweeping along the compound wall.

Anita sighed and looked around. She had been impulsive to think she would find anyone here, even Emily. The doors to the shrine were locked, the temple was officially closed for worship until late in the afternoon, and even Emily couldn't be so enamored of Kali that she'd sit in the sweltering heat and stare at a pair of closed doors. The leaves rustled in the light breeze. Anita turned and took the path around the compound, to the lane leading into the trees.

This was a bad time to be dropping in on anyone, Anita knew, but she began to feel she was running out of time. The police were treating Jean's death as an accident, which meant that anyone connected with her death could leave the country and probably never worry about facing any charges. This fear whirled through her head as she moved up the path, quickening her step, making her heart beat faster.

The families would be preparing the midday meal, the women in back cooking, and the men still at work. Anita passed to the last house, where the youngest of the three sisters lived. She rattled the open gate, to announce her arrival, but no response came from inside. Calling out hello, Anita entered the compound and approached the house. She leaned across the small veranda and knocked on the half-open wooden door, again calling out. Her calls grew louder and louder until she heard another voice.

"Aarilla?" someone called. The youngest sister came around the side of the house, a white tea towel thrown across her chest, another tucked into her mundu across her stomach, like an apron. She wiped her hands back and forth across the one at her waist as she came forward. "Oh, it is you. Yes, yes, yes." She gave a broad smile, waggled her head, and stopped at the end of the veranda.

Anita offered a greeting, and explained her interest.

"Prasadam? But the temple is making it. We are cooking there." She frowned, confused by Anita's question.

"I thought perhaps you might be making it here, at your house, and taking it there," Anita said.

The woman laughed, then shook her head. "No, no. Not here. There."

"Didn't I see you with ingredients yesterday?"

"Ah, the shopping. Yes, I am helping with that. Some we are donating, my sisters and I. It is the festival, you know. It is our offering to Kali." She waved her hand at the other houses in the row, with a little blush moving up her face, proud of her gift but not too proud, a little embarrassed too. "We are all giving." She nodded to the area behind Anita, who turned to see Moosa standing sentry at the end of his yard. He was watching them with such a bored expression on his face that Anita felt a little dead herself.

"What is the troubling?" Moosa asked.

"No troubling," Anita replied. "I was just asking about the prasadam."

"Especially made," Moosa said, stepping through the brush onto the lane. Anita almost groaned—the last thing she wanted was a detailed description of how prasadam was prepared.

"It is our gift for the festival week."

Anita turned back at the sound of another voice and met the gaze of the sister who lived in the middle house, the one who made the failed insect repellent. "I was just wondering about the prasadam," Anita said, moving closer to the other house. The baked-brick wall between the two houses was so melted down from the monsoon rains that in some parts it was no more than a dirt doorsill between the properties. Anita moved toward the lowest part.

"Their gift." Moosa moved parallel on the lane, ready to launch into an explanation at any time. "It is customary. You know these things, yes?"

"It is not a rich temple," the middle sister explained. "A modest gift means a great deal."

"Yes, indeed," Moosa said. "In fact, we are not having sufficient quantities of oil for the last two nights of the festival."

"That would be tonight and tomorrow night." And now the third sister, the oldest, appeared from the middle house and hurried across the ground. "Kali always rewards the generous."

Three women stared expectantly at Anita, and she suddenly realized she was all but committed, but she had no idea how much the oil for even a single evening might cost. She also knew that all she had to do was wait. "Could I have a glass of water?"

"Water? Yes, yes." The oldest sister snapped her fingers and sent her youngest sister scurrying back into her house. Anita offered the others a wan smile as she waved her hand in front of her face.

"Yes, very hot," the middle sister said.

The youngest one reappeared a moment later with a small bottle of water, handing it to Anita. It was unopened, and Anita twisted off the cap and took a large gulp. She edged closer to the wall, and the oldest sister smiled, seemingly alert to the next step.

"You must sit," she said, and motioned Anita to the veranda behind her. Anita stepped over the wall and followed her to the house, accepting a chair on the veranda.

This is going to cost me at least Rs 2,000, Anita thought.

"This is a very fine temple run by all of us who live here," Moosa said, growing more and more somber by the minute. It seemed to Anita that the more serious the discussion about money, the gloomier he got. "We are painting it freshly this year."

"Yes, I noticed. I live here." This seemed to mean nothing to Moosa, and he continued to describe all the work that had gone into fixing up the temple for the annual festival—the new paint, the patched concrete steps, the little roofs over the images at the cardinal points, the new roof on the offices, new bells on the shrine doors, improvements to the stage behind the temple compound. "So much work."

"I suppose the prasadam is special this year also," Anita said, after draining the water bottle.

The youngest shook her head, equally solemn. "No, no, the same. The same."

"The fruit and rice balls," Anita said.

"No, no rice balls."

"No rice balls?"

"No rice balls."

"Are you sure about that?" The three sisters and Moosa all agreed that no rice balls had been offered to Kali.

They must have noticed Anita's disappointment because the youngest said quickly, "I will get for you. You like these and I will get."

In a moment she knew she should be ashamed of, Anita wondered just how much she could milk their eagerness for her donation. This was surely when con artists were born—at the unexpected flash of opportunity. But she had bigger worries. Marge had been quite clear that Emily had given her rice balls as prasadam and had even remembered their taste, mostly for its sweetness but overall lack of taste.

"Yes, I like rice balls—the little ones with raisin and cashew bits in them. But I can get them myself—you needn't bother—I just haven't seen them around." Anita looked hopefully from face to face while the women chattered among themselves, naming each shop along the nearby roads.

"It is no trouble," Moosa said in English. "These people don't mind work." He smiled reassuringly, and Anita realized the sisters didn't understand a word of English.

"Which shop was it?" she asked the youngest. The girl told her and Anita wrote it down in her notebook. "I'll go by there later today on another errand." She stopped herself from putting away her notebook. "Hmm, what sort of donation would keep the oil lamps lit for one evening puja?" All four faces grew animated and figures flew among them, some high, some low, some made Anita wince, and some she truly hoped were closer to the reality.

"I'll take a check to the temple board president this afternoon," Anita said.

As soon as the transaction was settled, Moosa returned to his backyard, and sauntered up to his house, ready for a good meal and the opportunity to tell everyone he met how he had extricated a large donation for lamp oil from the niece of the owner of Hotel Delite. When she was confident he was not going to return, Anita turned back toward the middle house.

"How long have you been in business here?" she asked the middle sister. "The Nuisance Works. How long have you been here?"

"Ah, a couple of years." She shrugged. "We shall sell our stock if we are not selling to the shops."

"Could I take a look?"

"You are wanting to buy?" The oldest sister drew forward.

"No, not really. But I have a reason for asking." Anita didn't want to tell them the truth, her hunch that someone had been in and made use of their supplies, but neither did she want to lie to them. Something like that could come back to haunt her. The three sisters glanced at each other, seemed to come to an agreement, and gave her smiles and nods.

"Go on, go on," the oldest one said, ushering her into the house. "Go on, go on," she said, ushering Anita through the house and out the back door and over to a shed. The middle one pulled open the door and pointed to the bottles and jars and boxes of liquids and powders, all with warning labels and cobwebs.

"Do you mind if I look?" They didn't, so she did. On a rickety wooden bench were lined up a variety of chemicals used as pesticides, ammonia, bleach, lye, and other items. Anita recognized a bottle of insect repellent, an old spray can, jars of green powder that reminded her of the green coils that burned like incense, giving off an odor and smoke offensive to mosquitoes. She turned a bottle here, read the information on a paper packet there, noted the bottles of DDT. Trying not to breathe through her nose and holding the dupatta over the lower half of her face, she looked quickly at a carton containing empty bottles set on the floor. Able to tolerate it no longer, she backed out of the shed.

"Am I the only one who's been in here, other than you and your families?" Anita took deep breaths of the humid air. She wasn't sure exactly what she was breathing in there, but she wanted it out of her lungs and the rest of her body. She felt flushed and light-headed all of a sudden. "Has anyone else been in here?"

The sisters muttered excitedly to each other. "No, no one." They delivered this decision quietly.

"Yes, one." The youngest one pushed forward. "The one who was looking for a particular chemical."

"Which one?" Anita asked.

"The DDT."

"But we are not having good DDT. It is too expensive for us," the oldest one said. "We are having a poor mixture."

"I am telling her, but she is asking to look. She is having many cockroaches in her room, she says." The youngest one turned to Anita. "Such a problem for the foreigners. They are not accustomed to cockroaches. And chelandi also."

"So what did she take?" Anita asked.

The youngest one shrugged and looked to her sisters. "Nothing. She is not finding the DDT she wants, and she said she will look in the shops for something."

"I see." Anita ducked back inside and made a mental note of the individual jars and bottles that had smoothed-over surfaces, partly cleaned of spider webs, dirt, debris. It seemed to her that perhaps a dozen bottles had been moved or opened, including one marked DDT. She reemerged in the open air, again grateful for a deep breath. "When was the last time you made up any of your insect repellent?"

The sisters again muttered among themselves. "Two months," the middle one said. "Maybe three months. We have no sales." Again, she shrugged.

The three women accompanied Anita to the lane, thanking her profusely for her donation to the temple festival, assuring her that Kali rewarded the generous, and the temple Board would also be grateful. And by the way, did she know . . . ? The women began to list the names of the Board members, just in case Anita wondered who to give her check to—or perhaps as a reminder that many would know of her promise to donate.

"I'll go do it now," she promised, "this afternoon." It was getting late and she was hungry. "About the woman who came for DDT. Do you know who she was? Have you seen her around here before or since?"

"There are so many," the middle one said.

"Perhaps you saw her at the temple," Anita said. "She might have been there. One of the women staying at our hotel has been going regularly, twice a day at least. She feels she has been called by Kali." She began to describe Emily.

"Oh, I know who she is. She is asking the priest many questions," the youngest one said. "She wants to know everything." She described Emily to her sisters.

"Yes, that's her," Anita said.

"No, she did not come here." The middle one was definite. "No, not that one."

"Are you sure?" Anita couldn't hide her disappointment, but the sisters were certain.

The youngest one moved closer and laid a hand on Anita's

arm. "So, do you have cockroaches? It's not so bad. We can help."

Auntie Meena will kill me, Anita thought after she managed to slip away.

CHAPTER NINETEEN

Anita made her way along the path leading down the hill into the back of the resort. She was relieved to leave the sounds of Lighthouse Road and its traffic behind as the tall trees with thick branches closed over her. Even the radio blaring from the stage while the workmen prepared for tomorrow night's Kathakali performance seemed quieter than the din of her thoughts and the auto traffic.

Emily had given the rice balls to Marge, but she had not been to Nuisance Works and puttered around inside the shed. Someone else had. But who? The next corner Anita turned seemed to cut off all sounds from the radio, and she was plunged into silence, with only the sound of her own sandals slapping on the concrete walk to accompany her. The tiny tea and snack shop along the walkway was open, and as Anita passed she caught sight of a young girl's feet as she lay napping on the floor, curled up on a towel. Anita called out a greeting to the girl, who answered softly. On a whim, Anita sat on the step leading into the shop and leaned against the wall.

"I have to sit and think for a minute," she told the girl. But instead of thinking, she rested her head and closed her eyes. All this business with Jean and Marge was getting worse instead of better. Marge had not ingested anything accidentally and was quite clear Emily had given her the rice balls, and the doctor was quite clear that those rice balls had contained the chemicals that had made her sick. The Nuisance Works had all the chemicals as far as Anita could see, but Emily had not been known to go there. Could the sisters have been wrong? Could Emily have approached the house from the rear, gotten into the shed, and taken what she wanted?

Anita stood up, walked around to the rear of the tiny shop, and studied the back of the hill as it rose up behind the shop and stage area. Anything was possible, but the more she looked, the less likely it seemed. She returned to her seat, lowering herself with a steadying hand on the glass case. Inside were the usual assortment of biscuits, cookies, and packaged sweets. Next to stacks of these were little trays of sweets—miniature cupcakes with pink or yellow or green or blue icing, balls of cane or brown sugar and nuts and spices. Anita leaned closer. And there, in the middle of the tray, was an assortment of small rice balls.

"Those are rice balls." Anita stood up and tapped her index finger against the glass counter. The little girl also stood and stared at the inside of the case. "Do you always carry these?"

The girl looked perplexed but nodded yes.

"Did you have them four or five days ago?"

Again the reluctant nod. "They are very good. My grandmother makes them."

"I'm sure they're wonderful." Anita stood, stretching out her back. She felt like a ton of worry had been lifted off her shoulders. Of course she would find them here. They were part of the standard fare of local shops catering first to Indians and then to foreigners. The foreigners tried the sweets, then bought the cookies and biscuits.

"Do you want?" She started to slide open the door to the case.

"Do you sell these to foreigners?"

The little girl twisted up her mouth to say no but instead wiggled her head. "Not so often."

"How often?" Anita's mind was racing with warnings—she didn't want to lead the child into giving the answer the child thought was wanted. Anita had to have an answer she could trust. The child frowned at the question and seemed to think it over.

"Not so often."

"A few days ago?"

The girl nodded.

"Do you remember who?"

The girl paused to think then nodded again.

"Who?"

"I am not knowing the name. She is a guest here at the resort."

"Describe her."

"She is foreign."

"And?"

She shrugged. "Foreign."

"The one who is beloved of Kali?"

The girl smiled and cupped her hand over her mouth to hide her giggling. She shook her head, still laughing.

So, it wasn't Emily, Anita said to herself.

"Who?"

"The one who is called by Kali a few days ago—her name is Emily."

The little girl repeated it. "She is very nice."

"Have you met her?"

She nodded. "She buys colas from me. Sometimes she practices saying hello to me in Malayalam. Namaste she says. But she says namaas tee." Again she giggled.

Anita shared in her delight, then said, "If Emily didn't buy, who did?"

"Ah, it was her friend. The one who rushes here and there. So much rushing about." She smiled as though Anita should know at once who she was referring to.

"Can you describe her? Please try," Anita added when she saw the girl's discouraged expression. "I really need to know."

"You really need to know?" Anita nodded. "Go there, to Shree Jagat's house. He knows how to describe her. She is the one who got lost and wanted to take the lane through his property to the temple. He sent her back here. Many times she got lost, but he is kind and many times he sent her back, and he is walking with her to make sure she is finding her way."

Anita hurried down the path, skidding around its twists and turns, then turning left away from the resort, as the path went to the right, and she went left, past a small house on a high plinth. She followed the path into a yard, through that, and out into a small opening at the foot of the hill. High above she could see festival decorations. Ahead was a small house set in a clearing, with no compound wall, no garden, just a small house with a few chickens in the yard and the usual household equipment—a washing stone, two grinding stones, aluminum pots and pans drying on the ground at the side of the house, and debris scattered farther in among the trees.

Anita approached the front door and rapped. She knew no one was home—she knew the minute she entered the clearing—not a sound came from the house: no radio, no television, no voices chatting and laughing, no children playing or babies crying. No, the locked door was simply another manifestation. This house was empty.

Anita left the clearing and regained the lane, following it down to the canal, and then along the rear of the shops, to a lane near the southern end of the shopping arcade. She nodded to a woman cleaning pots behind a woven-mat house, and emerged onto the beach, the open front of the house crowded with brightly colored cloth bags, skirt wraps, and blouses swinging in the light breeze.

"If I can't find Shree Jagat, I'll settle for Emily," Anita muttered to herself as she headed up the walkway, passing the women selling fruit, the tourists strolling past restaurants looking for the meal of the day. On the sand, a few feet away, a mangy dog stood in the heat, apparently unsure which way to go. Anita cringed, instinctively looking around for someone to take the animal away. The tourists passed by, either ignoring it or saying *hello, puppy, hello, puppy.* When she didn't see a constable nearby, Anita moved along, leaving the dog and the tourists to fate.

"If I were Emily, where would I go?" Anita stared down the length of the walkway, at the old woman with a pile of grasses on her head, the man selling multicolored lungis, the young boy selling atlases and maps of India, the woman selling necklaces of shells purchased in Indonesia or China, the touts promising great adventures of beauty on trips into the hills and elephant rides and elegant dining at a tea plantation.

"This is where I would go." Anita looked up at the wide stairs leading up to the Beachview Café. "Just the place." And I hope she's here, Anita heard herself thinking—I'm starved. I need lunch. She climbed the stairs and emerged into a large, open room filled with tables in the front half, looking out over the walkway, the beach, and the ocean stretching across to Africa. The back wall was lined with a long high counter behind which food was prepared.

Anita scanned the tables, and the blond and brunette and red heads nodding over food, coffee, conversation, newspapers, and books. At the southern end she spotted Emily's four traveling companions finishing off what looked like an elaborate meal. Anita wondered if Emily had been the fourth member of the group, rather than the fifth, would her friends have abandoned her so thoroughly? Did they reject her less for her sudden falling in love with Kali, and more because four was such a comfortable number for a group? One of them, Pam, looked up, caught Anita's eye, and waved. Anita waved back.

Not wanting to appear quite so obvious, she rummaged among the European and American magazines littering a broad table, and selected an old news magazine. Flipping through it, she continued to inspect the customers. And there, next to the wall along the stairwell, hidden behind an especially prolific potted palm, sat Emily. With her head hidden by fronds, and only her back visible to anyone's searching eye, Emily might have gone unnoticed for the entire day, except for an especially diligent waiter. She leaned over her cup of tea and scribbled in her diary as Anita came up behind her.

"Uh, hello." She seemed startled to see Anita and quickly shut the diary, capping her pen and slipping it into her purse. "I was just reading." She drew a magazine closer to her, covering the diary.

"Mind if I join you?" Anita sat down without waiting to be invited. She had no illusions that she had interrupted the other woman during an especially private moment, probably more on her relationship with Kali, and might have to apologize—but later. Anita took a deep breath and waved to the waiter. She realized it would be a good idea for her to have something to eat for a couple of reasons. One, she was starving, and unlike some people, if she didn't eat, the hunger pangs didn't go away. They just got worse. And she couldn't dull them with water or a piece of hard candy. Two, because she was hungry, she was in danger of becoming testy, and she was already a tad testy because Emily had lied to her. So, she had better eat first, or she would accuse the other woman of something, and then they'd have a row and that would be awkward. No one would talk to her if she gave in to her testy moods. Anita ordered curd rice and fruit.

"I try to eat something new every day." Emily glanced at her plate. Anita speculated that she had had fried potatoes and onions, but said nothing. "Something I can't get at home, you know."

"Makes sense." Anita glanced through the menu again, even though she had already tried everything they offered. The food was good, reasonably priced, and the setting was fabulous. She could eat stale crackers here and be happy. She closed the menu and pushed it away from her. A burst of laughter drew the attention of both women. On the other side of the stairwell Emily's friends were wending their way among the tables. Pam noticed them and broke away from the others. She nodded to Emily, then turned to Anita.

"We're doing the Suchindram Temple trip tomorrow, then we'll nap before we leave. We're all set. Meena got us a car." She paused and looked down at Emily. "You can come, Em, if you want." The smile was perfectly polite, the face expressionless, but the voice flat. Anita could just imagine what it had cost Pam to extend the invitation, and her deeper intent was barely tickling the surface, but it was there. Emily couldn't have missed it.

"Thanks, Pam." Emily seemed shy in her friend's company. "But tonight there's another procession, a smaller one, for a large family that has its own Kali image. They don't do it every year, and the priest told me about it. I'd hate to miss it. They're going to let me watch them get the image ready for the procession and then let me follow along." The information came flowing out of Emily in a spate of useless details, leaving Pam, if not overwhelmed, at least rebuffed.

Pam rolled her eyes. "Whatever. Bye, Anita." She hurried down the stairs to catch up with her friends.

"It was very nice of her to include you," Anita said, wondering at her own need to smooth things over between the five friends.

Emily gave her a pitying smile. "Do you think I'm that frivolous?"

Anita decided that Emily was a bit deeper than she had at first thought. Not because she declined a trip to a beautiful temple to the South, nor because she had felt something special at the Kali temple. No, Emily surprised Anita with her questions and comments about the Indian world around her and especially those about her brother.

"I brought Marge home from the hospital this morning." Anita rearranged the plate placed in front of her, and settled in for lunch. Emily apparently didn't consider Anita's statement worthy of comment because she continued flipping through her magazine and gazing out over the beach.

"Did she have a virus or food poisoning?" Emily asked, breaking a long silence.

"Actually, in a way, she did. Have food poisoning, I mean."

"That's too bad."

"Yes." Anita decided the café had a new chef—the curd rice was the best she'd had in ages. She must remember to ask who the chef was, just in case he might someday be open to another job, when the hotel needed someone. "She mentioned where she'd been for dinner and the prasadam she'd had."

"You should check the restaurant."

"I think they did."

"So how did it happen?" Emily gave her an open, quizzical look.

"The prasadam."

Emily gasped. "I don't believe it."

"It's true. The hospital's been testing and testing and testing. And it's true."

"That's an awful thing to say."

Anita leaned back in her chair and gazed at the other woman.

203

She was playing the role of the naive foreigner quite well, at least she seemed to be doing so. Anita wasn't sure. Could her behavior be sincere? "You gave her some of that prasadam, didn't you?"

"Well, yes, but . . ." Emily was obviously confused. "But I had it too. And I didn't get sick."

"You had the cooked prasadam that the priest hands out."

"Yes." She looked like she was reliving that moment, folding her hands together in front of her, her palms shaping a small cup. "I've never had anything like it."

"And the rice balls."

"Rice balls?" Emily frowned then shook her head. "No, I didn't have any rice balls."

"You're sure?"

"Positive. I'd remember."

"Marge said you gave her rice balls. She remembers that particularly."

Emily's hands fell apart as she rested her fingers on the edge of the table, her head falling forward and tipping to one side. She seemed to be thinking hard. "Well, you know, I did." She turned to Anita. "Candy said they were blessed, special prasadam, and that they were for Marge. Marge had asked for them."

"When was this?"

"I don't know, near the end. Almost everyone was gone, and Candy was still there and she said she was supposed to give the rice balls to Marge, but she forgot and would I do it because she wasn't going back to the hotel right away."

"You got the rice balls from Candy," Anita said, to be sure she had heard correctly.

"For sure. She didn't want to run after Marge and asked me to take them back to the hotel. I said I would." Emily rested her hands on her lap and rubbed them down her thighs. "Are you all right, Anita?"

"I'm not sure."

"It's very hard here, isn't it? I mean, you're half Indian and all, but still. It's like we're living in an alternate reality here."

Startled by this sudden outflowing of philosophy, Anita tried not to show her feelings. She still had questions for the other woman.

"When did you give Marge the rice balls?"

"At the top of the road. She was still there when I left the temple. She was talking to Jean about something. I think they were having a disagreement."

"What makes you think that?"

"Marge was tired and Jean wasn't, and Marge kept telling her she should focus on what she was here for, something like that. And Jean just put her off."

"Did they go back to the hotel together?"

"Oh, yes. They stopped talking as soon as I came up to them, you know, the way people do when they're embarrassed and don't want to be overheard. So I gave her the rice balls, and she just took them."

"What did she do with them?"

"She offered one to Jean, but Jean just shook her head. I don't think she approves of non-Hindus taking prasadam."

"But Marge does?"

"I guess so. I don't really know. She didn't say much, just thanked me."

"She put them in her purse?" Anita was finding Emily's narrative frustrating and her overall attitude exasperating.

"Oh, no, she ate them. She popped one into her mouth, and then I guess she ate the other one on the way down the hill."

"You saw her eat them?"

"Shouldn't she have?" Emily looked puzzled, as though she hadn't realized what she'd just said. "We can't know what we're supposed to do here, can we? It's like we're drifting through on a separate plane and reality is entirely different from what we're seeing."

"It's a different culture, that's all."

"You think?" Emily considered the idea. "Maybe. That dog, for instance. That mangy one wandering the beach. If that happened at home, half the beach would be on their cell phones calling the police to come and get it. But here, no one pays any attention. It's like we stop thinking here." Emily clasped her hands in front of her chin and rested her elbows on the table. "We have to learn a new language, a new reality. Did Candy really ask me to do that, or did Kali arrange for me to do that?"

CHAPTER TWENTY

Anita was not prepared to accept that humans had no responsibility for Jean's death and Marge's illness. Kali punished those who had known sins; she did not serve anyone seeking revenge. And Balabhadrakali was a gracious version of the Black Kali most people were familiar with. No, Kali had nothing to do with Candy's artifice, it seemed. Anita finished her meal, paid the tab, and headed back to Shree Jagat's house, hoping he was still home for the early afternoon rest.

When she rounded the corner, she was relieved to see a man napping in a chair on the veranda. She approached along the path and called out a hello when she was still twenty feet away. He turned his head toward her voice and opened his sleepy eyes, but made no move to sit up. Anita called out again as she drew closer.

"Yes, what are you wanting?" He sat up. "Ah! Anita! Come on, come on." He waved her toward the house, and she climbed the steps and took the chair he indicated. He called into the house, and a moment later his wife appeared in the doorway, smiling and nodding and offering fresh lime juice. Anita accepted, and the other woman disappeared inside again.

"I passed the snacks stall and the girl said you were looking for me," Jagat said. The lime juice appeared during the niceties.

Anita took a sip, considering the tart flavor just right except for something added she couldn't identify. She looked up to see the woman smiling expectantly. "There's something in this."

When Anita looked puzzled, the other woman slapped her knee and laughed and tapped her husband's shoulder.

"A secret ingredient," her husband said with obvious pride. "You think about it, and tell us what you think it is." The wife returned to her kitchen, pleased with her guest's reaction.

She took another sip, let the liquid rest on her tongue, but couldn't quite get it. "This is going to take some time, I can tell." He laughed and repeated her words to his wife inside. "Actually, I came to see you with a question." She put down the glass, and repeated what the little girl at the snack stall had told her about the foreigner trying to find a way up the hill, the one Anita had thought would be Emily.

"Ah, yes, that happens, but not so much now. The paths are well marked, and there are so many of them now."

"Do you remember a young woman coming through here perhaps three or four days ago, maybe five days ago?"

"Ah, yes, big smile." This clearly delighted him and, he waved his hand in a gesture of enthusiasm. "She is certain this is the way, and I am telling her once, twice, even thrice, she is lost. Not this way." He continued to describe his encounter with this young American woman, with the short brown hair that looked like a bowl had been left on her head, sun blisters on her forearms, and a row of tiny little earrings made of stones in different colors running up the side of one ear. There was no doubt, this was Candy. Candy had tried to get up the hill behind the Nuisance Works and been turned back every time.

Anita headed for her gallery after her visit with Shree Jagat. Listening to him and his certainty had left her more and more depressed. She had been sure it was Emily, and then perhaps someone else, but Candy? Why on earth would Candy be interested in harming Marge? Anita turned into her lane, unaware that she had a scowl on her face.

"Ah, Chinnappa!" Anita greeted her friend and neighbor, the tailor next door.

"What is wrong?" Chinnappa asked. "You have trouble."

Startled by his reaction, she hurriedly told him all was well; she was just stuck on a problem.

"You should abandon such problems and stick to your work. You are a photographer, not a police officer." He snorted and set the sewing machine whirring.

A little meekly, Anita asked, "What're you making?"

"The usual," the old man said. He held up a long, thin tube of fabric that looked like it was intended for a waist tie, but for someone with a hundred-inch waist.

"I've never seen you make anything like that before."

"Ah, you have, but perhaps you have not noticed. These foreigners get larger and larger."

"If you say so." She unlocked her shutter, pulled it up, and listened for the sound of Peeru's feet. She was not disappointed. Peeru jumped up onto the gallery floor, saluted, and quickly went about his work of setting up the gallery—easels, framed photographs, bulletin board, matted photographs in a bin, table and chair for Anita, and a towel for Peeru. Every time she saw him, he had a different towel, and she figured he probably knew every laundry line in the area. "Have you had a meal yet?" He shook his head no, and she sent him off with rupees and an order, none of which she would eat.

"He will steal you blind." Chinnappa's muffled voice reached her, and Anita thought she detected just a little less hostility in it this time. Perhaps the old man was mellowing. "Probably poison you too." Well, perhaps not. Hard to say.

Anita flipped open her cell and called the hotel. She had a few details to sort out before she could move forward with the next phase of her plan. It didn't make sense as far as she could tell for Candy to want to poison Marge, so there must be a reason somewhere. But where? She reached Ravi at the registration desk, and after a few minutes he assured her that, yes, Candy was still booked in the hotel, her passport was still in the safety deposit box, and her belongings were still in her room. She showed no signs of going anywhere—her possessions were in complete disarray throughout her room. Ravi's disapproval came through loud and clear. Anita punched off.

"Tonight, madam," Peeru said, presenting himself to her with a large, folded banana leaf, "we are doing much business."

"Not tonight. Have your lunch, Peeru."

"But, madam, tonight is good business. You must be here."

"Not tonight, Peeru. What's the matter with you?" Peeru backed off, his face flooded with confusion and embarrassment.

"He wants to get paid more," came the hostile voice from next door.

"Is that it?" Anita leaned over and whispered. "Do you need money?"

Peeru began to look annoyed, then bowed his head, and allowed as how he did have need for funds.

"You only have to ask." She reached for her purse.

"I prefer to earn it." He waved away the purse and settled himself on his towel to eat his meal. "Let us work tonight. Much activity these evenings."

"Not tonight, Peeru. I want to watch the little Kali procession over near the hotel."

"Oh." Peeru looked despondent. "Please?"

"What is the matter with you? And I'm not asking you, Chinnappa," she added before he could offer his own tart opinion.

During the middle of the afternoon, when the heat was oppressive and fewer foreigners were wandering the lane, Anita left the gallery in Peeru's hands and headed off to the Internet café. Some obvious questions had been nagging at her over the last couple of days, and now another had grown larger, crowding out almost everything else. Who was Candy?

Yes, Anita knew what her passport said. Candace Arabedian, born in Illinois, USA, with a passport less than three years old, who had taken a long trip to Thailand over a year ago. Thailand and India. But she had given rice balls to Marge, and if Anita's investigation had any validity, she was probably the one who had purchased rice balls and contaminated them with the chemicals at Nuisance Works. But the chemicals weren't enough to kill anyone, and wouldn't Candy know that? And if she did, why bother? Why did Candy want to hurt Marge? What was the connection? Marge certainly didn't seem to know who she was. Had Jean?

Anita logged on, and began to Google various versions of Candy's name. She scanned down the list of sites—amazed at the kinds of sweets there were in the world. One site after another gave her nothing but useless information. She continued on to the last of four pages, and there in the middle of the fourth, she paused at one entry—Missionaries Raise Funds for Burmese Refugees in Thailand—and below this was a list of names, including C. Arabedian. Anita clicked on the site and read the announcement, which was a mixture of praise for the young people starting out on their holy work and a diatribe against those who would rest comfortably in their homes while others needed them. Anita scanned the list for other names that might be familiar, but found none.

The group was a mix of young people from the West Coast, most living in the major cities and connected with universities. Some were students, some were employees, and some seemed to just be part of that floating community that hovered on the edges of a university or college campus. Anita tried various other configurations of names and topics she had heard Candy discussing, but nothing more came up. The closest Anita came was the missionary site, and no other site even listed Candy's full name.

After another hour of searching, Anita logged off. Was it possible this was the same young woman who was staying at Hotel Delite? Candy never mentioned doing any work in Thailand, and certainly with all the gossip Jean provided about her work in Burma, Candy might have been encouraged to say something. But she said nothing, if that was her listed on the website. Most people never even showed up on an Internet site, never became famous enough to appear in a column in a local weekly newspaper, so Anita shouldn't be so surprised if she found next to nothing on Candace Arabedian.

Anita left the café and wandered back to her gallery. Three women blocked her path at the intersection with a narrow lane as two encouraged the third to give the beach one more try. Anita was ready to dodge around to the right, and an Indian man moving toward them, his head bowed down, ducked into an open shop. The three foreign women broke into shouts of encouragement or protest, their voices jumbled together into nothing but spurts of noise.

"It won't kill her to take a swim," one of them said to Anita as she passed by. "Tell her."

Anita shook her head but smiled as she passed them and the shop, the man re-emerged, and the women fell into step behind her, two reassuring the one that she'd be so glad she tried the water that she'd want to swim every day. "And it's not at all cold!"

Anita had heard that sentiment a hundred times—and she never knew how it was meant. It's not cold and therefore not refreshing. It's not cold and I feel like I'm taking a bath. It's not cold, so there must be jellyfish. It's not cold, so I don't have to worry about getting in and being miserable for the first half hour. It's not cold, so you can enjoy it forever. Anita picked up her step as she heard the women jostling and laughing behind her, two keeping one calm and committed. She turned into her gallery, and the women passed on.

"Hello, hello! So this is your place?" Candy hopped up onto the gallery floor and peered around. She reminded Anita of a goose whose neck seemed to jolt ahead to get the body to follow. "Can I look?" Candy didn't wait for a reply before she began flipping through the bin of unframed photographs, all the while continuing with her nonsensical gossip about the weather, a trip to Trivandrum, the food, whatever apparently came into her head.

Peeru remained at her side, ready to answer questions or hold a photograph for her closer inspection. He followed her step for step, just out of her line of vision, looking a bit worried that she might not buy anything. Anita reached down for a day-old newspaper and scanned the front page, ignoring Candy's chatter. The removals were going ahead in Munnar, one property owner had gone to court to protect his investment, the government was unmoved, and piles of rubble were being cleared away from state-owned land. The tourists would have to go elsewhere.

"These are so cool," Candy said when she'd made the circuit of the small gallery. "I don't know which one I like best." She glanced around the space again, running her eyes over the hanging photos, though not focusing on any one. "I'll have to come back. It's sensory overload."

"Not too much," Peeru said.

"Huh?" Candy barely glanced his way at the sound of his voice. "I'll be back," she said to Anita. "It's too much to take in all at once."

Anita smiled as Candy marched off down the lane. Whatever Candy was, she was exhausting. Just listening to her talk when she was supposedly calm could be overwhelming.

"Don't worry, Peeru. You didn't lose a sale. She didn't mean to buy anything anyway," Anita said. She offered the young boy a reassuring smile, and gave herself over to thinking. The lane was empty now, Peeru lay down to nap on his towel, and the familiar hum of Chinnappa's sewing machine filled the lane.

CHAPTER TWENTY-ONE

Anita held up the small photograph neatly wrapped in old news-paper and tied with string. The woman took it gingerly and swung it in the air.

"Lookit, Harry. Isn't that the wildest? They're so good at recycling everything." The middle-aged woman smiled merrily at the parcel before her husband took it from her. Still shaking her head, she lifted her long, red silk skirt off the ground as she glanced down at the step to the lane.

"They're poor, for god's sake, Elaine." He slipped the pack-age under his arm and offered his other hand to his wife. "I'm hungry. Let's eat."

"Why, Memsahib?" Peeru turned a confused face to her.

Anita shook her head, not wanting to explain the exchange—not even confident that she could. She nodded to another woman in khaki shorts and a white blouse holding up a framed photograph, turning it this way and that, and moving it into and out of the light. Peeru skipped over to offer his help.

"Busy this evening?" Anand appeared at the edge of the gal-lery, his hands resting in his pockets, sunglasses pushed up on his forehead.

"Some." Anita was surprised at how glad she was to see him. All of a sudden, the mild sense of accomplishment at selling a number of photographs that had been slightly marred by the insensitive comments of some of the customers evaporated, and she felt lifted off her feet. This must be what levitating feels like, she thought, if there is such a thing. She was somewhat skeptical of the many gurus who plied their trade of securing wisdom and enlightenment for anyone who wanted it, but she was never in doubt of the transformative power of feelings of affection or dislike. She stood in awe of the way feelings could move people in and out of sanity and rational behavior. And here was Anand to prove it.

Anand, she thought. So far he was behaving like the perfect suitor. He showed up when he was expected, dressed perfectly, and treated her like the only person around, as though the evening, even the world, was rearranging itself for her, and it was the most normal thing in the world. His conversation was always of interest, and if he ever strayed into a topic that seemed to bore her, he dropped it and moved smoothly into something else. He said only wonderful things about his parents and family and her family. He was nice to Peeru, friendly with Chinnappa, acknowledged all the shop owners she nodded to, and was far too perfect to be real. But he was so easy to look at and seemed to understand her so well that she was willing to accept the disillusioning details that were sure to come up soon. At such moments she was glad she didn't have any money to invest—she'd lose it all for sure.

Anand jumped lightly onto the gallery platform and found a chair near the back. He settled down while Anita dealt with another customer. Every now and then she turned around to see if he was all right, and each time he looked up from the newspaper and caught her eye and smiled, a warm, easygoing, reassuring smile. And then Anita wondered why Auntie Meena disliked him so much. She couldn't really see something that Anita didn't—it wasn't possible.

"I thought we could get something to eat, but I think you're too busy this evening," Anand said when Anita turned away from the half dozen tourists studying photographs.

"The dinner hour can be good or terrible, and I can never tell which one it'll be." Anita pulled her chair back near his and sat down, her body turned toward him but her eyes watching the customers. Peeru was keeping up well, but when it came time to take credit cards or cash, the customers wanted Anita.

"Are you ready for tomorrow evening?" Anand asked, the newspaper resting on his lap.

"You make it sound like something momentous is going to happen." Anita was glad she didn't have to look too directly at him—she was starting to feel uncomfortable. When he had first broached the idea of having his family and Anita and her aunt attend the Kathakali performance together, she had tried to see the wisdom in it. The evening would give Auntie Meena a chance to see that Anand was just a normal young man with a normal family, and there was nothing for her to worry about. But now that the evening was almost here, Anita began to feel like squirming every time she thought about it. She had this feeling that everything was going to go disastrously wrong just because Meena couldn't stand the idea of everything going right. She was getting so odd lately.

"Not momentous, but certainly not the usual evening."

Anita turned to him. "What does that mean? Should I be worried?"

Anand sighed, raised his hand toward her face, then dropped it when he saw a tourist coming toward them.

"How much is this in Canadian dollars?" the man asked. "Betsy, where's your converter? That kid doesn't know what it is." He stared at Anita but she couldn't tell how much of his question was for her or his companion. She rose and checked the tag, and did a quick calculation in her head. "Jees, you're not cheap." He backed away, still holding the photograph.

"Anand, you're making me worry about Auntie Meena," Anita said, returning to her seat.

He shrugged. "I was only thinking about the man following me, and what you might think about my parents."

"They're your parents. Like mine are my parents."

"Yes, they are." He gave her an expression she couldn't decipher. "I just want you to know that they are very decent people. A little odd, maybe, but really decent people. I'm very fond of them." He seemed to come to a decision then, and sighed happily. "They will like you very much."

"Now I am worried."

"And they will love Auntie Meena."

Anand left Anita both tingly and unsettled. She was dying to meet his parents, to get a look at the people behind the man she was falling in love with, but his reluctant warnings—and that's all that she could call them—had left her nervous, worried, uncomfortable. He was trying to tell her something without actually telling her anything, and she felt incredibly obtuse for not catching any hints about what it might be. What on earth was wrong with his parents?

Anita tried to imagine an older Indian couple that was—what? Criminals? Deathly infirm? So traditional that they wouldn't eat anything they hadn't cooked themselves? Or perhaps they were ultra modern—living the fast, modern life with trips to Bombay and New York, Western fashions, lots of foreign investments. Somehow nothing seemed to be right. Whatever there was about them that made Anand want to warn her, she couldn't guess what it was.

"You are worried, Memsahib?" Peeru stood before her with a frown and tense shoulders.

"No, I'm just fretting. Nothing serious," Anita said as she began the process of closing up the gallery. A few minutes later she handed Peeru some money for a late-night snack and jumped down onto the lane.

"You're still here, Chinnappa," she said to the old man when she pulled down the shutter. He grunted. "Why don't you go home?"

"Ah, what is home?" He turned his hands palm upward in a gesture of hopelessness.

"You've never talked like this before." Anita rested her hands on her hips and frowned at him. "Are you all right? Can I help?"

"What can you do? How do you fight karma?"

"You are in a mood tonight, Chinnappa."

"Mood? Do we not live and die by our karma? Look at that sniveling boy. Is he not destined to a bad end?"

"No, Chinnappa, he is not. And you should not talk like that about Peeru. He's my friend."

"Ah, he's a sneak."

Anita was about to scold Chinnappa when the two of them, Peeru and Chinnappa, broke out into a loud squabble, shouting insults at each other, waving their fists, and stamping their feet on the ground. Disgusted, Anita turned away and headed for home. She was tired, and it had been a long day, made longer by her frustrations at figuring out what had happened exactly to Jean and Marge, and not figuring out who Candy was.

It was night now, and tourists were settling into other activities—conversation in a lounge, reading, enjoying a movie screened in an open-air garden. Lights made the hotels and lodging houses sparkle, and the night air carried shreds of conversation. Couples called out to each other to hurry before the good fish was gone, a woman called down from her balcony to a friend in the courtyard below, quiet voices flowed from shops where other vendors were closing up—tailors bringing in the many cotton blouses and skirts left to dangle in the breeze throughout the day and catch gusts of sand, men putting away rows and rows of little tchotchkes that had spent the day on an ironed square of khadi cloth, the low-end coffee shops whose samosas and puris and bowls of curry didn't appeal to evening diners, children whining about going home and mothers grabbing their hands and hitching the water jar higher on their hips.

The night grew quieter the farther Anita went from the beach until, all at once, she realized, this part of the resort was asleep. Somewhere ahead she heard a voice, low and slow, and footsteps moving, then stopping. No one seemed to be hurrying here. But there was a rustling in the brush nearby and when no animal broke cover Anita's step faltered. The sounds were familiar, sounds she heard every evening, but the sequence was off—it was supposed to be, first the sound, then the sight. Tonight the experience seemed to be broken. Anita glanced around her and felt the night grow quieter. This was her home territory—a place she knew so well she could walk through it with her eyes closed and never fall into the canal, never trip over a loose brick, never miss a step or take a wrong turn. And yet, yet . . . she quickened her step, feeling a bit ashamed as she did so.

Anita walked quietly, hastening along the lane and turning toward the canal. A lot had happened along here over the years—a young tourist was found murdered in the canal one season, sometimes a dead animal was pulled from the waters, but mostly the waters bred mosquitoes. The lane was wide enough here to walk safely day or night, and Anita hurried on, eager to be more out in the open. She turned the last corner and a man stepped into her path. A knife glinted in the moonlight.

Anita gasped, quickly composed herself, and tried to step around him. He blocked her path, moving from side to side until she stepped back.

"What do you want?"

"Come!" he whispered, then jerked his head toward the lane, walking backward. Anita turned to break away but his hand shot out and hard fingers squeezed around her arm, leading Anita along the lane, across the canal to where she had met the beggar woman. That's when she recognized him—he was the man she'd seen in the lane across from her gallery, hanging around, possibly following her, but always avoiding letting her see him directly for longer than a moment. When she'd chased him and he got away, she convinced herself that that was the end of it—that he had given up. After all, there was no reason for anyone to be interested in her—she had little money, no power, nothing of importance in her life.

She opened her mouth to shout and in a nanosecond the knife was pressing on her skin—she could feel the cartilage push into her throat. "Who are you?" Her voice came out in a rasp of sound.

Despite her repeated questions he motioned her on, waving the knife in front of her. She watched him, trying to guess what was behind all this, but realized it didn't matter. What mattered was that he took one step, motioned her to catch up, looked over his shoulder, then turned back and waved the knife—and he repeated his pattern for ten steps, never altering it by even half a minute, a few seconds. She counted in her head each step in the sequence—five seconds, fifteen, six, and on and on. He was a machine without even realizing it—rigid in behavior and goals. He was taking them down the lane that ran above the old paddy fields with clumps of dry land every twenty feet where the lanes had been built over the boundaries. If he led her past this, he would have her in a dirt area well beyond the resort where no one would hear her if she called out—if she could—or be able to find her. He must have a car or van out there, Anita thought—that's where I heard a motorcycle start up when I chased him.

Moonlight caught a flash of color off to her left, but no one came forward—light on a rag lost in the swamp. Where I'm going to be, she decided, if I don't do something soon. The night was thick here, the romantically sparkling hotels and lodging houses blanketed by deeply sweeping trees and branches, locking her in as much as locking others out. Not even the footfall of another reached her. She watched him, the knife. She was afraid of knives—had always been, ever since she reached into a drawer for something and felt her hand tingle. It happened too fast for her to feel the pain until she extracted her hand and saw the sliver of flesh hanging from the side of her hand. She was never careless around knives.

She put the image out of her mind, kept her eyes on his head, noticed that as he turned forward his grip loosened just enough to slip a blade of grass through. Anita swung her purse and hit him hard on the side of the head. It knocked him to the ground. She stamped hard on his twisted ankle, hearing a gratifying crack. She kicked out her foot to knock the knife into the water but he bent around, caught her ankle and turned it, sending her to the ground. She hit the cement hard. She was too stunned to move away when she looked up and saw him looming over her—he fell on her, pinning her arms. She kicked up, her knee hitting his side, and pressed her fingers into his eyes. Somewhere in her mind she heard voices, but they seemed distant, like sound carried in a fog. With a final surge of strength, she pushed him away, but he grabbed her, began to choke her and she jerked her legs away, letting herself fall into the swampy water.

She fell face first and came up spitting water and slime, covered with the muck of abandoned paddy fields. He grabbed at her hair but his hand slid off and she pulled away. Above her the shouting grew louder and when she turned she saw two figures pounce on her attacker. A flash of color whipped through the air—a rope was flying above her like a lasso. Anita staggered to keep her footing in the muck, plunging through the swamp for more solid ground, and higher ground, especially higher ground—she was waist deep in water and only eye level with the walkway. Her attacker was yelling and threatening, but the two men seemed to have the best of him. Anita struggled closer to the walkway. When she saw her rescuers she almost lost her balance again.

"Chinnappa? Peeru?" She waded closer. "Is it you?"

Chinnappa spit out orders to the boy. "Tie it here, this way, no, this way. Yes, like that. Here, get this. Good. Tighter." The attacker yelled. "Put that over his mouth—yes, good. Pull it tight. Tighter. Let him suffer."

Anita reached the walkway, stretched her arms onto the cement, and hoisted herself up, sprawling exhausted in the dirt. She was soaked and sore. Her hand went instinctively to her head and she looked at her palm—it was covered in blood. She was bleeding. She must have landed harder on the cement than she thought. She got to her knees and now she could see what Chinnappa and Peeru were doing—they were tying up the attacker with lengths and lengths of cloth.

"Stay there, Memsahib," Peeru said, hurrying over to her. He was soaking wet also. So was Chinnappa. "We are taking care of all matters."

"I can see that." Anita raised her hand to her head again. "What are you doing here?"

"Get the bag!" Chinnappa yelled at Peeru. The boy jumped away from Anita and into the water and disappeared from Anita's sight, then reappeared, throwing a heavy plastic bag onto the walkway.

"What is it?" Anita asked.

"Karma," Chinnappa said. "We are telling the constable we have great concerns about this man, but he is not listening. Only a curious tourist, the constable is saying. No, I am saying, not so. Yes, so. Hah! You see? Not an innocent tourist now." Chinnappa stepped away from the bound and trussed man as though to admire his handiwork.

"He has been following you, Memsahib." Peeru stood alert on the other side, ready to pounce if Chinnappa told him to. "But no one is listening to us, so we are having a plan."

"This is a plan?" Anita wobbled on her footing, her hand going once again to her head.

"Yes, yes. I am saying we must capture this man and Chinnappa is saying no, we must throw him to the dogs." Peeru stood up and beamed.

"So we are doing both." Chinnappa gave Anita a sly smile. "Stupid boy!" He yelled at Peeru. "Make ready!"

Peeru jumped for the bag and dragged it closer to the man, who was now looking frightened instead of angry. He had ceased squirming and fighting the rope and was watching the old man carefully.

"But first, Chinnappa," Anita said, slowly getting to her feet, "ask him why. Why was he following me? What do I have that he wants?"

"He is evil," the old man said. "What reason does such a one need? It is his karma to do evil."

"But why me? He must have a reason for threatening me with a knife?"

Chinnappa considered this, shrugged, and kicked the man lying on the ground. "Good for nothing, eater of meat and ashes, defiled by liquor and women, what do you want?" He kicked him again. The man began to speak but his words were muffled by the gag in his mouth. Chinnappa pulled a small cup from his pocket, knelt down and filled it from the swamp, and stood over the man. "If you shout I pour this down your throat. Yes?" The man nodded. Chinnappa motioned for Peeru to pluck out the gag while he stood over him with the cup of water.

"Go on, talk," Anita said, leaning over him. "Why were you following me?"

"Let me go and I will tell you everything. I can help you," he said, his black eyes piercing her, desperation wavering under his confident promises.

"Hah!" Chinnappa kicked him again. "I will break your legs, lying thief."

"No!" Anita said. "Tell me the truth. This old man will drag you through the swamp and let you drown if you make him any angrier." This had the desired effect—both Peeru and the man were terrified.

"All right, all right. But you will let me go?"

"You will not die here," Chinnappa said. "Unless you choose to."

"I will tell you." The man swallowed and said slowly, "We are not wanting you, not until your friend is dying. She is the one we are watching." The man cast malevolent looks at Chinnappa and Peeru, and the old man raised the glass and began to tip it. "All right, all right. She is having items we want—they are worth much money and it is my job to get them."

"What items?"

"Medical items. We know she has them."

Anita brushed the wet hair away from her eyes and tried to think. She couldn't recall seeing any medical equipment in Jean's room. "We haven't found anything like that. You made a mistake."

"My boss doesn't make mistakes."

"Who is he?"

"Oh, no, no, I cannot tell you." The fear in his eyes was unmistakable.

"He was wrong, he made a mistake, and I will tell him so."

"And so did you," Chinnappa said, leaning over and pouring the water into his mouth. The man began to spit and Chinnappa motioned Peeru to stuff the gag back in.

"We'd better call the police," Anita said. She was suddenly very weary.

"Not us," Chinnappa said. "Let someone else."

"No, not us," Peeru echoed cheerfully. He untied the plastic bag and tipped it up, letting thick slabs of raw and rotting meat fall out. Anita felt her nostrils twitch and her stomach heave at the smell.

"What is that?" she said.

"Goat and mutton!" Chinnappa said. He pulled out a rag from his lungi, and used it to pull out a piece of rotten meat and lay it on the man's chest. The victim began to shout in a muffled sort of way, squirming and pleading as Chinnappa covered his body with pieces of rotten meat. One especially rancid piece he wiped across the man's head and face.

"What are you doing?"

"He is a vile man, a dog, an eater of excrement," Chinnappa said.

"All right, I get the point. But what are you doing?"

In the distance she heard a low growl, then a rustling, then a bark. Anita stepped back and peered into the darkness, turning around full circle at the sounds growing around them. The darkness was alive with the sounds of animals on the move, and they were all coming closer and closer. Anita stepped away from the man.

"You don't mean to leave him here?" she said.

Chinnappa turned to her. "He meant you harm—serious harm. Yes, we leave him here. The noise of the dogs will alert the people hereabouts and they will call the police. We remove his gag as we go." He finished arranging the meat, reaching down into the swamp to wash off his hands, leaving the rag, and then tossed the bag into the water. "Now we go." Peeru leaned down and pulled out the gag.

"Come!" Chinnappa ordered when he saw Anita hesitate.

"He is evil." Peeru tugged at her hand.

The three of them hurried down the walkway, back to the lights and sounds of the resort. Behind them Anita could hear the howls and growling of animals moving in and the man bellowing for help, then whimpering as a dog drew near, mangy and hungry and unwilling to be put off.

Anita turned to look behind her one last time, and in the distance she thought she heard a splash. Had he thrown himself into the swamp to get rid of the meat and the dogs? Had he thrown off a piece of meat tempting a dog to jump in after it? Chinnappa tapped her on the arm and nudged her to keep going.

CHAPTER TWENTY-TWO

Chinnappa and Peeru led Anita through the lanes and alleys until they reached the last shop on the beach, a young boy sleeping on the doorstep to keep potential thieves away. The beach was quiet with only the occasional tourist strolling in the dark. The dancers who had been brought in to entertain at the promontory that connected the two crescent-shaped beaches were long gone, and the braziers extinguished and carried off. In the distance they could hear a burst of laughter that seemed to unsettle the night air, until it finally sank again into silence.

Not until Anita stepped down into the sand did she realize how cold and wet and sore she was. Her ankle throbbed and she wondered if she'd actually broken it when the man twisted her leg, throwing her off balance and onto the ground.

"You are injured?" Peeru whispered at her side.

"I'm all right." She patted his shoulder and pushed herself forward, then stopped. "I think we should part here, Chinnappa. Nothing's going to happen to me between here and the hotel." She nodded to the paved lane a few feet ahead.

"Is that woman known to you?" Chinnappa pointed to a figure standing at the bridge over the canal where it narrowed before flowing in front of the shops and onto the beach; she was waving to Anita.

"Yes, I do know her." Anita waved back. "She's probably going back to the hotel." She noted that Candy turned and waited for her at the bottom of the lane. "What will you do now?" she asked Chinnappa. "You know the police will be looking for you."

"No, Missi, not us." Chinnappa smiled, smug and confident. "If he sends the police to us, what reason will he give? No, Missi, we have been in my tailoring shop all evening working hard to repair the damage this stupid boy has done." The old man gave the boy a gentle slap on the side of his head.

"I thought you hated each other," Anita said.

"We do," Chinnappa said.

"Yes, we do." Peeru straightened up and threw out his small chest, doing his best to appear insulted.

"Okay," Anita said. "I'm too tired and sore to care right now."

Anita limped to the lane and began the ascent. She often noticed how steep the lane seemed depending on how tired she was—some days it was just a little steep, and she wondered why people complained, other days it was much too steep for the tourists and she wondered when the government would step in and make modifications, though she couldn't imagine what those would be. Tonight it was the steepest she'd ever known it to be. She wondered if she'd actually make it to the top.

"Yes, Candy, I'm sure I look awful." Anita knew that anyone seeing her would be dying to ask what had happened—she was just grateful that it had happened so late at night when far fewer people were around to see the results. Her hair was matted with slime and blood, her clothes were soaked and torn, her body was bruised—she could feel a large one growing along one side of her face where her cheekbone was especially tender—and she was limping because her ankle kept sending shock waves up through her leg. "I had a run-in with a mugger, you might say."

"I sure would say." Candy oohed and aahed over Anita's injuries and opined that you never could tell what you'd run into in a resort.

That, thought Anita, was an understatement, but she did her best to adopt her hotelier's facade while Candy rattled on about her visit to Trivandrum, the traffic that had surprised her—especially the noise—and the great meal she'd had at a small restaurant near Chalai Bazaar. "Did you just get back?" Anita asked when her tale seemed to have reached its end.

Candy laughed. "Oh, no, I got back hours ago. I was just trying to persuade a couple of friends to come watch the Kali procession with me tonight, but no luck."

"That's too bad." They were close to the top and Anita was incredibly relieved—she had missed half of Candy's chatter because her ankle was bothering her, but by now she had started to hope that maybe it wasn't broken—twisted, definitely, but probably not broken.

"I really wanted to see it," she went on. "It doesn't happen that often, I'm told."

"Every year," Anita said. "It's the annual festival. But I don't think their procession is tonight."

"I meant the family one—it's not every year, is it? It sounded so special I really wanted to see it."

"Oh." They had reached level ground and Anita could feel her ankle begin to tolerate pressure and weight better. She was on the verge of crying with relief. She hated the idea of having to hobble around for a month or more while her bones mended—anything that held back her free movement turned her into an unpleasant, frustrated harpy—a veritable Kali.

"So, I guess I'm stuck." Candy made a face and flipped her hand a few times in cavalier frustration.

"You might try Emily—she's interested in Kali." Somehow Anita couldn't bring herself to go further than that, a sign of just how tired and done in she was.

"She's weird." Candy made another face, and Anita left it.

"You probably won't be able to get any good pictures—it'll be too dark."

"Bummer! The decorations are so cool!"

"The what? Oh, yes, the clothing—it's reflective of the goddess and her nature. It's not really decoration. She has to have certain colors and designs and the rest of it. It's all fixed in the sacred texts." Anita rattled off the standard reply.

"Wow, that is so cool."

And the same is true for a lot of Christian images, Anita thought to herself, wondering not for the first time why Americans seemed to discover the more obvious features of a religion only when they came to India. She found it hard to believe she had ever considered Candy a suspicious person in Jean's death—the woman didn't seem to have the brains to observe the world around her. "Didn't you see things like this in Thailand?" Anita asked.

"Well, no, not really. I mean, I wasn't around festivals and things like that."

"No, I suppose it might seem a little suspicious for a missionary to start going to Hindu festivals, wouldn't it?" Anita was gratified to see Candy wince, then blush. "Would you like to tell me about it?"

"Ah, what exactly?" She looked blank.

"About your months in Thailand, which you forgot to mention."

"Oh, that. You're right, I should have, I mean, Jean and Marge kept talking about it, so I probably should have mentioned it, but really, I just got caught up in what they were talking about. I mean, Jean was really, you know, imposing." She shrugged, and turned to gaze out over the narrow beach where the waves crashed, sending spindrift up into a small canyon.

"You should have let me know afterward," Anita pointed out.

"I wasn't much of a missionary, I guess." Again she shrugged.

"I can't believe those are all those little boats. It looks so danger-ous out there. Do you ever wonder what we look like to them?"

"I don't think they pay much attention to us out there—they're too busy fishing for the few fish left. And watching out for sharks."

"Oh. I'm sorry I didn't mention it. I hope it didn't do any harm?"

Anita shook her head, much more concerned with the expres-sion on the guard's face when he saw her limping down the lane. He swung open the gate and hurried toward her. She was quick to allay his fears, not bothering to say goodnight to Candy. Anita made her way up to her suite, relieved to be alone.

Auntie Meena pulled and twisted and would not rest until she had bound her niece's ankle in the tightest bandage she was capable of winding. She checked it half a dozen times, even unwinding and redoing it twice. Anita supposed this was the least she could expect, considering the look on her aunt's face when she burst open the door to Anita's suite and got a good look at her. Anita thought the poor woman would collapse on the floor in a heap, but she should have known better. Auntie Meena, for all her melodrama and histrionics, was a woman used to coping with distress. She went into overdrive. "I think you must be very careful, so very careful, until a doctor has persuaded me that this is mended and safe for walking." She leaned back on the stool and studied her handiwork. "It will have to do. No, it can be made better." She leaned forward, ready to undo her handiwork, but Anita put out a hand to stop her, gripping her ankle beneath the bandage. Anita would not have believed a certified surgeon could do a better job.

"Thank you, Auntie." Anita swung her foot off the bed.

"No, no, you're not done yet." Meena was on her feet, her fingers crawling all over Anita's head. "There is blood!" She bustled into the bathroom and emerged a moment later with a first aid kit and numerous washcloths. Anita resigned herself to more medical care, but at least she was going to get her hair washed.

"Perhaps I should call in Dr. Govindan," Aunt Meena said. She stood back to give Anita another appraising look, her distress replaced by a scowl, as though she were sizing up slightly unacceptable vegetables in a market. "You are really looking very damaged."

"I am very damaged, Auntie." She gave the other woman a warm smile. "But I feel much better. So much better, in fact, that the fog is clearing out of my brain." She pulled the cotton blouse over her head and limped back into the sitting room.

"It is time for supper. Come with me."

Anita shook her head. "I think I'll just stay here and call over for something before they close the restaurant. I don't want much."

"I am thinking that is not good, Anita. You should have certain foods."

"You can warn the cook for when I call. Tell me, now, what did your friend at the consulate say?" Anita let herself fall onto the settee and plumped a couple of pillows behind her. It felt so good to sink into something soft and cool.

"Ah, not so much." Meena pulled a chair closer to the settee and sat down, leaning forward with her neck arched and her eyes fluttering. Anita noted how tired her aunt was, the result of both anxiety and overwork. Perhaps it was time for the pair of them to go off visiting for a while.

"Well, tell the little that you got."

Meena straightened up and studied her niece. "Nothing that will do you any good at all, nothing, I assure you."

"Just tell me, Auntie. I promise to think it's completely

unimportant."

"Hmm. All right. Yes, the consulate knew of this boy, this missionary. He registered with them when he was traveling through Madras."

"Chennai," Anita said absently.

"Yes, that. And he seemed very sweet, one of those naive young Americans who has a heart to teach others." She sighed and looked down at her entwined fingers. "How does this come about, Anita? Such young people coming to Asia to change people?"

Anita shrugged. "Did the consulate people know anything about what happened to him?"

"My friend knew a little bit, not much. He comes from a good family in America; he was not a boy in trouble ever before. She was certain of that. And he insisted he was not a drug person and they had made a mistake. A mistake. But who is listening?"

"What did your friend say?"

"She is not saying one way or the other. She is saying it is difficult when young Americans get into trouble because they are not understanding the gravity of the situation. And this is true, I am thinking. But more than this she does not know."

"How did he die?"

"Ah! This is a question without an answer—perhaps suicide, perhaps violence in the prison, perhaps shock and sorrow. Answers are not coming."

"So we don't know who he really was—missionary or dealer. Innocent or guilty."

"Ah, who knows these things? Sometimes our fate is a surprise even to us."

"I think, Auntie, you are tired, and so am I."

Chapter Twenty-Three

Anita pushed the double doors open as wide as they would go and leaned on the balcony; below were rocks polished to a shimmering gold under the moonlight. Just to the left was the terrace with a few diners lingering over their meals. Their laughter and soft voices trailed through the breeze, caught in the palm fronds. The waiters tidied up the other tables and shooed away a few aggressive crows. She closed her eyes and felt the tension, the worry, even the fear slip away from her, as though it were flowing right out of her fingertips, into the ocean below. She felt wonderfully clean and calm.

And yet, not much had changed. Peeru and Chinnappa had surprised her—no, shocked and amazed her—with their foray into the criminal world. And now that she was relaxed and safe, she didn't have a single worry about the man left tied up and at the mercy of a pack of wild dogs. They would take their meat, perhaps fighting over some of it, lick the juices off his body until someone came along in response to his cries, and he would, wisely, probably never return to the resort. Anita barely gave a thought to her lack of sympathy for him.

But he did leave her wondering. She still had a slew of unanswered questions, but at the moment she had no ambition beyond resting and curling up under a soft, clean sheet. The evening was young but she was ready for bed. She turned back to the settee and stretched out, resting her feet on an embroidered stool. She really should get into bed and go to sleep, but she hated to let go of the day and this feeling of well-being. It must be some kind of hunger in her, something that kept her from letting go when she was tired, even exhausted, willing to try again another day. Instead, she laid her head back, slipped a pillow behind her neck, and stared out at the stars.

She might not have heard the light tapping on the door if she had been asleep in bed, but she wasn't asleep in bed; she was still lying on the settee, a little stiff but still half awake. She pushed herself up and looked at the clock—ten-thirty. Several lights were shining in the room. No wonder someone thought they could knock on her door at this hour.

Anita opened the door to the bright smiling face of Candy and the harsh glare of a flashlight.

"I hope I didn't wake you," she said, glancing at Anita's rumpled clothing.

"I was just falling asleep on the settee."

"Oh!" Candy peered past her into the suite. As warm and as generous as Anita was, she rarely if ever invited any of the hotel guests into her private apartment. She just wasn't one for quick, short-term friendships. She pulled the door closer to her, and waited for Candy to continue. "About this evening."

Anita blinked. She hadn't thought Candy knew anything about this evening except that Anita took a bad fall and was badly bruised. Had she seen something?

"When we were walking up the hill and I told you about my being in Thailand." Candy's eyes drifted from side to side. She was almost as tall as Anita, but she had an odd way of slouching, as though she had practiced the walk of a hip teenager for so long that her body had molded to a certain bending form, and she came off looking much shorter than Anita. When she walked she bounced from side to side, her hips and waist swinging out, but her shoulders moving the least. "I wanted to apologize for not being more open." And as if to prove her sincerity, she looked up with a broad smile and somewhat abashed expression.

Anita thanked her for her honesty and stepped back to say goodnight and close the door.

"I really mean it, and I want to tell you about my being there and what happened. Because it does have something to do with Jean." She paused, looked around as though searching for the rest of her speech. "I met Emily over there."

Anita froze. Her mind began to spin with the possibilities, one fragment latching onto another, a sudden web of what-ifs and perhaps. She struggled to keep her face neutral, a mask of nothing more than mild curiosity and courtesy while she tried to figure out how to deal with this new development.

"I know they're leaving soon, so I thought I should tell you— everything before they go." She shrugged, as though apologizing for another lapse. She held up her camera and binoculars. "I was going out to see the procession tonight when I saw your lights on. The guard said the procession was coming down that road over there and wouldn't get here till almost eleven, so I figured since you were still up I'd just let you know." She made a face, embarrassed for having imposed on Anita but childishly admitting it. She held up the camera again. "Do you mind? I really want to see the procession. They're so different from anything I get to see at home—I mean, my family is so Protestant it isn't funny." She nodded and smiled ruefully.

It took a moment before Anita realized she was being asked to go with Candy to watch the procession while she told her story about Emily in Thailand. Anita suddenly felt very tired, and sick and disgusted, but whatever had been driving her since Jean's disappearance stirred, and she found herself putting on her sandals and closing the door behind her.

The gate to the hotel compound was still unlocked, since it

wasn't yet eleven o'clock, but Anita guessed that no other guests were still out as she and Candy stepped onto the lane. The guard concealed a smile as Anita nodded to him—she knew what he thought of the foreigners who were silly enough to go traipsing off in the dark to watch a procession they could barely understand.

"Now, this is what I've figured out so far," Candy said as she led the way away from Lighthouse Road and down the lane to the beach. They passed the steps to the sand and climbed to the old gate left from the years when a private estate covered this part of the coast. The boulders were arranged as a series of steps, but since they were installed long before foreign tourists came to the area, they were not easy to climb. Anita moved to the side, to let the ambient light better illuminate the path. All the while Candy babbled on about the details of the procession she had gleaned from taxi drivers and restaurant waiters.

"Are you going to Thailand after this?" Anita asked, trying to get back on the track that had originally enticed her to leave the comfort of her living room.

Candy let out a laugh that was part giggle. Anita wondered if she was nervous about admitting her interest in a Hindu procession, since she had made such a point of her family's Protestantism. Anita stood on a boulder and looked up at the other woman.

"I don't think I'll ever go back there," Candy said, shaking her head. "Not me. It was too traumatic."

Anita climbed up onto the next boulder. "How did you meet Emily?"

Candy was over the boulders and onto the sand, which offered little purchase. She stretched out her foot and put her weight on it, but slid back down. "I made it up here easily today."

"When there was daylight," Anita said. All the locals knew

this area was not the best for walking; it was convenient to the village nearby. "You were saying, about Emily."

"Yeah, Emily. She came out to help her brother." Candy reached out and grabbed a tuft of grass just as she was about to slide down again.

Anita almost told her to take to the other side, where small, flat stones continued the steps upward, but she was struggling herself to get up the path and also trying to follow the conversation and line up Candy's statements with what she already knew. Unfortunately, she had a splitting headache and every part of her ached every time she moved a limb. She could barely pull together a basic sentence let alone follow Candy's meandering thoughts.

"Man, this is so awkward." Candy clambered up to where the path became easier to negotiate. Anita followed her along the steps.

"She told me he got into trouble there," Anita said. Despite the ambient light from the many hotels, the area was dark, a bleak night with black scrub, pockets of black ash—no street lights illuminated the area, no small fires marked the edges of the path.

"Oh, yeah, he sure did." She held up her camera and began sighting it, turning as she did so, from the road to the ocean. "I hope I get some pictures. It has a built-in flash but I never know if they're any good."

"Drugs are pretty serious business over here," Anita said. "So, how did you meet Emily?"

"I told you. She came over to help her brother. I knew her brother."

Anita knew where the path went through this part of scrubland—she had lived here long enough to explore every inch—and she was watching Candy wander along its edge, first toward the fence and then closer to the cliff. "Be careful over there.

The ground isn't solid."

Candy looked down at her feet. "No?"

"How did you know her brother?"

"Oh, he was a missionary too—we were in the same group. Do you think some of those boats will show up—will they make a good photograph?"

"They're pretty far away." Anita's stomach was sinking faster than a shark with a fisherman in its jaws. "So you know what happened to him? Was he using drugs?"

Candy continued to hold the camera up to her eye and press the button controlling the lens. The low-level buzz of the lens moving in and out filled the night air, like an insect circling and circling, looking for the best place to land and sink in its poison. She lowered the camera and frowned at it, then turned her face to Anita. "They're so convenient, these little things, but I can't tell if the pictures are any good when I look at the screen. I guess that's not supposed to matter as much because you're supposed to be so impressed with being able to see them. Not like film, where you have to take it on faith that something will come out." She paused and laughed. "Faith." She raised the camera to her eye again. "We use that word a lot in America. You know?"

The evening had gone still. Anita looked around, and began to wonder if a Kali procession was indeed scheduled for this evening. There should be more people here, if this was in fact the route.

"I think we may have missed the procession, Candy." Anita started to turn away.

"Oh, no, we're early." She took a step closer to the fence. "You don't think Christians can appreciate a Hindu festival?"

"Tell me about Jake Lanier."

"Jake?" Her face softened, then hardened. "Jake never used drugs. Never."

"But that's what he was arrested for."

"Drug-related activities," Candy said, as though reciting something.

"Why don't you tell me what happened?"

Candy moved closer to the edge of the cliff, then stepped backward, holding the camera close to her chest. A pair of binoculars dangled around her neck. "They'll probably build a hotel here soon, won't they?" Her lips turned down and she seemed to grow sad, as though she personally were losing something valuable, were watching a piece of her own life and history fragment and dissolve.

"Depends on who owns the land."

"Everything depends on something else. Everything's linked, he said. Who we are, how we think, how we live, what we do. It's all one piece. Yeah." Her whisper became a snarl. She tipped the camera back and forth in front of her. "I signed on with Jake because he thought we should do this work before we talked about our own future he thought we'd really get to know each other."

"And did you?" The bitterness in Candy's voice unnerved Anita.

She shrugged. "I got to know a lot of things." Her voice trailed off, and she stood unmoving for a moment before her body started fiddling again, as though she were a doll with a motor running inside her, sending her limbs into a series of random actions.

"Candy, what happened to you and Jake?" Anita took a step forward, drawn by the young woman's tone of sorrow.

"Nothing happened to me." She pulled on the camera strap with one hand, feeling the woven fabric run through her fingers.

"All right, then, to Jake." Anita was beginning to think that Candy had nothing to tell her—just a moody woman who

241

couldn't sort out her own life.

"He helped out a friend—at least that's what he thought he was doing." Candy swung around to face Anita. The young woman's face was transformed—her eyes wide and wild, her mouth twisting and opening, her fingers sharpened into claws and trembling as she waved the camera in her other hand. "What would you think if you opened someone's mail and found a box of syringes? What do you think they would say in Thailand? Well?" She took a step forward. "Yeah, needles, you know, those things we find on the streets and call the police to come pick up. Those things that can kill you or at least leave you diseased for life. Yeah, those."

"Candy . . ." Anita called to her, reaching out a hand, but couldn't bring herself to move any closer—something held her back. The woman was struggling to speak.

"He couldn't explain them—he didn't know they were coming!" Her mouth twisted again and though tears formed in her eyes and slithered down her cheek, she stared out at Anita without a sound.

"Why did someone send him syringes?"

"They were supplies. Supplies! He was going to hold onto some supplies for someone—he was doing a good deed."

"Didn't he know what was coming?"

"He thought they were sending sleeping bags and camping equipment. Like for a trekker." Her face hardened. "They used him. They didn't bother telling him what they were doing—they just sent stuff. And when he got picked up, they did nothing. Nothing!"

"Candy," Anita said, holding out her hand, "who is *they?* Who was sending him things?"

"Can't you guess?" She took a single step toward Anita, her whole body now a coiled spring, her slouch a mass of energy ready to explode.

"Jean." The name was barely a whisper between them—Anita stared at Candy, at her defiant, angry face, tears caked down to her chin. She hadn't noticed her clothing before—she was wearing the same outfit she'd worn almost every day. It must have cost Candy a small fortune, in her world, to get back to Asia on a second trip. In the distance a drum sounded and a horn wailed; somewhere was a procession.

"Jean." Candy mimicked Anita's matter-of-fact voice. "Yes, Jean."

Anita shook her head back and forth. Was this all a misunderstanding? Did someone die because of a misunderstanding? She studied Candy's face, wondering, trying to think fast, but stumbling over the odd bits she knew about Jean's and Marge's lives. "What did you do when he got arrested?"

"I called the States and one of my friends tracked down Jean. It took a while—she hadn't left the country, but she wasn't at work anymore. But I got hold of her and I told her he'd been arrested and she needed to prove to the authorities that he wasn't into drugs. She had to show them her medical credentials." Candy's arms stiffened—she was reliving those moments on the phone, Anita knew, every syllable that bounced from one continent to another and bounced right back. "She wouldn't do it. She kept saying, 'Who are you? Who are you?' "

The wind shifted and the sound of the procession was carried away. They were surrounded by silence in darkness again.

"So you went back to the States to get help," Anita said, recalling the dates in Candy's passport, the fragments Emily had shared.

"I went back to the school. I knew they'd help him. Ha! I knew! I was sure of it. He was a straight-A student, his grades were awesome. He was tight with his professors. They loved him. He started a ministry for kids in the downtown, taking them to sports games and tutoring. They loved him. But not when he needed them, not when he was in trouble."

"Tell me what they did," Anita said, watching the other woman. Candy seemed to go wild, then calm down, then lose her bearings. Anita feared Candy wasn't entirely conscious of what she was saying anymore.

"What they did? More like what they didn't do. They didn't do anything. The school completely abandoned him. They said if he was doing things illegal, then he was on his own. Their mission was too important to be sacrificed for one foolish student." Candy gazed down on her camera, her grip relaxed, her tears dry, her breath slowing. "Jean arrived in Thailand— she sent me an email, said it was out of her hands, and then she went straight on her way. She met her contacts and she wouldn't do anything."

Anita was putting the pieces together, but even now that she understood it, it seemed bizarre. Stranger things had happened—she listened to the tourists all the time talk about the odd tangles they got themselves into—but this one was ugly as well as bizarre. "Listen to me, Candy." Anita spoke softly, and was relieved when Candy looked into her eyes, wary, challenging, but attentive. "Candy, she thought her supplies were stolen—she saw them in the market. Marge told me."

"She used him."

"But not the way you mean."

"You're splitting hairs."

"You made her pay with her life for an accident," Anita said.

"She cost him his life."

"And Marge?"

"Marge!" Candy waved this away as though Marge were just a fly. "She wasn't in any danger. It was just bug repellent." She began to pull on the strap again. "She was in the way. I wanted to be sure she was out of the way—I had to make sure that if I got Jean to go for a walk with me that Marge wouldn't interfere."

"And that's why your light was on so late at night?"

"Oh, you saw that?" Candy nodded, a small smile spreading across her face. "Yeah, I came back and she was just getting sick. I was going to sleep in her room, just to be sure. Not that it mattered. I got Jean to go out with me."

Just like you got me, thought Anita. And now we're at a stand-off—you're on the cliff, and I'm not budging from the lane.

CHAPTER TWENTY-FOUR

"Let's go back, Candy." Anita reached out her hand again, stepping back along the path. She had heard too much to do anything but get back to the hotel and call the police. They might not believe her, and they might not be able to stop Candy from leaving the country, but Anita wasn't going to let Candy walk away without at least making some effort. "You've told me what you brought me out here to tell me. You killed Jean to take revenge for your boyfriend's death in an Asian prison. It was an awful thing to have happen, but it's over. Let's go back."

"I'm not going back." She pushed a button, slipped out the memory disk, and tossed it to Anita. Anita dropped her flashlight and caught the memory card in her cupped hands and pressed it to her chest. Then Candy began to slowly wrap the camera strap around the camera. "I've taken lots of photographs—things for my family. Could you send them the disk?"

A feeling of ice-cold damp encased Anita—Candy, standing there with the camera in her hands, winding the black cord and looking up every now and then at the ocean shining blue-black in the dim moonlight, her face a mask. "Talk to me, Candy."

"Here!" Candy held out the camera toward Anita, then just as abruptly pulled it back and threw the camera out into the water, watching it sail out over the rocky outcroppings until it disappeared into the night. They heard a light, distant splash. She turned to Anita, gave a defiant smile, and pulled off the binoculars and threw those. They fell into the blackness below the cliff. Anita heard a single crack, then a splash. The binoculars had hit a rock on the way down.

"That makes it easy," Candy said. "That rock first, then the water." She stepped toward the cliff.

Anita rushed forward, threw out her arms, ready to tackle Candy around the knees. But Candy was ready for her, turning, hunkering down, and flipping Anita onto her back and sliding her to the cliff edge.

"You're such a do-gooder!" Candy said, pushing Anita toward the cliff. "I knew you'd try to save me. You're such a sucker."

Anita stared up into Candy's face, smirking, satisfied with her trick, which, Anita had to admit, really worked. Her legs dangled over the edge, her back had landed on the overgrowth beneath which the soil had already given way. To her left was the overhang of the fence, beneath her feet—nothing. Anita grabbed at a scrub, praying the roots held long enough to let her get a purchase. Her other hand scrabbled in the dirt for something—anything—to hold on to. She managed to get turned over onto her stomach and threw out a hand toward the fence.

"I'd tell you not to bother, but you seem to have this idea—batting your head against a stone wall is your idea of fun, I guess." Candy planted her foot firmly on Anita's hand, pressing down until Anita could hear her fingers crack. The scrub held, but pain seared through her fingers.

"You thought I was going over the edge, didn't you?"

"Let me up. We can talk."

"Do you think I would give my life for someone like Jean? She killed Jake! She killed him! She might as well have held a gun to his head." Candy stood up and leaned hard on her foot. She placed her other foot on Anita's head and pushed down.

All right, Anita thought, what is down here? If Candy's going to push me off the cliff, I have to think about what else might be around here. Anita tried desperately to remember what she had seen the last time she'd been here, looking for signs of Jean and her accident—or what she thought might have been her accident. She remembered the rocks below—those tall, sharp pinnacles that could impale and kill in an instant. She thought of the binoculars—that horrible sound of glass breaking against rock. Candy's foot pressed hard on her head and Anita felt herself sliding. She waved one foot in the air, searching in her blindness for some leverage. There was a ledge down here, just beneath the overhang, but it couldn't be enough to hold her. Could it?

Through the darkness came the sound of a drum. The procession. Maybe they were coming this way, maybe they would be coming down this lane, maybe they would pass just a few feet away from her. She opened her mouth to scream, but Candy knelt down and shoved sand into her mouth. Anita choked and coughed and snorted, spitting sand every time. She let go of the ground and tried to reach for the fence. She managed to swing a foot up until Candy kicked out. In the miasma of fear and desperation that filled her brain, Anita took note that Candy avoided getting too close to the edge—she knew it wasn't safe. Odd the way the mind works in a crisis, Anita thought. Oh, god, I hope my last thought on this earth isn't about something as grotesque as Candy.

"You're lucky Jean didn't take you over with her," Anita said.

"Jean was stupid." Candy was sitting on the sand, pushing at Anita with one foot planted on her head. Even if Anita could find something to grab, she couldn't fight Candy's entire body weight pressing against her. The wind shifted again, and Anita felt a warm breeze ruffle her pants. How nice, she thought, I'm going to fall to my death on one of the most pleasant evenings of the year.

"Yes, she was. And you may only think you killed her. You're so angry with her that if she fell off the edge because she got too close, that doesn't mean you did it." Anita tried to control her breathing—she was breathing so hard and heavy that she felt she was drowning in sand. She had to keep Candy calm, so calm she lost her sense of panic and hatred.

"What are you on about? You think I didn't kill her? I did. She had it coming."

"That doesn't mean you killed her. You were angry, but maybe she just fell off the cliff by herself. Just because you thought about killing her doesn't mean that you really did."

"You're not tricking me with all this being reasonable." Candy was breathing heavily also, and Anita thought she felt just the slightest lessening of pressure on her head. She moved her right leg farther to the right, stretching it beneath the cliff to the last post of the fence, which she was pretty sure was sunk deep into the ground in anticipation of the unstable cliff someday leaving the end of the fence dangling over the ocean.

"No one's going to hold you accountable for an accident." Anita swung her foot farther—nothing.

"Don't you think it's a little late to offer me amnesty?"

"You're a Christian. You believe in forgiveness."

"Not anymore. They left him in that prison. They didn't believe me for one minute. No one believed me and no one helped."

"You're angry. I understand. We have plenty of time to talk."

"No!" Candy shouted and stood up. She waved her arms like a windmill, her rage spinning faster and faster. Anita's leg hit metal—she calculated it was closer to her knee than her foot. But how close? The breeze brushed against her, moving harder off the water. She closed her eyes, felt again for the metal, and prayed her fingers weren't broken—she was going to need all of them to grab hold of the bar and hang on. Anita looked up at

Candy's twisted, raging face.

"Kali! Oh, Kali!" Anita cried out.

Candy glared at her, turned automatically at the sight of Anita's expression locked on something behind her. There, in bright red and yellow and shiny black loomed a larger than life image of Kali, blood dripping from her fangs, rocking closer and closer to Candy as its bearers leaned in to see what was happening.

Candy gasped and cried out, then whimpered as she bolted away—shocked, surprised. For a moment, poised in the air, Candy looked terrified, then confused as she stumbled to regain her balance along the cliff edge. Anita felt the ground crumble beneath Candy, then beneath herself. She loosened her grip just as Candy's foot came down on her shoulder, and made a desperate reach for the iron rod. Her hands closed around the rusty iron. She closed her ears to the sound of Candy's screams, of her body hitting the rock and splashing into the ocean.

The many hands reaching toward her couldn't help Anita one little bit if she couldn't get herself out from under the cliff before it collapsed on her. The muscular hands with the long fingers couldn't reach her, and she couldn't let go of the bar to reach them. The iron bar sunk into the soft ground could only bear so much weight, and it wasn't meant to hold hers when the ground was giving way.

Anita tipped her head back as much as she dared and tried to get a look at the fence. Just above her were long arms reaching for her, and behind the man with the arms were two more holding down his legs. Kali, her vibrant reds glowing in the moonlight, rested against a bush and watched every movement, every twitch, every drop of sweat. Behind her stood another half dozen attendants, ready to rush to whatever needed doing. Anita closed her eyes and prayed.

The iron bar gave a tiny squeal, as though it was pulling against something metal—the fencing above. Anita felt her feet, one braced against the sand with her ankle turned so far it began to hurt, and the other pressing against a small outcropping of stone. The sandal on her right foot was torn and hung on her foot precariously—she had loosened the straps to better accommodate her aunt's bandage. She couldn't stay like this—she had to move.

She heard a crash above and looked up. She could only get a sliver of the scene but she saw a man climbing down the fence, inside the compound. To her right a goat meandered closer, curious about the odd behavior of humans. He stamped his hoof and a shower of sand and pebbles fell past her. Don't look down, she told herself over and over. Another hand reached out through the opening between the fence sections. The goat bleated. It was now or never.

Anita pulled her foot back and swung. Her sandal flew off and her toes hit the cliff. Her ankle sent a shock of pain all the way through her body, exploding in her head. She squeezed harder against the cliff, almost pulling the iron bar toward her while she tried not to scream.

"Once more," the man above her said. He pushed a section of fence closer to the edge, and motioned her to try again.

Shivayashivoo, Anita thought. She closed her eyes and swung her leg. Something caught. She looked up, straining to see what had happened, what was holding onto her foot. Her bandage was caught on the fence, and a powerful hand reached out and grabbed her ankle. She gasped in pain and gratitude. The tears fell.

"Let go!" The two men held her leg and another two now held them from falling. Anita looked below, where a mass of colorful cotton billowed in the waves, a limb glowing in the moonlight appeared and disappeared. Farther out were two

251

boats paddling in toward the shore, fishermen already coming to help with the body. "Let go!" Softer this time. Anita looked up into the eyes of a stranger, reassuring, confident, matter of fact. It occurred to Anita that this was nothing compared to what he faced every day, every night, just trying to make a living. She closed her eyes, said a prayer. She let go.

The light cotton blanket couldn't possibly slip off her shoulders because Anita was holding it in a death grip. The owner of the house and fence had come out to investigate the unexpected appearance of a Kali procession on his property, taken one look at Anita shaking so hard she could barely stand, and rushed back into the house for a robe or a blanket. His car was immediately brought out, but Anita refused. Nothing was broken, she insisted. She was just scared—terrified, if she was being honest—and all she needed was to go back to the hotel.

He would drive her to the hotel.

But no, that would alarm Auntie Meena. Anita thanked him profusely, and in something of a daze of pain and terror and relief, promised to return the blanket in the morning. The man looked to the fishermen for help, but they could only shrug.

The attendants picked up Kali and returned to the path, helping Anita along, slow step by slow step. When they came to the steps to the beach, where they had intended to take Kali for a late-night swim, two of them carried Anita onto the hotel. If nothing else, this gave her time to prepare for Auntie Meena. Anita was going to have to come up with a lot of good answers if she was ever going to be able to leave the hotel alone at night after this.

Chapter Twenty-Five

"I do not understand, Anita. I do not understand." This was only the fiftieth time Aunt Meena had said this, shaking her head, her eyes darting from table to teapot to notebook and back around again. Whenever she frowned like this Anita knew the other woman was trying to get at the idea, the story she'd just heard, and couldn't quite make sense of it, so she had lapsed into a quiet lamentation, repeating over again and again that she didn't get it, it didn't make sense, and what on earth had happened.

Anita took a deep breath and braced herself for another recitation of the confusing web of events that had left an American hotel guest, just a young woman, Candy Arabedian, rocking on the ocean in the middle of the night, battered again and again against the rocks while fishermen jockeyed into position to pull out her body. Safe once again on hard ground, Anita could hear the fishermen's voices far below, her one glance down had given her far more than she wanted to know of Candy's end, and even now as she put the pieces together for her aunt, it all seemed surreal. Her bruised and battered body, her now badly twisted ankle, her scratched and bloody legs, and her bruised and perhaps broken hands were like a strange out-of-body experience, so tied were they with feelings of terror and surprise and life flying out of control. She rested her bandaged hands in her lap, and lifted her chin.

"It was just an awful need for revenge, and it drove her crazy,"

Anita said. She kept trying different ways of phrasing it, to make more sense of the irrational, but nothing seemed to work. Words, no matter what they were linked to, were ever so much more tidy and sane than the life they described.

"She might have killed you," Meena said, her hands lightly clasping Anita's forearms. She looked down at her niece's hands and winced.

That was the general idea, Anita thought, but couldn't bring herself to say it. Instead, "She was after Jean. She gave Marge poisoned rice balls, knowing they'd keep her tied to her bed for a while, so she couldn't call on Marge for a late night chat or a cup of tea or something. Remember, even you noticed how close the two women were throughout their stay—planning everything together in great detail, going over every possibility. Candy saw that too."

"So poor Jean was lured away and pushed to her death." Meena sighed deeply and her eyes watered. This was something Anita loved about her aunt—her fussiness and nosiness might drive everyone nuts, but she alone would feel the loss of another life and shed a tear; she alone would think every life worth living, and every life lost worth grieving. Anita couldn't fathom the depths of her aunt's compassion, but she knew how deeply it affected her own feelings for her aunt.

"And then Candy came back and sat up all night to make sure Marge, in her ailing, didn't call for Jean. That's what confused me when I came up the stairs that night. I turned left, to the room that had a light on—I could see it under the door— and then I realized my mistake and turned right to Marge's room. I think Candy even considered sleeping in Marge's room, just to be on the safe side, keep her quiet through the night. There was a sleeping mat stashed in the laundry room that didn't seem to belong to anyone.

"Candy was driven. As soon as Jake Lanier died in prison in

Thailand, she blamed Jean and went after her."

"And was she not to blame?"

The first time Anita had explained the confusion surrounding the medical supplies sent on ahead to Jake in Thailand, Aunt Meena had stiffened, her head rose and shoulders with it, and she had looked down her nose at Anita like Kali herself. Meena knew the danger of accepting mail for strangers—nothing good could come of this. But it wasn't the syringes, Anita had explained, it was the failure of anyone to come forward and vouch for him—the failure of Jean to see more than someone trying to take advantage of her, the failure of his sponsors to insist on a more thorough investigation, the failure of the police to hold onto the confiscated property, instead of letting some of it filter into the marketplace where Jean saw it and became enraged.

Anita paused. Part of her had to agree with her aunt—because Jean was willing to take risks, she expected others to do so too. And because she was committed to what she regarded as an unassailable humanitarian purpose, she didn't see the risks as all that serious—she was an American on a mission of mercy. The most she faced, in her view, was confiscation of her property and deportation. She was one of those foreigners whose brashness and good luck protected her from the realities that crushed most other people.

"Well, Marge will go home wiser but alive," Meena said. She leaned back in her chair and stared at her teacup.

Anita had let her aunt fuss over her for hours last night, dragging in a nearby doctor from one clinic and a nurse from another—no one was taking her niece anywhere that put her beyond Meena's control, so Anita was bandaged and treated and advised in her own suite. She was left to sleep, but couldn't keep the sun from waking her, and so she rose at her usual early morning hour, wandered over to the main hotel for breakfast, and tried her best to calm her aunt, who was trying her best to nurture her niece. The guests gathering for breakfast knew only that a terrible accident had befallen Candy, and that was all.

"Hello?" Anita turned in her chair at the sound of the greeting. Out in front of the registration desk was Emily peering in at them. Anita went out to her. Emily gasped when she saw Anita's hands in their bandages and the bruises and cuts on her face.

"So, is it true?" Emily asked. "About Candy? Someone said she tried to kill herself by jumping off the cliff and you tried to stop her. Did she really?"

Anita knew it had been too much to hope for the discretion of the fishermen—too many had seen what had happened, too many had helped pull her back from the brink, too many had collected Candy's body and transported it to the police morgue. Too many people, too many families, and far too violent an evening to keep quiet. "Yes, that's sort of what happened." Anita avoided her eyes, surprised at how much the lie hurt her, but she didn't want to say the vile things about Candy that were true of her, not now, not now that it was all over for her and for Jean.

"She was the one who pushed Jean off the cliff, wasn't she?"

Anita started. "Why do you think that?" Anita heard Meena gasp behind her.

Emily shrugged. "A lucky guess, I suppose. All that bubbly enthusiasm—it sounded kind of phony to me."

"So what will you do now?" Anita said. "Will you go home from here?"

"I guess so. My ticket is for tonight, and my friends are getting packed." She managed a wan smile, glanced at Meena, then took a deep breath, as though she was starting in on a completely different topic. "I've been asking about coming back and staying, and I know I have to have a certain amount of money and things like that, but I'll be back next winter. I have to come back, I can't leave after what has happened to me, not after what Kali has done for me, and even though it's so far away I know it's the right thing and I know I'll get back here because—"

Meena leaned over the counter and rested her hand on Emily's face, running her cool, soft fingers across Emily's mouth. "Yes, of course, you will, child. And we will want you to come here. This is your home in India, right here."

"Now where are you going?" Aunt Meena said as Anita headed for the door.

"A little shopping." Anita limped out the door and up the lane before Meena could stop her. Certainly she didn't feel like wandering around the resort this morning—she really did feel tired and battered and sore and just generally worn out—risking your life could be very exhausting. But there were a few details she really wanted to clear up.

"Memsahib!" Peeru came running down Lighthouse Road, his arms swinging so far, his scrawny, spindly legs so twisted in his hurry that she thought he might just fly up into the air. "Memsahib! You are safe? You are well?" He rushed up to her, and so distraught was the boy that he even grabbed at her arm. "Yes, you are safe?"

Anita calmed and comforted him, resigned as she was to the news of her adventure the night before having spread through the resort. Shop owners came to their doors and nodded to her, in silent respect, children stopped playing, hawkers stood silent as she passed, nodding and smiling. She was embarrassed, surprised, appalled, and felt like sinking into the sand. Anita did her best to nod but she could barely get her eyes off the ground. She felt herself turning four different shades of red.

"I want to go over here," she told Peeru.

She led him near the first shop set up on the sand—a

makeshift affair made of woven palm-leaf mats and sandbags selling all sorts of purses and beach accessories, the trader's specialties since he had first opened several years ago. When it was time to close for the evening, he lowered a woven mat shutter and tied it into place, then he went to sleep in a small lean-to in the back. Anita greeted the shopkeeper, who couldn't believe his good fortune—the hero of the resort was stopping to shop at his establishment—he would be rich!

"The lean-to? You want to see the lean-to?" He blinked twice trying to absorb this peculiar request, looked at Peeru, as if to make sure the lady hadn't lost her sanity during her trial the night before, then shrugged.

"I'll meet you there." Anita waved and continued on, coming to the sandbag steps leading up to the walkway. But instead of turning left, she turned right, and headed down the narrow lane, passing a small hut housing a family, whose kitchen in the back was open to the elements. Anita turned right onto the dirt path, leading behind the kitchen to the lean-to. This was larger than it sounded, and was really a one-room hut with a kitchen outside. The shop owner stood next to the doorway, looking at his modest dwelling. His wife emerged unsure of whom to ask about this strange encounter. No one came around here—this was the private area for the shop owner and his family.

"Why, Memsahib?" Peeru inched closer to her.

"I'm thinking." Anita moved closer, staring at the back of the shop. The rust-red soil had been packed down by thousands of footsteps back and forth, during cooking and cleaning and visiting, and showed no signs of having been disturbed at all.

The shop owner's wife motioned her toward the door, but Anita declined to enter with a smile and a shake of her head. Nearby were a number of men and women inching closer, to get a look at what was going on. Anita knew they were thinking she had been mentally damaged the previous night, and now she was going to be the oddball on the beach, the freak who wandered around while the shop owners told skeptical tourists about the night she had been rescued from falling off a cliff and had never recovered. But these thoughts were like clouds unable to form because of a high wind tearing everything apart, and she continued her search, moving closer and closer to the back of the shop.

Anita knelt on the ground, where the mats rested against sandbags. She pushed her hand through the overlap between two mats and had the satisfaction of feeling her hand brushing against a bundle of cloth bags and something made of straw.

"'There is something in the back of your shop that doesn't belong there," she said as she stood up. I can't quite tell what it is, but I think I know." She held up her bandaged hand to explain her uncertainty. "Can we look out front?"

"Yes, yes!" The shop owner hurried around front, and Anita followed.

The shop was small, barely eight feet square, with a small section in the center for the owner to sit. Anita climbed in and began to rummage among the bags and mats placed around the shop. White cloth bags embroidered in bright colors with tiny mica mirrors hung from the bamboo bars, bags in dozens of bright colors were stacked high on grass mats, mats of many colors were stacked along one wall.

"What are you desiring, madam?" The shop owner held up a number of bags, but when none of these caught Anita's attention, he pulled out a few more. Anita ignored him, working her way to the back and gently pulling the stacks of bags away from the wall.

"Just what I thought." Anita pointed into the pile.

"Which one?" The shop owner was beside himself with delight—he was making a sale to the hero of the resort—he would be rich—everyone would come to his shop now. "That one?" He frowned and pulled out of the pile a nylon bag with a zipper across the front.

"It's not for sale," Anita said, standing up and taking it from him. "This bag belongs to someone else—it was hidden here a few nights ago. I knew it was missing but I just couldn't find it—and then I realized what must have happened to it. She hid it." Anita held Jean's bag in her hands.

The disappearance of Jean's bag had been nagging at her, and it wasn't until this morning that she realized where it could be. Candy would have been foolish to keep it, or throw it into the trash, but she had few choices. If she burned it, someone might investigate the ashes, but if she left it to get lost among hundreds of bags, who would notice? It was a little different in style and materials, but it was similar enough to be hidden in a shop. And that's what Candy had been doing that day when Anita and Anand saw her coming down the lane, the lane that tourists didn't use because it was too far away from hotels and restaurants; this little lane was just for the workers. "Thank you," Anita said, turning to the shop owner. "You've been a great help."

The shop owner stepped back and nodded and bowed. This wasn't as good as making a sale, but it was good nonetheless. And really, it was much better that she hadn't gone insane hanging over the cliff—such things are such a burden on the family.

Once again down on the sand, Anita turned to the store and reached for a temple hanging—a bright red and yellow cloth tube that would swirl in the breeze and remind her of kinder things. "I'll take this." She handed over the rupees to a doubly surprised shop owner and handed the purchase to Peeru. "For the gallery."

Chapter Twenty-Six

"Are you almost ready?" Anita watched her aunt Meena fussing with her pallu, pulling it up and draping it over her head, then pulling it down and fluffing it and letting it billow out behind her. She was wearing a raw silk sari purchased in Bombay some months ago—an expensive indulgence unlike her—to save for a special occasion. It gave Anita an inkling of just how nervous she was about this evening. "Relax, Auntie, you'll like Anand's parents, and you'll enjoy the evening."

"No, I won't." Meena looked so distraught and saddened that Anita began to believe her, but before she could say anything, Meena began to mutter about her makeup.

"It's fine, Auntie, truly." Anita reached over and squeezed her hand.

"No, it isn't." Meena shook her head and began to cry softly. She lowered herself into a chair and looked sadder and sadder, little wisps of hair flying out with every sniff. Anita drew a chair closer and sat down.

"Auntie!" She reached for her hands, took them in her own and stroked them. Meena's fingers wrapped around hers.

"I am so ashamed. So ashamed." Meena continued to cry, her sobs growing heavier and deeper now that she had embarked on her confession.

Anita didn't dare ask why. She just held onto the trembling gripping hands and waited.

"I do not trust. It is true, isn't it? I do not trust." She let go of Anita's hands and reached inside her choli for a handkerchief. "It is so hard. What do you know about these things? You are sometimes more American than Indian. How can you know how your family feels?"

Anita didn't know where this was going and how they had gotten here, but she knew what some of the landscape would be. Meena had never accepted the fact that Anita's father had not kidnapped her mother, held her at gunpoint, and forced her into marriage. In her aunt's view, Anita's mother was little more than a hostage. Even when Anita told her that her mother had moved out of the house once when her father had insisted on buying a small business just for fun, and moved back in only after he sold it, Meena was convinced her beloved older sister was secretly downtrodden, even when they argued over the telephone for hours about visits and purchases and which cousin should undertake which journey to investigate which potential new in-law. No, Meena could not imagine Anita's mother as a free woman.

"Okay, Auntie, tell me what is worrying you this time?"

"You do not understand the ways of your own people." Meena avoided Anita's intense gaze, letting her black eyeliner streak her cheeks.

"Which ones?"

Meena clucked and shook her head. "Do you remember your great-aunt Shanta?"

Anita frowned, trying to see an imaginary family tree with a single branch named Shanta. She had a vague recollection of an old woman missing most of her teeth, white hair sticking out like electrical charges, knees as thick as wood apples, skin as rippled as laughter. "Sort of."

"Her husband was dead by the time you came along." Meena gave a great sigh—the sign that she was at the outset of one of her uplifting stories. Anita gave a smaller sigh—a sign that she was resigned to listening to it—and tried to soften it with a smile. "She was married a long time, but not early in her life."

Okay, thought Anita, here it comes. What good Nayar lady does not marry early in her life? Maybe there's a juicy story here. Anita's attentions perked up. "No?"

"No. She fell in love with a college student at university." Meena looked suitably grieved.

"That's nice."

"No, it was not nice. It was not nice at all!"

"Okay. What was not nice about it?" Anita struggled to appear interested and loving.

"He was a Nambudiri." Meena lowered her voice and her eyes, forcing Anita to lean closer to hear her.

"You're joking."

"No, it is true."

"That's not what I mean."

"It is what I mean." Meena's chin jutted out, and her eyes flashed, just in case Anita didn't appreciate how serious this matter had been.

"But that was—what?—a hundred years ago? She must have been ninety when I met her and I was a child, barely in school."

"That is exactly what I mean!" Meena's hand shot out and she grabbed Anita's wrist. "Listen to me! It was love, they said. Such love! All through university they were in love. And they went to graduate school and into university posts. Still they loved each other—virtuous, devoted, passionate. Even their parents began to believe them. And it was a time for everyone talking about a new world, a new way of living." Meena closed her eyes and pressed her fists to her breast, as though she were personally reliving the experience.

"So what happened?" Anita tried not to be suckered into the story, but she gave in.

"One day a man came to her with a paper. It announced the

boy's engagement to a good Nambudiri girl." Meena's eyes squeezed shut tight and she gasped shortly. "Poor Shanta! She almost went mad!"

"You should write novels!" Anita leaned back in her chair. Really, her aunt was too much—she would go to any lengths to get her way when she didn't like someone.

"You should not make fun!" Meena was fierce. "After the wedding, he came to her, to poor, devoted, innocent Shanta, and offered to have a sambandham marriage. A sambandham!"

"Hmm. Well, he certainly had nerve." Anita rarely heard anyone talk about the traditional Nayar marital arrangement that was similar to common-law marriages, without some of the complications. A man and a woman who liked each other agreed to a relationship and the man visited the woman's home. If she grew tired of him, she simply didn't let him in again. Life could be so simple sometimes.

"How can you joke?"

"I'm not joking. He had nerve, and poor Shanta must have been devastated. Is that why it took so long to marry her off?"

"She would have no one after that. It took years. And then she was old."

"Still, she had children, didn't she?"

"Not relevant." Meena waved away this detail. "You must understand me."

"I get the point. You think Anand will just lead me on because since he's a Nambudiri when it comes to marriage, he has to marry within his caste."

Meena grabbed both of Anita's hands. "You do understand. I knew you would. I knew my efforts were not wasted."

"What efforts?" Anita held onto Meena's hands when she tried to pull away. "Auntie? Tell me. All that money you've been spending—all those sums that look like you've hired another staff person. Is that what this is about?" Meena tried to pull away. "Auntie! Talk to me!"

"It was necessary. It is important that I know who these people are!"

"But he's a friend of your cousin-sister's daughter's husband! You met him at their house. You have to know who he is!" Anita shook Meena's hands. "You liked him. You asked him for help, remember?"

"Of course, I remember. But I didn't know he was going to invade my family!"

"He has not invaded your family. Oh, this is silly!" Anita stood up, pushing the chair back. She was startled at how upset she was to find that her aunt had been spying on Anand and his family. She was even more surprised at the shame she felt and the worry at what Anand's parents would think about this. "I can't believe this! You spent a fortune to spy on Anand's parents like they were common criminals."

"Alas, it is true."

"Let's just hope no one noticed your spy hanging around."

"He was very discreet, a professional. Certainly I paid him enough." Meena winced at the recollection of the bills, giving Anita a moment of relief that her aunt had returned to her old self.

"Maybe we should just get going. The Kathakali performance is going to start soon. Why don't you go fix your makeup," Anita said, an offer of peace if not of forgiveness. She just prayed she'd get through the night.

"What are you doing?" It was Meena's turn to wonder what was going on when she returned to the office. Anita was examining a pharmacy bottle. "What is that?"

"Cipro. It's an antibiotic. It's a huge prescription with Jean's name on it." She turned the bottle over in her hands, then replaced it and picked up another. "These were in the hotel safe."

"Leave it. We do not have time for that." Meena was once again the radiant matron in her best sari, gold jewelry, and makeup. She didn't look like she'd had so much as a minor worry in the last twenty years. Not for the first time Anita marveled at her aunt's inner resources, not to mention those of the boudoir.

"They have Jean's name on them. How did they get in the hotel safe?"

Meena shrugged. "Oh, look at the case." She leaned over and tapped a slip of paper taped to the top of the case. "That's Ravi's signature. He must have put them in and given her a receipt. Come, let us go."

"Typhoid capsules."

Anita heard a sharp intake of breath from her aunt. "Did she feel so unsafe in this country?"

Anita shook her head. "No, I don't think she felt unsafe at all. I think these weren't meant for her, though she might have taken a few Cipro if she needed them. No, I'm guessing that these are part of the supplies she was taking to those villagers in Burma." The thought of an entire village waiting patiently for the large foreign woman to show up with her medicines and bracing goodwill sobered Anita and she replaced the bottle in the box. "They're never going to know what happened, just that she didn't show up."

"What are you talking about, Anita?" Meena pulled the pallu around to the front of her sari and tucked the end into the waist. "We should be going. Look, it is after nine o'clock."

Anita brushed her hand over the bottle tops, the treasures of the Western world, the possibly lifesaving gift of a stranger. "I think we should put these away. I don't know if the heat has ruined them or not, but I can check tomorrow." She reloaded the box into its slot. "This would mean a lot to those villagers."

"Come. We will be late."

They followed the sound of the drumming, up Lighthouse Road to the temple lane, where the crowds grew thicker, then down the lane, past the temple, to the clearing with a makeshift stage set up at the far end. The ground had been cleared and was now covered with families and foreigners settled on mats or light plastic or folding chairs. New arrivals jostled for space among those already settled, children hopped through the crowd, chasing and being chased. Anita watched the Indian families settling in among the westerners, wondering how long before the westerners, in need of "space," were edged to the outside.

"Ah, there he is!" Meena nudged Anita and nodded to Anand in the distance. He had arranged chairs in front of the stage, where they would have a perfect view. The people immediately behind them, sitting on the ground, might not be able to see anything, but Anita and party would be fine. Meena took a deep breath and started to inch her way through the audience. "Where are his parents? I don't see them."

Anita studied the crowd around Anand. A few feet away were a group of foreigners following the rapid-fire talk of a man apparently giving a lecture. A tall, lanky man with wet hair plastered to his forehead and wearing a lungi leaned over them. Next to him were a redheaded woman in a sundress, a man and woman in their fifties in jeans and T-necks, their short black curly hair framing their faces, a man with a long brown ponytail reaching down the back of his white shirt to his khaki shorts. The small group seemed to be following the guide's every word as he pointed to various parts of the stage, then to the temple, and again to the stage and the rooms behind where the actors were preparing.

"Ah, there," Meena said, nodding toward the chairs. An Indian couple in their sixties, in sari and dhoti, were tugging at the chairs, pulling them into better positions. Anand leaned over and spoke to them, and the couple turned away. "What is happening?"

"It doesn't look like those are his parents." Anita was beginning to pick up on her aunt's anxiety. The group had disappeared around the back of the stage, to get a better look at the actors getting ready, Anita guessed, and Anand was alone, with no one who looked the least bit parental nearby. Meanwhile, Anand smiled at Anita as she and Meena drew near.

"Welcome, Auntie Meena." Anand greeted Meena warmly, telling her what a pleasure it was that she could join them, and how much he hoped she would enjoy the evening. Having had her good cry and having relieved herself of all her fears and superstitions, Meena was ready to be generous.

"I am so looking forward to meeting your parents." She smiled and blushed. "It is so unusual to meet this way, isn't it? But we are modern, are we not?" She gave a half-hearted giggle. "Are these our chairs?" She turned around and rattled the arm of a molded plastic chair. "So very nice of you to think of these things."

Anand settled Meena into her chair and she continued to look around for the Indian couple who had been the object of her obsessive attentions for the last several weeks. In her excitement she had forgotten the small fortune she had spent on the investigator, the pages and pages of reports telling her nothing at the end of every two days, her fears that he would learn something horrifying about the parents, and her fears that he would learn nothing. By this point she was just as curious as Anita to get a first glimpse of this Indian couple. The sound of laughter caught Anita's attention, and she turned to see the little tour group returning to the front of the stage. The guide accepted tips and melted into the crowd.

"Fascinating tour as always. The things these fellas like to tell us—all these myths. Such rot." The man in the neatly pressed jeans and red T-neck, long sleeves pushed up to the elbow, just as were his wife's, smiled broadly at Anita and Meena. "And you must be Mrs. Nayar." He leaned over and took her hand in a firm handshake. Meena's mouth hung open only for a second before she snapped it shut and jerked back her hand. The man introduced his wife, she of the jeans and red T-neck, and they settled into seats beside Anita.

Anand knew his job. Amid signs that the performance was not about to begin soon, he told Auntie Meena a delightful story about his childhood traveling around the country with his grandparents while his own parents were out rabble rousing.

Anand's father leaned closer. "I have been so eager to meet you, Mrs. Nayar. I mean to draft you. My dear wife and I are engaged in the most satisfying protests against Government corruption."

"And we are succeeding." Anand's mother leaned over also, her hand resting on her husband's jean-clad leg. "Government is applying pressure."

"Yes." The older man's eyes twinkled and widened with excitement. "Government is spying on us! We have proof!" He lowered his voice and looked positively gleeful. "We have a most attentive shadow—wherever we go, Mrs. Nayar. Just imagine, wherever we go—for several weeks now. It is most gratifying." He and his wife leaned back and continued to congratulate themselves on the success of their efforts.

Meena's face drained of color but she managed a thin smile, her head and shoulders stiff. She looked like she hardly knew where to turn.

"Just think, Auntie, someone has been following Anand's parents around for days!" Meena refused to look at her niece.

Anita shook her head and grinned. "It must have cost someone a fortune."

"Pop has been really eager to meet you," Anand said. "He is so glad I've become friends with someone like Anita. He was worried I'd end up conventional, like most of my other relatives." Anand gave his most winning smile, but Meena was still too disoriented to even notice. "They're so conventional, and he thinks it would truly hurt my mother's feelings."

"Hurt your mother?" Meena couldn't fathom a mother being hurt by discovering she has had the joy of raising a conventional son.

"Well, it would feel like I was rejecting her." Anand spoke softly, following Meena's confused glance.

"But you would never do that, would you? You are true to your heritage, yes?"

"Exactly."

Meena nudged Anita and leaned closer. "You see?" she whispered. "True to his Nambudiri heritage. This protesting business is nothing, just a pose." She turned again to Anand. "Yes, heritage is important."

"My attitude about such things is important in our family." Anand looked over at the woman in question and Anita felt a thud of surprise at how deeply he cared for her—all the game playing disappeared in a flash, and he had only warm affection in his eyes. "Yes, Auntie Meena. You probably don't know this, but she was an orphan. My mother grew up in an ashram for abandoned children. No one knows who her parents were, but you know how things were back then. Higher castes didn't abandon their children, as long as they were legitimate. My parents met in college and fell in love there."

"An orphan?"

Anita had no idea what might have come after that because the drums drowned out whatever it was Meena was trying to say. An orphan? How had Anita missed that, or had she? She couldn't recall Anand mentioning that. Meena didn't say anything, just sat quietly, a barely concealed look of distress on her face, her hands tightly gripping her purse. Anita guessed what her aunt must be feeling—the massive confusion around how she should feel on learning that this woman had no known caste—not a good one, not a bad one, not a non one, nothing.

"Is your mother unwell?" Anand's father leaned past Anita, a worried look on his face.

Anita squeezed her aunt's hand and turned to Anand's father. "She always gets a little sad at these plays. She's so moved by the story of Rama and Sita."

"Hmm. Shouldn't be," he said, leaning over the side of his chair to make himself heard to Anita. "Rama and Sita. Sentimental claptrap. You know the great writers couldn't stand the idea of a woman showing any resourcefulness, and in the end they had to change the story in the epic. So, what did they do? According to them, Rama abandons Sita in the end. Not a good sort. No, bad form, very bad form." He leaned back in his chair, his face the perfect expression of disapproval.

"I hear you had some distressing events recently," Anand's mother said. "A nurse died?"

" 'Fraid so." Anita explained briefly about Jean and Candy.

"Those poor villagers," the other woman continued. "What will happen to them now?"

"Good question," Anita said. "I've been thinking about that myself. It's really been bothering me, so I've sort of decided to go into Burma myself in Jean's place, just to deliver the medical stuff. I have all her notes and a map."

"Oh, admirable, very admirable." Anand's mother beamed her approval.

"Good girl!" His father said, with a firm nod of his head.

"Not without me, you're not," Anand said.

Auntie Meena, overwhelmed by the turn the evening had taken, burst into heart-rending sobs.

ABOUT THE AUTHOR

Susan Oleksiw is the author of the Mellingham series featuring Chief of Police Joe Silva, who was introduced in *Murder in Mellingham* (1993). Oleksiw introduced Anita Ray, an Indian-American photographer, in a series of short stories, including "A Murder Made in India" (*Alfred Hitchcock Mystery Magazine*, 2003).

Also known for her nonfiction work, Oleksiw compiled *A Reader's Guide to the Classic British Mystery* (1988), the first in a series of Reader's Guides. As consulting editor for *The Oxford Companion to Crime and Mystery Writing* (1999), she also contributed several articles.

Oleksiw trained as a Sanskritist at the University of Pennsylvania, where she received a PhD in Asian Studies, and has lived and traveled extensively in India.

Oleksiw is a co-founder of Level Best Books, which publishes anthologies of crime fiction by New England writers.